THE 13ᵀᴴ PLANET

ALSO BY THE AUTHOR
Your Heart Knows The Way

THE 13ᵀᴴ PLANET

ELLIE SHOJA

Peace Unleashed
Los Angeles, California

Peace Unleashed
Publishers since 2019
Los Angeles, California
www.PeaceUnleashed.com

Library of Congress Cataloging-in-Publication Data

Names: Shoja, Ellie, 1981- author.
Title: The 13th Planet / Ellie Shoja.
Description: First edition. | Los Angeles: Peace Unleashed, 2020.
Identifiers: ISBN 978-1-7341304-1-6 (ebook)
                  ISBN 978-1-7341304-2-3 (paperback)
                  ISBN 978-1-7341304-3-0 (hardcover)

First edition 2020

Cover design by Zsófia Vera

Dedicated to my mother, who in the midst of storms, found a way to keep us dry.

Thank you for your unconditional love and support.

PROLOGUE
descent into dark

It was not her first time on Easter Island. In the beginning, Isha had frequently found herself on this remote rock that never failed to remind her of Favadan, the home planet she had left behind. It wasn't that this place looked anything like the uninhabitable Sorufii Desert or the bottom-less Cliffs of Navili-ya, whose massive craters could be seen from any of Favadan's three moons. The similarities between her home planet and this strange terrain were more metaphorical than literal. It was the way the ocean seemed to hold its breath between waves, the almost indecipherable hiss of the wind through the low grass, the pregnant stillness that shrouded the island during its darkest hours. Fleeting moments of Isha's earliest years as a Newform were captured in the details of this place. It was no wonder that as centuries of separation drifted by, Isha had found it increasingly difficult to spend time in this particular corner of the blue planet that the Council of Elders had decided to call "Thaia."

In reality, Thaia and Favadan could not have been more different. As the first planet to awaken, Favadan was the oldest and wisest in this young Universe. In her wisdom, Favadan had given birth to the Kouri, a being so complete, it held the knowledge of an entire planet within its corporeal form. Even before her awakening, Favadan had been a place of peace — a hub of interstellar creativity that welcomed all cooperative life forms. After her awakening, Favadan had become a conduit of knowledge, inspiring many races to return to their home planets and assist in their own awakenings. This was perhaps a result of the tempered calm of the Favadani, which was in stark contrast to the lawless turbulence displayed by the humans of this planet. Isha had compassion for these beings at first. They were nothing but children, after all, and as children, it was understandable that they would be influenced more by their creature instincts than by the sentience they had recently acquired. Thaia was young, and it made sense that in her youth, she would be reckless and her offspring would be dumb, deaf, and blind.

Still, no amount of study, logic, or intergalactic exploration could have prepared Isha for the shock of actually living among an unawakened race. Even her extensive guardian training had proved inadequate in painting a realistic image of the unbridled waves of violence that plagued this planet. It hadn't taken long for Isha to wonder if there was something intrinsically wrong with Thaia. Was it normal for a planet to be constantly on the brink of annihilation? Few were the humans who did not spend the entirety of their days in a defensive stance, ready to pounce at the gentlest rustle that stirred the shadows of their haunted minds.

Isha's fingers curled around razor-edged rocks, and her toes pressed into shallow grooves of the cliff from which she dangled. She closed her eyes and listened to the shatter of the waves below. If she listened intently, deep beneath the roar of the ocean, in that split second which separated one wave from another, she could almost make out the faint familiar buzz of a swarm of be-ings that did not belong to this sea — that did not belong to this planet.

Ominous words of a homeless man she had encountered two years prior rang inside Isha's mind.

Everything will burn! the man yelled. *Boom! Boom! Boom! Everything will burn!* At the reference to fire, his eyes widened as he gestured toward the sky.

It had been Thaia speaking through him. Isha was certain of this. Thaia was warning her and pleading for help. All exist-ing knowledge — and there was an abundance of accumulative knowledge among twelve fully-awake planets — suggested such a communication could not, should not, be possible. Yet there Isha had stood, receiving a message from Thaia and sensing deep within her consciousness that something was very wrong.

The wrongness remained with her still, but it had evolved in the six hundred and eighty-three days since the man's forebod-ing declaration. Even a feather becomes a burden if you carry it long enough. But this message was not a feather. It was an entire planet shrunk down into a marble; a whale of a secret swept into her home on the back of a whisper. The longer she held it, the more the wrongness expanded inside her, like a parasite claim-ing its host. Isha wondered how much longer she could hold on before it consumed her entirely.

A gust of wind slapped Isha's back. She opened her eyes and softened her hardened shell. Her chin-length black hair fluttered atop her head like a bird in distress. Pressing into her fingers and toes, she pushed her pelvis away from the mountain, and looked down between her legs. Two hundred feet below, a wave explod-ed against the lava rock, leaving behind a layer of foam. With spider-like agility, Isha crept down the cliff toward the ocean.

When a dozen yards separated her from the jagged rocks below, she launched herself backward. A blink before impact, she hardened, and her rigid frame punctured the water like a bullet. In all of her three thousand years on this planet, she had never gotten used to the sensation of liquids against her outer membrane. And of all liquids, she most disliked ocean water and its countless curious organisms ready to force their way into her. Maintaining a stony shell would save her the trouble of expelling them later, even if it did limit her range of motion.

In these clear waters, her eyes made out details hundreds of feet away. She broke off a boulder the size of her own body and allowed its weight to pull her down into the belly of the sea. Her eyes scanned nearby grooves for anything unusual. Periodically, her bare feet encountered urchin-covered outcroppings. The pressure she used to push against these was minute, yet its force was enough to thrust her body downward.

Her feet gently lowered onto the sea floor. In front of her, a narrow opening led into a cave beneath the island. Releasing the boulder, she squeezed through the entrance and followed the familiar buzz of thousands of microscopic mechanics into the pitch black of the cave. Even against her stony shell, she could feel the subtle collective vibration of the Moli-orath.

What are the implications?

By the time Isha came into being, Favadan had been awake for hundreds of millennia. All existing forms had been remade thousands of times in the New Knowing. There were no longer any first-hand accounts of the pre-awakening days. All new-forms knew about the Moli-orath upon their arrival — many having had experiences with them in previous incarnations. The way of the Moli-orath, which was only in its experimental stages before Favadan's awakening, was now a part of its modus vivendi

— the planet's way of life.

Isha's gifts were recognized upon her arrival. She was selected for Moli-orath training when she was just old enough to control her new limbs. To her parent's pride, she had not only mastered her command over the living machines faster than anyone in her class, but she had also established herself as a powerful Channel, capable of translating information into frequencies beyond those of her kin. She knew this was how Thaia communicated with her now. And this was how Isha would stop whatever sinister plot she unearthed.

Her fears were confirmed deep inside the cave. A glittering ball of light appeared suspended in blackness — brightest at its core where the concentration of the Moli-orath was greatest. In the center of the light, an egg-shaped object, four inches in diameter, was wedged inside the lava rock so completely only small pieces of it peeked through open crevices. To a human, this device would be indistinguishable from the black rock that housed it, but Isha recognized it as a Potouyel — a rare housing device forged of an indestructible material only found on the expired planet of Bofsho-ghool, the Dead Giant.

How many years have you been hiding here?

She ran her fingers along the mouth of the stone where it touched the object. The thin layer of algae that covered the lip of the opening must have taken centuries to grow. But no algae grew on the probe itself — another confirmation of its alien origin. Whoever had placed it here had gone through much trouble to ensure its security. Still, too many of the mechanics had already separated from their Potouyel and were bouncing aimlessly around in its immediate surrounding — a sign of prolonged lack of supervision.

The Moli-orath grew restless as she worked. The ball of light expanded to encompass her body. A few lone explorers landed on her hardened shell, feeling for any opening they might find into her. The idea spread among them almost instantly. They may have been abandoned, but their connection remained intact — a sign of a unifying host consciousness.

Isha brushed them aside and was surprised by their lack of attention to her will. She split her focus and commanded them to cease and encountered a complete lack of obedience. They pushed and probed, bit into her stony membrane, and tried to break the barrier of her skin. Isha closed her eyes and pushed back, her will a focused beam of consciousness. The Moli-orath paused an instant and resumed their attempted incursion.

Enough! Isha commanded. A ripple of energy ran through her, and forced the Moli-orath away. The lava rock shattered in her hands, leaving within her grasp only the unbreakable alien device. The light of the Moli-orath dimmed as it became a thin shell around her. Even the glow of the Potouyel in her hands diminished as those still trapped within it retreated into its core.

They may be unruly, but they are still Moli-orath. And Moli-orath are made to obey.

Inside! she demanded. Now!

The Moli-orath did not go. Those surrounding her relaxed as if ignoring her.

Whom do you obey? she asked but did not receive an answer.

Isha was acutely aware that all her experiences on this planet, all her years of training that preceded this mission, all her years of study from the moment she first claimed this current form —it *all* had culminated in this precise moment of complete concentration required to probe the uncooperative device in her hand.

Isha peered at the object, pushed her consciousness into it, inspected the microscopic machines as her mind floated alongside them inside the thing she held. She demanded answers and encountered silence.

She expanded her awareness inside the device until she was the thing itself. Tugging at their consciousness, she attempted to make their minds her own. The Moli-orath resisted. Then she saw their shells, thin and translucent, shielding each of the mechanics against precisely this form of interrogation.

A secret where there should be none.

She thought once again of the toothless man's doomsday prediction. With all the intensity available to a powerful Channel, Isha translated the image of the man into every frequency within her vast range, and projected this complex frequency band into the device. If she had broadcast this image into the universe in this way, every race on every planet would be able to receive it in its entirety. No matter who had created these Moli-orath, no matter what their host consciousness consisted of, they would be able to see and process this scene that had created such turmoil inside her. Isha hoped that in their response she might find a clue. She became still as she held the projection.

Recognition rippled through the Moli-orath. Isha heard the words "not yet" click through them like a wave. The thin shell of light that surrounded her became thousands of lines as the Moli-orath darted into the device she held, and the thing became dim and obedient in her trembling hands.

Everything will burn! She heard the phrase echoed in a million mechanical voices inside the device. Was this truly its purpose — to destroy Thaia? If so, who among the Awakened could have devised such a plan that was in direct opposition to their mission of peace?

Isha pushed the Potouyel into her pocket, recognizing it for what it was: a weapon capable of destroying this world. A feeling of utter loneliness, the like of which Isha had never before encountered, spread inside her. To be awakened was to not know loneliness. It was to be anchored in the universe as a fetus is anchored to its mother, with its umbilical cord intact. Yet, in this moment, Isha felt severed from all that made her belong.

Can it be stopped? It was a rhetorical question.

But as though in answer, a school of more than a hundred translucent fish, each less than a centimeter in length, swam into Isha's view. When they were in front of her, they moved in a zigzag pattern that was uncharacteristic for them. Isha recognized the pattern. It was the gesture that contained both a plea for help and gratitude for being saved, given by one Favadani to another, after finding himself stranded on the exposed ridges of the Sorufii desert during the heavy air before a Wudi storm.

Give me life, the gesture said, and *I will repay the debt when I have life to give.* Like so many ancient customs, it had become obsolete after Favadan's awakening.

Isha accepted the plea with a nod of her head. It was only appropriate for her to respond with a human gesture.

I will give you life, if life is at stake, she thought; though inside her, she felt the crushing weight of a promise she knew she may not be able to keep.

1
nightmare is the beginning

Nathan Bradley woke with a start, and for a moment he did not know where he was. His heart pounding, he tried to slow his rapid breath. The feeling of despair which would soon turn into a steady hum of depression was overwhelming when he first awoke from the nightmare.

He had learned a great deal about nightmares in the last few months. Mainly that he had known nothing about them before. *Nightmare* was one of the most misunderstood words in the English language, he had decided. How long ago he decided this, he did not know. The days had begun to blend into an endless chain of internal dismay since his education on this subject had begun.

Before he was properly introduced to the true meaning of *nightmare*, Nathan had been guilty of the same usual mistakes most people make on the subject. A nightmare was a jealous girlfriend who cut up all your clothes when you were two hours late and your phone died and you didn't have a way of letting her know. Or it was a two-year-old who had a melt-down on an airplane during takeoff. In his ignorance, nightmare could have been a place if it was dirty enough or an event if it was boring enough. Anything he did not want to do could easily be a nightmare to accomplish, and any performance that didn't fit his exact mood or expectations was often a nightmare to sit through.

Nightmare was, of course, none of these things, for the simple reason that all these scenarios lacked the main defining element that made a nightmare what it was: the abject ability to make life a living hell.

People, Nathan realized, created illusions of nightmares in the absence of tangible threat to their actual wellbeing. And without such threats, they often demoted the word to encompass mere inconveniences and marginally frustrating situations.

Nathan's education on the subject of nightmares had begun with a single disturbing dream, which he had mistakenly labeled as a *nightmare* that first night. It wasn't until weeks later that he realized the dream had turned into a nightmare only after it had taken over his life. If that first dream was a nightmare, he had reasoned, what would you call a thing that completely obliterates every aspect of life? There had to be word that described the nightly recurring horror that had turned his life unlivable, which didn't simultaneously mean *the temporary disturbance of a night's sleep*. No. If *nightmare* was the persistent assault he endured every time he closed his eyes, which had in a span of a few excruciating months sucked all the life out of him, then all other uses of the word had to be wrong.

Nathan sat up, gripping the steering wheel with numb fingers and buried his face inside his elbow. Tilting his gaze upward, he peered at her third-floor window. The light inside the apartment was still on, curtains still drawn. Inside his pocket, his phone buzzed impatiently. Staring at the cracked screen, he contemplated what he might say if he actually picked up.

A few days ago, Nathan had made the mistake of confiding

in his brother. If anyone could understand his impossible position, he had reasoned to himself, it would be Pic. Nathan had been wrong. Instead of understanding, Pic had extended to him the same self-righteous criticism Nathan had come to expect from practically everyone else in his life.

Nathan cringed as he remembered Pic's final advice: *Stop stalking the girl.* As though he'd heard nothing of what Nathan so painstakingly poured into the open Guiness bottles that separated them. The bottles had once been full of beer, but Nathan made sure to empty them so he could fill them with his fears. It hadn't been easy filling so many bottles with so much of his pain, but he had done it, and in the end, it had been for nothing.

Who the hell are you to judge? Nathan thought as he shoved the phone back into his jacket pocket.

Cocooning himself inside his gray blanket, Nathan reclined back in his seat. He stared blankly at her window and struggled against the weight of his heavy eyelids. Exhausted as he was, Nathan fought back sleep and the nightmare it would bring.

———

Nathan's eyes popped open. Disoriented. 3:17 AM.

The dream he'd had was new, unprecedented. She was sitting under a tree, next to a lake. When she saw him, she gestured for him to join her, took his hand and placed a small rock into it. Then she smiled. Nathan felt the warmth of her smile trickle down his spine. When he opened his hand to inspect the rock, a butterfly flew out from between his lax fingers, lingered a moment and disappeared inside a distant flower. She laughed then, and he woke to the musical sound of her laughter. It filled his car for the briefest moment before dissolving into the deep shadows of the night.

Distracted by the dream, Nathan almost didn't notice the front door of her apartment building slide open and her unmistakable silhouette step onto the sidewalk. Nathan sucked in a shallow breath and stopped breathing. His wide eyes were fixed on the outline of her. Every cell in his body was on alert. By the time his brain could make sense of the scene, she was halfway down the hill. His breath returned — fast, loud, short, shallow.

He stumbled out of the car and found it impossible to think. She was already a fading dot being swallowed by the dark near the bottom of the hill. He ran after her, leaping from one foot to the next — his downward momentum amplified by gravity and the pull of her body. The hill tapered to flat ground at the bottom and helped him come to a stop. She was nowhere in sight.

Nathan's heart accelerated when he realized he didn't know which way she had gone. He circled around, looking down every street, squinting, and wishing he had driven instead of chasing after her on foot. Did he not know how fast she walked? Then he *felt* her — that unmistakable tug he had felt the first time he laid eyes on her. It was an invisible tether that bound him to her.

He ran down a dark alley until he found himself one street away from the ocean. His eyes searched the deserted street and the long stretch of empty beach beyond it. He spotted her walking toward the pier and ran after her.

His heart pounded inside his chest as his hurried steps closed the gap between them. Once on the pier, she seemed to float over the weathered planks. He stopped in mid-step the instant she reached the dead end of the pier. Blood drained from his face as his mind wrapped itself around the flaw in his plan: *what if she turns around?*

She did not turn around. Instead, she bent down and lifted a large box that he only now noticed onto the railing. From her pocket, she produced a rope, long and with some girth. One limb at a time, she lifted herself onto the railing, and sat next to the box with her back to him. She twisted at the hip and tied the rope to a hook at the top of the box. Then she curled her body, pulling her knees into her chest, and tied the other end to her ankles. Nathan's gaze shifted back and forth between her busy hands and the box until a new realization took form in his mind.

It's not a box, his mind determined. *It's... it's... a concrete block?*

Nathan was suddenly aware of the crash of waves beneath his feet. Before he had time to fully process what was happening, she slid herself close to the concrete block, and shimmied it off the railing.

"NO!" Nathan's voice ripped through the clamor of waves. Before she was sucked into the ocean, her head snapped toward him, her eyes glazed with shock. Then she was no longer there, sitting on the ledge.

Had he imagined her? Just now, standing there? Had she been real?

Nathan ran to where she had stood a moment ago, looking for proof that she had really been there. Without pausing to think, he boosted himself onto the railing and jumped into the abyss.

The water hit Nathan's body like a bed of daggers. A few feet below the surface, the current of the sea washed over him. He took off his jacket and let it float away behind him. With all his strength, he pushed his way down, wondering if his eyes were still open, hoping his hand would graze hers at every stroke.

His head throbbed. His chest ached with the impulse to breathe. *Where are you?* He repeated in his mind until he could no longer think. He needed air.

In mid-stroke he turned and began to swim in the direction he thought was up. Panic overtook him. The sea pressed against him, squeezed him. It seemed to drip acid into his nose and eyes as it crushed his ribcage and pressed his temples until he felt his head might explode. Nathan opened his mouth to scream and inhaled the burning water.

Then, it was over. All that was around him faded, the pain inside him dissolved, and Nathan floated off into darkness and defeat.

2
savior and the saved

The thought that he might be dead did not cross Nathan's mind. He knew he was alive the same way he knew it every moment of every day. He simply didn't question it. He didn't question his lungs when they inflated on their own accord, or the lightness of his head, which seemed to be floating weightlessly inside its own personal vacuum. His body felt impossibly large and lacking joints, and even this seemed entirely normal. Now that he could finally stretch, he could see how crammed he had been, living in such a small body for so many years.

How does anyone do it?

Nathan felt lucid, as though he had just woken from a long sleep. Whatever clarity he experienced, however, was fleeting. It faded from him as he became aware of his leaden limbs, glued heavily to the ground. Slowly, he registered the cold air on his physical arms and the throbbing in his physical shoulders. The lightness he felt slipped away and dissolved entirely into the familiar sound of nearby waves.

Nathan's eyelids flickered open. Squinting against the brightness, he tried to make sense of the blur of colors that dizzyingly danced in front of him. A hand, slender with long fingers, pulled away and came to rest on something blue. *Jeans*, he thought, *knees*.

His body jerked violently, and he was on his side, coughing up a mixture of sea water and vomit. His throat burned and his lips quivered with the bitterness in his mouth. When he looked up, he recognized her sitting next to him on her heels, her hands on her thighs, looking more like a porcelain statue than a person. He opened his mouth to speak, but the words scraped against his raw throat and got painfully stuck.

"What are you doing here?" she asked. Her plump lips, a shade too purple, parted to reveal a row of perfect white teeth.

Being this close to her was an entirely new experience. He no longer felt her pulling him toward her. The inconsolable longing he had felt for her was replaced by a general sense of ease. It was a homecoming of sorts, as though being near her meant everything would be alright.

"Why are you here?" she said impatiently. "Why are you following me?" The light of the early sun clung protectively to the wings of her long naturally-curled lashes and accented the green of her eyes.

"I…"

"How'd you know where to find me?"

"I…"

She got up abruptly.

"Wait," he said. "Please."

She stood looking at him, her clothes dripping. Nathan propped his knees underneath his body and shifting his weight onto the balls of his feet. Straightening his long limbs, he stood with an arched back on shaky legs. He was weaker than he had anticipated.

"Just —" he said. "Don't go."

He winced when his attempt at taking a step toward her resulted in a stabbing pain in his chest.

"Tell me why you're following me," she said more calmly.

"I wasn't—"

She seemed to be contemplating something. Despite her short small frame, the authority with which she stood in front of him, with her legs spread and her arms folded across her chest, made her frightening to approach. Nathan waited, unable to voice the pleas inside him. How could he tell her that he might not survive being separated from her? He wanted to beg her to not walk away from him. He didn't have the strength to chase after her. The more he searched for the words that could describe the agony he felt in her absence, the more the words scurried away into the dark recesses of his blank mind.

"You're in pain," she said.

Nathan nodded.

"Okay." Walking toward him, she wedged her tiny figure beneath his arm. A tingling aliveness entered him where her body made contact with his. Despite her small frame, she was able to support his weight without any visible strain. "You lead me to your home," she said, "and we talk along the way. Understood?"

Nathan nodded.

"Which way?"

Nathan hesitated. If he guided her to his car, how quickly would she realize that he was leading her to her own apartment? He considered leading to her to some other address in some other part of town. *But then what?* Eventually, he would have to find his way back to his car and risk running into her.

"Which way?" she repeated.

He looked down at her impassive face. Her eyes were a most unusual shade of dark green with splatters of yellow and navy blue. He bit his lip and formulated a plan. He would lead her to his car, he decided, and say that he lived a few apartments up the street. They were neighbors. That's why he was parked so close to her apartment. And he wasn't following her either. He was on his way home from a bar when he saw her jump off the pier and, well, he couldn't just do nothing, could he?

"That way." He pointed across the street.

"Begin with who you are," she said as they took their first step together. Nathan wasn't sure if it was the way she supported his body that made it so much easier for him to walk, or if it was the comforting heat of her touch. All he knew was that being close to her made sense. There was a rightness to it he could not explain.

"My name is Nathan Quinn Bradley," Nathan said.

"And why were you following me, Nathan Quinn Bradley?"

"I wasn't. I was just… walking home."

"Really?"

Nathan fell silent. Could she tell that he was lying? Had she seen him in his car outside of her apartment? Had she seen him behind her, hiding in the shadows of buildings and in strange doorways? He remembered Pic's advice from when they were kids, *If you want control over a conversation, you'll need to ask the questions,* and he decided to take control of the conversation.

"What's your name?" He asked.

"Isha."

"Were you trying to kill yourself, Isha?"

"No."

"What were you doing then?"

"Nothing that concerns you."

"You should be dead though, right?"

"I was fine," she said. "You're the one who should be dead."

"Did you save me?"

"What do you think?"

"I think yes, but I don't know how."

"You are leading me to my own apartment, aren't you?"

Nathan stopped in mid-step, his face hot with anger and shame.

"It's okay," she said. "I suspected that much from the beginning. I just need to know why."

"No," Nathan said, "I mean, yes. But I—"

I live on that street too, he wanted to say. *Just a few buildings away from your place.* How would he know which street she lives on if he saw her on the pier on his way home from a bar? How would he know that he lived only a few buildings away from her if he wasn't following her? Was he supposed to know where she lived in this scenario? Nathan's mind twisted as his stomach churned with anxiety.

"It's okay," she said. "I'm not upset."

"I've had a rough few months," Nathan said.

"You and me both."

"I don't normally do this. I mean, I'm many things, but I'm not a creep."

"I know."

"How do you know?"

"Because creeps don't sweat so much."

He smiled for the first time in weeks.

"But I still need to know why," she said.

They resumed their slow walk toward her apartment. She needed to know why. The problem was that even Nathan did not know his reason for following her. He couldn't understand it himself. It was simply the way she made him feel, like there was nowhere else in the world for him to be but in her vicinity.

"When I first saw you," Nathan began, "I don't know how to explain it."

"Try."

"*Before* I saw you," Nathan corrected himself, "I was crawling out of my skin. For months, I woke up with this rage, this pounding, like this thing inside me was trying to tear itself out. It was… *hell*. Just, pure *hell*." Nathan's voice trembled but he pushed on. "And then, one day I see you sitting on a park bench and suddenly, I just… I could breathe. You know. I could—" He took a long deep breath and sighed to demonstrate.

"Seeing me gave you relief?"

"Yes. For the first time since—" Nathan stopped abruptly, unsure how to continue.

"Since what?"

Since the nightmare began, he wanted to say, but instead, he just shook his head.

"Why didn't you talk to me?"

"You would have turned me away."

"I wouldn't have."

"Yes. You would have. And I wouldn't have survived it."

They both stopped asking questions. Controlling the conversation, Nathan decided, was too much work. It required too much effort. She, too, retreated into herself. They walked in silence the rest of the way, each in their own faraway world. She didn't return to him until they came to a stop in front of her apartment.

"Relief from what, Nathan?" she asked.

"I don't know."

"If you don't know, who does?"

Nathan shrugged. "Honestly…" he hesitated.

"Just spit it out."

"I think… it might… maybe it has something to do with my nightmare."

"What nightmare?" she asked with sudden interest.

"Fire everywhere. People dying. The end of the world."

The intensity with which she stared into him confirmed the connection between her and the horror of his last few months.

"How do you know it's the end of the world?" she asked.

"I just do. When I'm in it, I know nothing will survive."

"I think, you should grab whatever food and clothes you have from your car," she said. "Can you be ready in a few minutes?"

"Are we going somewhere?" he asked.

"Yes."

"And if I refuse?"

"It's important that you do what you feel is right. Do you want to think about it?"

"No," Nathan replied. "No need. I'll go."

3
not of this world

As they drove, the dusty flatness of the desert that persisted outside Nathan's window was accented only by shrubs and cacti, grayed with prolonged lack of moisture. At dusk, low dust-covered trees rose out of the barren landscape like deformed creatures crawling out of the earth.

"You should get some sleep," she said when the sun dropped completely out of view behind them.

"I'm fine."

"It wasn't a suggestion."

Nathan's aching mind longed for rest. Despite his bodily fatigue, he was determined to keep himself awake. But drowsiness was like a fog that gradually seeped into his mind and slowly consumed it. He knew he was fighting a losing battle. Sleep always won in the end. It chipped away at his will until he was so helpless that he *had to* yield. Without the aid of his precious caffeine pills and energy drinks, Nathan's will presented little resistance to the tireless invasion of sleep. Eventually, all he could do was to let go and allow it to take him.

————

Nathan opened his eyes, and it was all that was needed to snap him into full awareness. Isha's outstretched hand rested on his head, filling him with a strange emptiness where his nightmare should be. He jerked away from her, severing their physical connection.

"You were dreaming." He thought he heard her say, though looking at her, he could not imagine her porcelain face capable of moving enough to form the words.

"What the hell was that?" he demanded.

A haze of confusion filled Nathan's mind, as though she had reached into him and shrouded his entire mind from view. Hidden as it was, however, Nathan still felt the nightmare lurking in the recesses of his subconscious mind, just beyond his reach. Nathan pulled the back of his seat up, feeling violated.

"I thought you needed the rest," she explained.

"What did you do to me?"

"Nothing."

"Then why ... I can't — you can't just—"

"You're right. I should have let you be."

"How did you do that?"

"Do what?"

"My thoughts — they're... I can't think straight."

"All I did was put my hand on your head."

"You did something, some weird mind control—"

"I think maybe you need to watch less television. Just... relax, okay?"

Nathan sank back into his seat. As he steadied himself, he wondered if he had overreacted. What could she have done to him anyway?

The desolate road now snaked through a dense forest that pressed against them on either side. Tall firs shielded them from the rays of the rising sun, their sharp tips glistening golden against the blue sky. Nathan remembered driving through precisely this type of forest as a child — his face pressed against the cool glass of the backseat window. How his parents had loved to take him on lonely drives that were punctuated by strange towns, dirty bathrooms, and old men doused in the scent of tobacco.

The car slowed and turned onto a narrow, unmarked dirt track. Their speed, which Isha had locked at above eighty miles per hour for most of the drive, slowed to a crawl as she drove them into the belly of the forest. Soon, the double track became narrow and unforgiving and eventually tapered off until it was no more than a path, overgrown on all sides and barely wide enough for the passage of a car. Low branches hit the windshield and scraped the sides of the car. Nathan gripped the assist handle above his door in a feeble attempt at protecting himself against the violent bumps.

She parked the car in front of a stream, gushing with cool, clear water, and got out.

"We walk from here."

Standing in the damp forest, Nathan's stiff body ached as he stretched. She stood by the open trunk, contemplating something. Nathan wondered if he should be scared of her and was astounded by the utter calm he felt. Why was he not concerned about being here? For all he knew, he was following her to his unmarked grave.

She grabbed a small chest from the trunk of her car and placed it on a nearby branch, which creaked under its weight. "You'll need your stuff."

Nathan grabbed his backpack from the trunk, deciding that someone who was planning to murder him wouldn't have stopped on the way to buy snacks and water. He eyed the chest.

"Want me to carry that?"

"No. It's too heavy for you."

He hated this reverse psychology bullshit. Now, he would *have to* carry the chest. He knew it, and she knew it, and he knew that she knew it. What he could never understand was why women couldn't simply ask him for what they wanted. Why they had to jab at his manhood when all they had to say was, "Yes. I would love for you to carry this for me."

He bent down, grabbed the handle and pulled. The thing did not budge. Nathan bent his legs, dug in his heels, and pulled with all his strength, turning red with strain. For all his efforts, the chest slid slightly. He might as well have been trying to lift a car.

"Seriously," she said. "It's fine."

She bent down, and lifted the chest with an effortless elegance that would have anyone believe it was made of cardboard and filled with feathers. Nathan was perplexed.

"Don't fall behind." Her voice snapped him out of his shock. He ran after her.

"How'd you do that?"

"Do what?"

"What is it? Magnets?"

"What?"

"The trick with the box? Are there magnets in there? You press a button, it gets immovable. Then you press another button, and deactivate it. That sort of thing?"

"No. It's just a heavy box."

"You have a patent pending or something?" He still couldn't understand.

She glided through the forest at an uncomfortably fast pace which remained unaffected by the unevenness of the terrain. He tried to keep up with her, stumbling across rocks, stubbing his toes on protruding roots. Hanging branches seemed to appear out of nowhere in the dawn light. He tripped often, and struggled to keep himself from falling.

"Fine!" He yelled after her when she was barely in sight. "I won't ask you about your magic trick… Just slow down! You're gonna get me lost."

She stopped and turned to face him. He stopped also, catching his breath. She started moving again.

"No. Wait. Just… give it a sec."

She waited until he took a step toward her, then resumed her pace.

Despite the chill in the air, Nathan was dripping sweat by the time he spied asymmetrical, moss-covered mounds sprinkled across the dense forest. The unusual structures swelled out of the earth like massive bellies of pregnant, prone giants. She waited for him within view of the strange lumps.

"What is this place?" he asked as he came to a halt next to her.

"I guess, you'd call this a village."

"And those things —"

"Homes."

"You mean people live here?"

"My people, yes."

"So… you're from… *here*? Like some wild Amazonian jungle person?"

"I guess you could say that," she said and started walking toward her village.

She led him around one large, moss-covered mound, revealing a log cabin entrance on the backside of what looked like a heap of dirt. A set of weathered stairs led up to a shaded front porch and a hand-crafted wooden door.

"Try not to get too close," she said as she opened the door.

Nathan stayed close behind her. They entered a dimly lit entry that looked almost modern with its polished walls and smooth, domed ceiling. They walked down a wide corridor that ended in a bright, circular glass room that provided clear, unobstructed views of forest in every direction. Nathan wondered how he had not noticed this room from the outside.

Sunlight flooded the room. The dome was made of a thick textured glass that was patterned like a turtle's shell. The glass, which connected the ceiling to the floor, looked alive with fluid veins that resembled running water.

The chamber was furnished only by a large round table made of heavy wood and seven evenly spaced wooden chairs around it. An exquisitely crafted marble statue resembling a person was placed in one of the chairs across from the entry. The statue was dressed in a loose-fitting green and gold kurta. A wig of long raven black hair covered its head and fell behind it in one thick braid, giving it a human-like appearance.

"This is Veda." Isha gestured to the sculpture.

The resemblance between it and Isha was striking. The same oval face, high cheekbones, thick lips. The statue's nose was more pointy than Isha's, and it looked less like a woman, although it did not look like a man either. Nathan wondered if the ambiguity of the statue's gender was intentional and admired the workmanship that had gone into making the hairline look so natural.

Isha pulled out a chair next to the statue and sat down. "Please, take a seat."

Nathan sat down across from her.

"Veda agrees with me about you." Isha said. The way she spoke of the inanimate object as though it was a person, the urgency in her voice — it made Nathan think of Jessica, his six-year-old cousin, who had made it a habit of announcing to anyone listening what Mr. Teddy thought at any given moment.

"Veda says you must learn about us."

Pursing his lips, Nathan suppressed a smile at the memory of Jess saying, Mr. Teddy says your armpits smell funny. And I agree.

"You must understand the gravity of this." Isha leaned forward in her seat. "Great danger comes with knowing what you are not meant to know. On the other hand, duty comes with necessary knowledge. Do you understand?"

Nathan did not understand. He had barely listened to her words since he started comparing her to a child. He nodded.

Her face relaxed, and she leaned back in her chair. She looked at the statue and back at him.

"We are not of this world," she said as casually as naming her favorite band. "We are not of this planet."

Nathan tried to process. What did she just say?

"Here." She leaned in and cupped her hands together in the air at the center of the table. When her hands parted, a small orange sphere the size of a marble remained floating in midair.

"This is Favadan. Where we are from — our home." She flicked her hands apart, and the sphere expanded, gaining detail and dimension.

The virtual planet that floated in front of Nathan looked like it was on fire. A magnificent crimson sea, velvety and dark, covered the majority of its surface and bled into fields made of every shade of orange, yellow, and brown. Blotches of a superb royal blue were splattered haphazardly across much of the surface, and golden streaks ran through it like veins. The planet rotated on an invisible axis, and a thin layer of foamy gas, shimmery and white, shifted and twisted like a shell around the solid mass.

Humor drained out of Nathan, and he found himself on his feet, backing toward the entry of the room. As the orb grew and filled the space, continents of glittering lights took shape and peeked at him through layers of atmosphere.

Isha too was on her feet, walking around the growing world toward him. When she stood next to him, she pointed at a narrow valley next to a thin winding river. "This is where my family lives."

Nathan jerked backward, startled by her sudden presence next to him.

He stood with his back to the dark corridor through which they had arrived. The suspended planet vanished in a blink.

"I didn't mean to frighten you."

His instinct was to run. To turn and run down the length of the tunnel, run out the door, run through the woods until he reached its end. Run back to civilization and to *people.*

His heart raced. Fear gripped him and turned into panic. He heard her voice — a faint echo in the distance, telling him to sit down. His body trembled — his mind a shamble. What would she do to him? Why had she brought him here?

"Nathan." He heard his name somewhere far away. "Nathan, calm down."

Not of this planet. The words twisted inside him, wrapping themselves around images of her, uprooting memories, transforming them until they morphed into a new kind of reality. A reality that should not exist. He remembered her sitting motionless for so many hours in the park, never eating, never drinking, the texture of her flawless skin — the very flawlessness of her — the overwhelming sensation of her touch.

He looked at the statue, and recoiled when he saw its eyes were open, their irises as green as the forest. Nathan pressed himself against the wall, wishing he could sink into it and out of this trap. He shouldn't have come here. He had made a mistake. He shouldn't have come.

"Nathan!" Grabbing his face, she yanked his head toward her, forcing him to look at her. The heat of her touch gushed through him like a stream, and washed away the panic that had overtaken him. His breath steadied.

"You're okay," she said. "You're fine. Now, sit."

4
the many voices of veda

It was a long while before anyone spoke. Nathan sat across from Isha and the genderless statue with its eerie unblinking eyes. He was fully alert. His back erect and his breath shallow, he kept his palms firmly glued to the table in front of him in a feeble attempt at retaining some semblance of a grasp on the physical world. Whatever they planned for him, he wanted no part of it. This much his decades of media-driven alien studies had taught him.

"The statue," he said at last, "its eyes... they look... alive."

"Veda *is* alive."

"If you say so."

Even before Nathan finished speaking, the statue's stone exterior transformed into flesh, and Nathan was hit by an invisible wall that knocked the air out of him and locked him into an immobile state of momentary paralysis. Nathan was unable to move, to breathe, to blink, to think. Someone was talking to him, but Nathan could no longer hear. Isha snapped her head toward the figure, and in the next instant, Veda turned into stone once again. Nathan gasped, grasping at his throat.

"What… the hell…?" he wheezed, sucking in air.

"Veda… is not used to visitors."

"Is this some kind of threat? Is that a weapon?"

"What?"

"I swear, I won't say anything."

"Why—"

"People will be looking for me. They know where you live. My friends. They know who you are. They can find you."

"Nathan, calm down."

"Don't fucking tell me to calm down!" Nathan spat. "What the hell is that thing?"

Isha got up from her seat. There was a scolding rigidity to her expression. She sat down next to him and took his hands in hers. Nathan felt her warmth trickle into him until his entire body tingled with a weightlessness he now associated with her touch.

"Veda is greater than you can imagine," she said. "Even now, Veda protects you by hardening. Don't let go."

This time, Nathan witnessed Veda's skin transform. *It softens,* he thought, *the skin, it hardens and it softens.*

He understood that it was her touch that protected him against Veda's snaking current, which Nathan was now able to see as fleeting scribbles of light reaching outward from the center of Veda's chest. The strands seemed to move independently from one another — each at its own pace and on its own trajectory. When they entered him, Nathan felt their curious inquisition as they explored his physical make up. Nathan reached his free hand above his head and watched it become translucent as it passed through a thin spiral of indigo light.

Veda leaned in, and the strands of light became somehow brighter, somehow more alive. "Isha thinks you were chosen,"

Veda said in a voice that was neither male nor female. "But the question is, does being chosen mean being able?"

"Why would Thaia send one who is not able?" Isha interjected.

No one sent me. Nathan wanted to say, but instead all he could do was stare dumbly into the dizzying tangle of light.

"A planet's choice speaks of potential, not of will," said Veda.

"His will must be present if he found me," Isha said.

"That was Thaia's will. His is yet to be tested."

Thaia. He had heard this name before.

"And the device?" Veda asked.

There's been a mistake, Nathan yelled at them in his mind and tried to remember how to translate his thoughts into words.

The strands seemed to respond to Veda's most minute movements. If Veda as so much as looked in a direction, they followed. When Veda stood up, they reached to the corner of the room before Veda began to move toward it. Once there, Veda grabbed the impossibly heavy chest that Isha had brought in the trunk of her car. The ease with which Veda lifted it with one hand onto the table without the slightest sign of strain made Nathan cringe.

Nathan had not noticed how beautiful the chest was. It was carved out of one single trunk of a tree with no visible seams. Its heavy, hand-carved lid was locked down with a leather belt. He leaned in to inspect the intricate carvings covering its every surface. Figures of men and beasts trapped in a never-ending battle protruded out of the wood as though they were trying to escape.

Veda returned to the seat across from him and hardened; the endless swirls that had occupied the room a moment ago were sucked back in. Nathan's body felt leaden in the absence of the energy that he now realized had made him not just light-headed, but somehow less heavy. As though he'd been floating and was abruptly dropped to the ground. The room, too, looked more drab and less alive.

Isha loosened the belt that passed underneath the intricately carved bronze handle, which featured two nude female figures — one with a serpent's tail instead of legs, the other with the wings of an eagle, each bent at the waist and reaching toward the other. The serpent woman twisted as her arms reached toward the sky to grasp the tips of the other's eagle wings. The eagle woman arched her back in her struggle to break loose. Nathan remembered the sculpting class he once signed up for on a whim. Like almost everything else he had done in college, he stopped attending class as soon as it became too difficult and his attention waned.

Nathan could not understand how the sculptor of this handle had worked such detail into the faces. How had he gone through the process of creating multiple positive and negative molds, and still ended up with perfectly strained muscles, minuscule veins on perfectly defined feathers, dilated irises, and a snake tail complete with scales?

Isha turned the chest so it would open toward him. "You ready?"

"Ready for what?"

She lifted the heavy lid, revealing an ordinary-looking rock resting on a silken bed.

"All this for a rock?" he asked, somewhat perplexed.

"What do you see?"

"I see a rock," he repeated. "What am I supposed to see?"

"What color is it?"

"Black. Dark green in parts."

"Is it glowing?"

"Glowing?"

"Look closely," she urged.

He looked, even though he did not understand what he was looking for.

Then, he saw. The faintest glimmer, almost too subtle to detect, as though a tiny dot of light was trapped inside the stone.

"You see them," she said almost to herself. "You really see them."

"I don't know what I'm seeing." He leaned in to get a better look. "Is it blinking?"

The light inside the rock seemed to pulsate and became almost imperceptibly brighter the more he stared at it. Nathan cocked his head and brought his ear closer to it. He could almost hear a faint buzz like the subtle hum of an air conditioner emanating from it.

"You hear them too," she whispered. "Remarkable."

"What am I hearing?" he whispered back.

"You might be the first human to actually see and hear them. No. You are the first human. *Ever.*"

Nathan looked up at her. The whole thing felt like a joke — a bad prank. In her face, he saw genuine awe, and yet what formed inside him was a feeling of dread. He could sense the formation of yet another set of impossible expectations that he would not be able to live up to.

When Nathan reached toward the rock, Isha was by his side instantly, pulling his hand away from it.

"Don't," she said. "I have to show you something." She closed the lid of the chest, and buckled the belt to secure it. "Come."

Standing at the doorway, Nathan felt he was seeing the room for the first time. The domed ceiling looked like the inside of a waterfall with wavy patterns flowing effortlessly down the glass walls. The perforations turned into intertwining roots when they reached the dark gray of the ground. The wavy squiggles smoothened into lines that came together at a single point in the center of the room, directly underneath the heavy table.

"Everything okay?" Isha asked.

"This is a ship," Nathan gave voice to a new realization that had started forming inside him even before he had consciously become aware of it.

"What makes you say that?"

"The hatch under the table where all those lines meet," he said. "I think, maybe, that's where the captain's chair used to be?"

"You're right." Isha smiled. "This is the control chamber of our ship. There was once a chair in the center of this room where Veda sat. But that was a long time ago."

"How long?"

Isha opened her mouth to speak but her expression quickly shifted into one of concern.

"Was I not supposed to know this?" Nathan asked.

"No…" Her eyes darted past him and came to rest on Veda's hardened body.

"I didn't mean to—" he began.

"Don't let go," she interrupted.

She draped herself around him like a cloak just as thousands of strands of Veda's energy whipped past them with such intensity that Nathan could barely keep from fainting. Nathan didn't hear the click of the front door, but he fully felt the relief of Veda's energy being sucked out of the room.

For a moment, he was confused to see Veda standing in the forest beyond the glass barrier. He did not need to hear what Veda was saying to know that something was not right. Despite the unusual events of the day, he was still unprepared for the sight he encountered when he followed Veda's eye line.

Six strange figures stood scattered among the trees, facing Veda. Their authority was undeniable.

Isha's arm darted up into the air. Her hand created a series of swift looping motions in front of her and the room, which had once been the control chamber of a spaceship, filled with the sounds of the forest.

"This human is only of concern to the Favadani," Veda was saying.

"It is of concern to us all!" The response came from a short hefty woman. Nathan recoiled as she straightened herself to her full height, which couldn't have been more than four feet. Underneath her loose-fitting robe, six unnaturally bent arms opened like the petals of a repulsive flower.

"What the hell?" Nathan said.

"Ma'ona," Isha responded. "She's a Magirian."

"Do you forget our pact?" Ma'ona's percussive way of speaking reminded Nathan of the bark of a dog.

"We forget nothing!" Veda's voice split into a dozen distinct voices, speaking in unison.

"Tell us, Veda, why is he here?" asked a tall black man with eyes as yellow as the sun.

"You will know in time," said Veda's many voices. "We assure you my friends, he is of no threat to us."

Even Nathan understood that the emphasis Veda placed on us was significant. It was the way Veda's voices merged into one as Veda spoke the word, percussive and sharp. Yet, whatever reassurance this provided, it was short-lived. When Ma'ona spoke again, her voice was a high-pitched hiss that almost brought Nathan to his knees.

"We shall join hands and learn your intentions." The sound of her shrill voice set flight to a flock of birds perched atop surrounding trees.

"Yes," the yellow-eyed black man's voice boomed. "We shall join hands."

"It's the only way," echoed a hunched gray-haired man.

"Is that good?" Nathan asked.

"Probably not," Isha responded.

"And you?" Veda's attention turned toward a ghost-like albino with white hair and deep sunken gray eyes. "What say you?"

A hush fell over them as they waited for the ghost-man to speak. A scrawny red-headed woman standing next to the ghost-man shifted from one foot to another, crossing her long arms in front of her chest.

It seemed strange to Nathan that none of the figures had acknowledged him and Isha standing only a few feet away, even if they were separated by a pane of glass.

"You don't have to be so stiff," Isha said as though in response to his unspoken question. "They can't see us." She pulled him directly to the edge of the glass and began to wave. "See?"

"What are you doing?" Nathan's instinct was to retreat. To hide under the table or behind a wall.

"It's not glass. They can't see us."

"I say, we returned to this site six hundred Thaian years ago," said the ghost-man.

"Here." Isha moved her hands into a series of gestures that seemed to grab and expand the image of the speaking man. What filled the window directly in front of them was a close up of the man's face, each feature as big as Nathan's body. From this proximity, Nathan could almost feel the metallic texture of the ghost-man's skin. He could easily see the swirling liquid inside his eyes and the slightly elongated shape of his irises.

"And all this time," the albino continued, "not a single human has been invited into our Viliov. If the Elder of Elders chooses to change this now, there must be good reason. You are the wisest among us, Veda, and the most complete. You would not jeopardize the Awakening when we are so close to its achievement."

"Who is that?" Nathan wanted to know.

"That's Thoma. The Elder Representative of Pari Pa'ari."

"I don't know why, but I don't trust that guy."

She smiled. "Come," she said and led him into the hallway.

A swift motion of her hand triggered a door in the ground, and the floor began to retreat, revealing an underground passageway that led into complete darkness.

"Go down the stairs and wait for me," she said. "I'll be there in a few minutes."

"What's down there?" Nathan asked.

"Something you need to see. Just, don't touch anything."

"What about…"

"The danger has passed. I will be down soon."

She returned to the control deck, leaving Nathan alone in the hallway. Looking into the cavity in the ground, he could only make out the first few steps. Beyond that was the black of the unknown. Nathan thought about following her and asking for a flashlight.

The door at the end of the hallway clicked open and he felt the rush of Veda's energy.

Too late, Nathan thought. Veda's chaotic current began to fill him. Closing his eyes, Nathan noticed his heartbeat was irregular and fast.

"This is it," he whispered to himself, though he didn't know what it was, and stepped into the darkness.

5

into the dark

The stairs were a bit too high and a bit too wide, as though they were built for people slightly larger than Nathan. He allowed his hand to glide along the glossy wall to his left, partially for stability and partially because the buttery sensation beneath his fingertips felt comforting. Every time he took a new step, a floor light came on next to his foot against the wall, which illuminated his current placement and shed just enough light downward to let him know he had not yet reached the bottom. He had climbed far enough down that he experienced Veda's energy as faint spells of lightheadedness that passed through him only sporadically.

There was a musky smell that became stronger as Nathan descended — a stale earthiness that made him think of a crypt. A thin film of dewy sweat accumulated on his upper lip and brows. With one hand on the wall, he fixed his gaze onto the ground, wishing he could see beyond the two or three stairs that were illuminated in front of him.

He stopped to look up the long staircase that stretched out behind him, its half-lit steps floating in a sea of black. The hatch at the top was a small far-away rectangle through which a faint light entered the chamber.

Where is she? he wondered as took another step. A light flickered on next to his foot, and revealed a small area of the white floor beyond the staircase. At last, he had reached the bottom. Nathan wondered if this sterile room with its thirty-foot velvety wall and smooth white steps was part of the original ship. Leaning slightly into the wall for reassurance, he glanced once more to the hatch in the ceiling before stepping off the stairs onto the ground.

A row of floodlights came to life along the edge of the wall and startled him. Their brightness was an assault, and Nathan had to shield his eyes with the heels of his hands until his vision adjusted.

The room he found himself in was much larger than he had anticipated. A banquet hall of sorts with too high of a ceiling. It was divided into two distinct parts. He stood inside an angular room covered entirely with a brilliant white surface that seemed to swallow the shadows that fell on it. The effect was disorienting — an endless white void that, if he squinted just a tiny bit, seemed to stretch out into eternity.

Thankfully, at least in one direction, there was reprieve from this unnerving sea of nothing. Ten yards in front of him expanded a magnificent domed cave with walls and a ceiling made of tightly packed dirt, held together by an intricate scribble of intertwining roots. The floor lights continued along the entire space, creating cohesion between the sterile white box and the organic cave.

In the center of the cave, a few feet from its walls, a massive eggshell-colored circular floor glistened like the surface of a lake during sunrise. As Nathan walked toward it, the floor revealed hundreds of perfectly round holes about three feet in diameter, which were punched into its surface in a precise pattern of rings. A distance of about two feet separated each hole from its nearest neighbors.

Standing at the edge of the shimmering floor, Nathan's eyes fixed on the nearest hole, which was filled with a smooth dark-green substance. The material that filled it did look very much like a rock, he decided, but then again, there was something non rock-like about it. Maybe it was too smooth to be a rock, or even too solid, if that was possible. If he hadn't learned about the existence of aliens just moments ago, and if he didn't know that he was now standing inside what used to be a spaceship, there would have been no question in Nathan's mind that what he was now looking at was nothing more than a hole in the ground inlayed with an ordinary rock. But everything had changed. Now, everything was suspect.

Kneeling, he lowered his hand and placed his fingers gingerly onto the smooth floor. Aside from the way it looked, he felt no difference between this surface and the wall he had grazed on his way down. He stretched his arm across it to the hole closest to him. Something — perhaps whatever the substance was that filled it — resisted his hand in a way that made him think of the push between two magnets. He pressed down with more force and felt the intensity of the invisible barrier increase.

What's in there? he thought as he stood up.

Nathan took a step onto the polished floor, which seemed to create a kind of pathway through the pattern of holes. Carefully testing his weight, he walked onto it. He could see no seams, no grout lines or blemishes in the surface, no chips at the edges of the holes. Slowly, he made his way to the center, and noticed the punched out circle that marked the mid-point was larger than the rest. The material that filled it was a lighter shade of green, and unlike the others, it did not look solid. A thick liquid swirled inside this hole like green lava.

Curious whether it would react the same way, he moved his foot over it and gently pressed down. The resistance he encountered was strong as though there was an invisible solid dome covering the hole.

"Hey! Don't do that!" Isha's voice cut through the silence of the room and startled him.

With one foot in the air, Nathan wobbled for a moment before he lost his balance and fell backwards. When he expected to find the ground, he was caught by what felt like a large rubber ball, and was bounced upward in the opposite direction. He flew forward, headfirst, into one of the dark pools. His face hit another invisible barrier, which felt like a punch to the jaw. The unseen fields that protected the circles caught him in mid-air, and bounced him up and away. Several similar hits and bounces later, he came to rest on his back on the hard ground that separated them, his body throbbing.

Isha's face slid into view.

"This is your fault," he groaned.

"I told you not to do that."

"You startled me."

"Are you okay?"

"Do I look okay?" He collected himself into a seated position. "What are these things?"

"Can you stand?"

"I think so, why?"

Gesturing him to follow, Isha guided him to one of the dark pools a few rows away. The larger hole that marked the center was now between them and the staircase.

"Tell me what you see," she said, her eyes cast downward.

Nathan's eyes darted from the ground to her face and back down.

"A hole in the ground," he said.

"What's in it?"

"Some kind of a rock maybe."

She knelt. He did the same.

"How about now?" she moved her hand over the hole. Nathan expected her hand to stop a foot above its surface like his had, but her hand encountered no resistance. When it was a few inches from the material that filled it, the thing lost its solidity, and began to stir. Nathan knit his brows as he tried to understand what he was seeing.

"What do you see now?"

"It... it's moving."

The mass inside the hole spiraled upward toward Isha's hand. When she pulled away, the substance became elastic and reached for her fingers. She lowered her hand and the rubbery substance wrapped itself around it, becoming more gelatinous in the process. Suddenly, her hand was glowing as though it was covered with something radioactive, or at least what Nathan imagined radioactive material to look like.

"It's so *bright*!" he said. She snapped her head towards him.

"Bright?"

"Yes. Like it's on fire. Well, a greenish fire, you know, if fire was green."

She laughed. "You can see their light?"

"*Their* light?"

"Tell me this," she said, "what do you see there?" she nodded toward the hole next to them.

"I've told you. A hole with a rock in it."

"It doesn't glow?"

"No."

"But when you look at my hand, you see light?"

"Yes."

The gel separated from her and dripped back into the pool, darkening and becoming solid.

"Moli-orath," she explained. "That's our word for them. Roughly translated it means *mechanics*. We're inside the recovery chamber of what was once our ship. It's one of the few rooms we kept before dismantling it. Each of us has a recovery pod. This one's mine. The big one in the middle belongs to Veda."

"Each one of these belongs to an alien like you?"

"Yes."

Looking at all the circles surrounding them, Nathan felt the room shrinking. There must have been over a hundred of them.

Isha lowered her hand into her pod and swirled it around. The gel danced around her touch, moving up and down her wrist, dodging her approaching hand, jumping over and through her fingers, but never quite touching her.

"Every pod is filled with billions of them," she continued. "They're too small for you to see. But to us, each Moli-orath emanates light and sound."

"What are they?"

"They're part machine, part living. They do what we need them to do. On my planet, we use them for many different tasks, from building and fixing things to growing crops. They're very useful as long as you can program them. *These*," she gestured to the room, "have been programmed with a very specialized task. When we get hurt or when we need to change our bodies, we enter our pods. The Moli-orath take our bodies apart, they absorb the damaged cells and use the rest to remake our form."

"They take you apart? As in take you *apart*?"

"Yes," she said. "Each pod is linked to one being. *These*," she lifted a handful of glowing gel towards Nathan, "have as many of my cells inside of them as I have in this physical form."

"Everyone on your planet can do this?" he asked. "So, no one can ever die?"

"Not exactly," Isha said. "It takes tremendous mental focus to control the Moli-orath, especially those designed for recovery. For instance, if I lost a limb or got a nasty gash I need them to fix, I'll submerge in my pod, and I ask them to remake the damaged area. But if I am unable to control them, they might take me apart completely. You have to remember that they are part living. If my will is weak or unclear, they will take the action their collective mind considers to be right."

"So, you have to override their mind?"

"Yes. Once they take me apart completely, the only thing that remains of me is my consciousness, dispersed between billions of organisms, each with its own mind. It feels like I am split among billions of spaces. In that state, my will has to be singular. If I am unable to focus, I may remain in that state forever."

"So, you, what, just cease to exist?"

"No. I still exist. But my consciousness, the part that makes me who I am will, with time, become part of the collective will of the Moli-orath that ingested me."

"Damn."

"You see how my mechanics react to me?"

Nathan nodded.

"They move toward me when I reach for them. They sense me. I could will them to take apart my hand and put it together backwards. It would be done." She paused. "The device you were looking at earlier," she said. "It is filled with Moli-orath."

"You mean the rock?"

"Yes. It's filled with them. I can see them. I can hear them. But they don't respond to me. They don't respond to Veda either. But…" Isha pulled her hand out of the pod and placed it on Nathan's. She looked into his eyes when she spoke. "When you reached for it, they moved toward you."

Nathan leaned away from her, taking back his hand. "What are you saying?"

"Those Moli-orath responded to you," she said.

"What does that mean?"

"That means you may be able to control them."

"Why would I want to? After what you just—"

"Your nightmare," she broke in. "What if it has something to do with that device?"

"I don't follow."

"Is it a coincidence that you started dreaming about the end of the world around the same time I found that device? I think Thaia is asking for your help."

There was that name again.

"Listen," he said, "I don't know who this Thaia person is."

"Thaia is not a person," Isha said. "Thaia is what we call this planet. You call her *Earth*. You felt compelled to follow me. What if it was Thaia pushing you toward me?"

"How does that even make sense?"

"How do turtles know where to lay their eggs? How do plants know to grow on certain trees for nourishment? Every being on this planet knows what to do to survive. To evolve. How?"

"That's… different."

"You are a part of Thaia, Nathan. She lives inside you. No matter how independent you think you are, every day her will influences you in ways your conscious mind cannot comprehend."

"I know what I felt. It was you pulling me."

"Maybe," said Isha. "But I wasn't tugging at *you*. I asked Thaia for help, because I didn't know what else to do. And in response, she sent you."

The possibility that Earth was responsible for his stalking this girl both disturbed and relieved him. If he accepted the notion that it was something other than his own will that had compelled him to follow her around, could he then stop feeling shame for his actions? Actions he would have categorized as a perversion in another person.

What of my free will? He wondered. *Am I not responsible for my own decisions? Or for the thoughts in my own head?*

"What you're saying is impossible," he said. "From the point of view of both common sense and science."

"Your planet is a fully conscious being," Isha informed him. "She thinks. She remembers. She creates. She lives. She is in constant communication with all of her offspring."

"If that's the case," Nathan said doubtfully, "why doesn't she just tell me what to do?"

"She did, and now you're here."

"You know what I mean. Why doesn't she communicate more clearly?"

"Your species is still very young. Her messages, they're like poems read to an infant. They're complete, but to the child they don't quite make sense."

"I'm the child in this example?"

"You, as in humans, yes." Isha got up. "Come on," she said. "There is much we must do."

At the base of the stairs, Nathan stood with his hand on the wall and his head spinning with an endless stream of questions

— too many for him to be able to focus on at once. The only thought he was able to vocalize was, "I don't understand."

"What part of it don't you understand?"

"Why am I here?" he answered.

"You want the truth?"

"Yes."

"The truth is, I don't know yet."

"Can I go home?"

"Do you want to go home?"

Nathan did not want to return home. He did not want to stay either. In a perfect world, the ground would open up and swallow him whole, sparing him the decision.

"No," he said reluctantly.

"Okay." She nodded and ascended the stairs.

6
a gift from veda

On his way up the stairs, Nathan glanced down at the strange cave-like chamber and the large circular floor with its rings of pods, each representing an alien from Isha's planet. He suddenly remembered the exact moment he had stopped believing in all things magical. God, aliens, fairies, Santa — they had all walked out of his life in unison the day of the car crash that took his cousin.

Lizzy. He thought as he strained to remember her face.

They were both turning six, and instead of celebrating together as they had all their lives, Nathan lay sick in bed, furious that they had decided to go to Disneyland without him. Lizzy could do anything she wanted for her birthday, true, but spending the day with Mickey and Pluto, getting dizzy on rides, and eating too much sugar had been his idea. She should have done something else. It was unfair.

The injustice Nathan felt was not because they had left him behind. Even then he understood that going to a theme park with strep throat was the opposite of what he needed to do. The truth was, he didn't want her to have a birthday without him.

And so, without the ability to understand or express his feelings, he resorted to crying. He cried because he couldn't swallow anything without a scraping pain in his throat. He cried because despite spending all day in bed for weeks, he was still sick. He cried because his head hurt all the time, and because he was not allowed to play with his friends. And then he cried because Lizzy and her friends went to his favorite place on earth without him, even though it was all *his* idea. And when she never came back, he cried because her death was all his fault.

Nathan didn't know what to do with this new information about the existence of aliens. He didn't know what to do with the memory of a dead cousin either. When Isha took his hand in preparation of their emergence into the hallway, he squeezed it gently, more as a comfort to himself than anything else.

The opening in the ground closed behind them, leaving no indication that a basement existed beneath it. Veda stood in the doorway of the control chamber, one long-fingered hand cupped into the other. The snaking arms of Veda's energy passed through Nathan and filled him with electricity and hope.

"Unfortunately," Veda said in a singular, genderless voice, "you cannot stay here. May I have your hand please."

"My hand?" Nathan looked to Isha for a translation as though Veda had spoken in a language he did not understand.

Isha raised her free hand and held it open-palmed in front of her. Nathan did the same with his free hand. She nodded once. "Now hold still," she said as Veda lowered an index finger onto his palm.

Though Veda's touch was light, it sent intense waves of heat into his entire body. The invisible circle that Veda traced onto the palm of his hand burned as though it was traced with fire. Nathan yanked his hand away. "What the hell?"

"A gift," Veda responded with many voices speaking in unison.

"What the hell kind of gift is that?" Nathan clutched his hand to his belly. He tried to blow into his palm, but the air intensified the pain. "God dammit!"

"Let me." With one quick motion, Isha grabbed his wrist in one hand and pressed the palm of her other hand into his. The fire that had been contained inside his palm shot into Nathan's arm. He struggled to free himself from her, but it wasn't until the heat had dissolved into him completely that she loosened her grip. Without releasing his wrist, she removed her hand from his, revealing a charcoal gray circle in the center of his hand.

"What is this?" Nathan demanded.

Isha waited for Veda to harden before she let him yank his hand out of hers. Nathan spat into his palm and tried to rub away the mark first with his thumb and then with his shirt. "What have you done to me?" He demanded of the hardened statue.

"It will help you control the Moli-orath," Isha said.

"Who said I want to control those things?"

"You'll need all the help you can get."

"I said I'm not doing that!"

"Nathan," she began but stopped. The way she looked at him, as though he had already failed, made him feel entirely helpless. Veda's eyes, too, looked disappointed as they stared at him through slit-like cutouts in an impassive hardened face.

Nathan saw his life as a literal chain that threatened to crush him under its unbearable weight. Every ring an event outside of his control, connected to other rings of unmet expectations, disappointed glares, shame, and judgement. Nathan wore his failings as armor. Except this armor was useless in battle, because it rendered him paralyzed and threatened to bury him alive.

"Do you really want to turn your back on this?" Isha asked. "Knowing what you know?"

"What do I know exactly?" He spat. "Nothing!"

"Nothing at all?"

Why was this happening to him? Nathan's face burned with the accusation of her question. Why did these things always happen to him? Why couldn't people just leave him alone and stop telling him what he should or shouldn't do? In this moment, he was certain of only one thing: he felt more confused, more lost, and more violated than was normal even for him.

"What I know is that you're not telling me everything," he said.

"What do you want to know?"

"Why me?"

"I don't know."

"What happens if I walk away?"

"What do you think happens?"

Nathan shrugged. Inside him flashed images of his nightmare. A world engulfed by fire and pain, and then by an endless permanent nothingness. He closed his eyes and swallowed the lump in his throat. How could he walk away?

"How will this thing help me?" Nathan held up his marked palm once he collected himself.

"It will help you focus your energy," Isha said. "You'll still have to do the bulk of the work yourself, but it's something."

"Are we ready?" A voice came from behind and took Nathan by surprise. He turned toward it.

A man stood in the corridor, his back to the entry. He was lit only by the faint light that came from the control chamber on the opposite end of the hallway. Nathan felt annoyed at the sight of an unannounced stranger at such proximity.

"It's okay," Isha said. "This is Kiras. He is a friend."

"Let's go," Kiras said.

Nathan had the strange feeling that an entire conversation took place in the silent look that Kiras exchanged with Isha. He suppressed the irritation of being excluded from it.

"He will be ready when the time comes," Isha said in a tone that claimed having the last word.

She exchanged one final glance with the hardened statue of Veda before walking out with Nathan in tow.

Outside, dusk had fallen. Dark clouds had set upon the forest, giving it an ominous heaviness. Nathan felt a knot growing inside his stomach. This was the same knot he had felt the morning of Lizzy's birthday trip. The same knot he felt before getting a rejection letter from his top choice for music school. The same knot that appeared moments before he stood steps away from Jillian Morena and made himself the laughing stock of the entire school for the rest of the year by asking her out on a date.

Nathan knew this knot well. He had spent the entirety of his life trying to avoid it. This knot, Nathan knew, was a warning. It warned him against trying anything new, against dreaming, against wanting more than the misery he deserved. It told him that he was destined to fail, that unhappiness was his way of life, and that something important, something he had allowed himself to want, would go terribly wrong.

7

the deer

"You okay?" Isha asked as she glided effortlessly through the dense forest. Periodically, Nathan spied Kiras's stiff frame through the trees outpacing them and could not help feeling that there was a twinge of condescension in the way she deliberately kept a slow pace. He wished she would march ahead and allow him to lose himself in the tangles of the twisting mass that had been growing inside his gut.

"I know it's a lot to take in," she said.

"Yeah." Nathan sped up to an uncomfortable pace which she matched with no strain. He felt restrained by her presence. He suddenly had the urge to push her into a ditch somewhere and flee. He recognized the absurdity of the impulse and felt angry at his own idiocy that had dragged him into this mess. He was angry at her, too. At her very existence, which invalidated so much of what he believed, so much of what he had suffered. A world in which aliens existed and Lizzy still died at the age of five did not make sense. He was angry because aliens were real and they let children die. He was angry because if aliens were real, then so might be God and Santa and unicorns, and they had all turned their backs on the suffering he had endured his entire life.

"If you have questions—"

"I don't." Nathan stopped walking. "I don't want to know anything. I don't want to know about you. I don't want to know about your planet. About your people. About how fucking amazing you are. How you've come to save us from ourselves. I don't want to know it."

Nathan felt his blood boiling. She reached to touch him, and he took a step back.

"Don't touch me," he said.

"Nathan, what's happening right now?"

"I'm coming to my senses, that's what's happening. I want you to leave me alone."

"You don't mean that."

"I absolutely mean that. I mean it three hundred percent. I want you to take me back to my car and leave me the fuck alone."

"Do you know what's at stake?"

"Not my problem."

They stared a long time into each other's faces. Nathan's face was on fire. He could barely see through the blur of his anger.

"Okay," she said at last. "We'll take you home."

It was in the relief of those words that Nathan realized he'd been holding his breath. They walked the next hour in silence. With every step he took, the anger he had felt dripped out of him. By the time they reached the car, Nathan was no longer certain he wanted to go home. In fact, he knew he didn't.

"Were all those buildings once spaceships?" He asked when he spied the glint of the car's blue bumper through the trees.

"Yes," she said.

"So that's a landing site then?"

"Yes."

Nathan glanced at her and wondered how he might win her back.

"So, what do you call that place?" he asked.

"Viliov," she answered, without looking his way. "Camp of Elders."

"Elders? Is Veda an Elder?"

"Yes."

"And what does that mean?"

"The Elder of a race," she answered in a disinterested monotone, "is the most evolved."

"So, Veda is more evolved than you?"

"Yes."

"How?"

"Veda is all things at once," she said. "The physical manifestation of my planet."

"What does that mean?"

"A being with an infinite mind and a memory that spans all of life."

"How?"

"How what?"

"Well…" Nathan said. What was he trying to ask? He decided to shelf the topic for the time being in favor of a more pressing question.

"Back at the cabin, the spaceship, whatever," he began, "you and Kiras, you were talking without words, weren't you?"

"Yes."

"How did you do that? I mean, is it telepathy?"

"No."

"What then?"

"Communication on awakened planets is different," she said. Then looking directly at him, she added, "but you don't care about these things."

Nathan felt the sting of her words. "Just making conversation," he said.

They walked in silence for another minute before he asked, "Are you talking to him now?"

"Yes," she answered.

Nathan's legs ached when they finally reached the car. In the driver seat, Kiras's hardened body sat like a marble figurine. Even though his face remained impassive, there was an air of impatience about him.

As Kiras bounced the car out of the forest in reverse, Nathan felt the weight of fatigue settle on him. It had been a long day, he decided. It had been a long several days and a long month and a long decade. As his eyelids grew heavy, something inside him released, and Nathan felt he did want to let go, even if he didn't know how. He wanted to let go of the undercurrent of depression that colored every moment of his daily life. And of the stabbing pain in his chest when he witnessed the joy of others. He wanted to let go of the numbness that shrouded him and the haze that blurred his vision even in the clearest of days. If aliens from another planet were possible and if magic was real and if God and Santa and unicorns or whatever could also exist, he wanted to be swept up by it all. Perhaps one day, he might even know what it feels like to be happy.

The thought was a long shot, an impossibility. It was like saying one day he might live on the moon, grow wings out of his spine or become the president. It was a fairy tale, a romantic comedy, an unfulfillable promise made by a con man. But then again, aliens had been impossible one short day ago, and here he was in a car with two of them.

Even as he longed for it, Nathan suppressed the bubbles of

hope that drifted up from the depth of his soul. *What's the point?* he thought, *I'll let everyone down, and then, I'll have to kill myself for real.* He melted into the seat, into the shame of what he was, into the voice that lived to remind him of his unquestionable smallness.

Please, he pleaded, *no nightmare.* It was his last conscious thought before sleep took him.

———————

Nathan was yanked out of his nightmare with the loud thump of an explosion, and for a moment, he didn't know if the sound belonged to the real world or to that of his dream. It was still the middle of the night, and the moonless sky was sprinkled with more stars than Nathan had ever seen. He pressed his temple against the cool glass of the window and stared at the glistening lights, breathing deeply.

In the passenger seat, Isha's hardened body reminded Nathan of the days he had spent staring at her from a distance. She looked so *alien* in this state — so incredibly not human. How had he not noticed this before?

Nathan leaned to his right to get a better look at Kiras who sat in the driver's seat in front of him, hardened, as he drove at an alarming speed through the narrow, windy road that snaked through the dark forest. Tiny, nearly imperceptible movements that controlled the steering wheel were the only indications that he was even alive. He was larger than Isha both by physical stature and by the authority that his sharp jaw line and short crew cut demanded.

When Nathan looked back at Isha, she was staring at him.

"You said Earth is awake?" he asked.

"No. I said she's alive."

"What's the difference?"

"All planets are alive, but it takes time and effort for them to awaken."

"Right," he said turning his attention to the blackened forest outside his window. "Thanks for clarifying."

"I thought you didn't want to know any of this," she said.

"I don't."

Nathan fixed his eyes on the thin layer of translucent fog that was shrouding the window. In his periphery, she continued to stare at him.

"Thaia has been conscious for billions of years," she said after a long while, "without being able to communicate with anyone outside of herself. So, she created and continues to create life." He turned to look at her. The new softness in her eyes, the subtle smile as she spoke — they were small changes, but provided him comfort. "At first," she went on in the patient tone of a middle school teacher, "life is simple: single cell organisms, plants, insects. Little by little life becomes more complex, until eventually, she creates a being that is self-aware and may, in time, be able to understand her mind. This is the process on all planets that are alive."

"So, Earth created humans."

"Yes, humans. And then one day, these humans will have a chance to sync with her. And when the minds of all the humans have perfectly synced with the mind of Thaia, she is said to be awake."

"And what happens to me?"

"You live happily ever after."

"No. I mean. What happens to me, Nathan, this person that I am."

"Your individual desire is supplemented with the will of

Thaia."

"Like a hive."

"No. Not a hive. You won't lose your individual identity. You'll still have your own thoughts and desires. Your own innate talents. But many of the things you thought were important won't be any more, because you will also know that you are one part of a much larger whole. Violence, jealousy, resentment, fear — so many human emotions that you've developed for survival — won't make any sense when you realize the creatures around you are a part of you."

"And then we live happily ever after as a hive that's not a hive," he said.

"Something like that."

"So, when's all this supposed to go down?"

"We'll see. Most planets awaken eventually."

Most, Nathan thought, sensing the sudden hesitation in Isha's voice.

"Most?" he repeated.

She turned away from him and looked at the road ahead. Nathan sensed a new kind of distance between them. A thick, palpable divide stemming from the millions of lightyears that separated each of their origins. He felt like she was no longer there with him, then. As though it was only the idea of her that sat in the car with him, and the real her was now somewhere faraway, perhaps somewhere outside of the Milky Way, on some world beyond the galaxies that were visible with even the strongest of telescopes.

What had she meant by *most*? He wanted to ask her, but instead, he uttered, "I don't think I should go home." He felt her relief as a wave of energy that passed through him and dissolved unceremoniously into the night.

For several hours they drove. Though he could no longer sleep, it was dawn before Nathan felt he could break the silence that had descended on the car. "It seems like a lot of work for nothing," he said, picking up on the tail of a thought that had been preoccupying him.

"What is?" she asked.

"The whole awakening business. Can't Earth just use whatever life she creates to give herself a voice? Can't she just use trees and monkeys to communicate?"

The brief patronizing look that was exchanged between the aliens did not escape Nathan.

"Not exactly," she said with the tone of a person who was explaining basic arithmetic to a child. "Most creatures are not complex enough to understand Thaia's mind, therefore it would be impossible for them to know what she wants them to do. To make an analogy, if Thaia is a supercomputer, most creatures are calculators. The function of a calculator is to perform operations of arithmetic. If you posed a question to it that goes beyond the realm of numbers, it wouldn't have the capacity to understand the question, let alone answer it. You couldn't, for instance, ask a calculator what an adverb is or how to use it in a sentence."

"So, more like that singularity thing?"

Isha exchanged another patronizing look with Kiras, who slowly shook his head.

"No," she said. "I'm not saying that humans will evolve into silicon-based life forms, or that Thaia is a supercomputer. I'm only making an analogy. I'm trying to explain why Thaia needs sentient offspring to awaken."

"Okay. So, what, Earth is *like* a computer and a deer is *like* a calculator?"

"Yes."

"So, what does that mean for the deer?"

"Like a calculator, a deer is limited by the type of information it can process. It will never be able to act on Thaia's needs or desires. For a planet to awaken, communication has to be two way and complete."

"So, calculators eventually evolve into computers. And the computers sync with the supercomputer."

"Yes and no," she said. "A deer is the end of the line for that species. Evolution is a tricky thing. Thaia has to be constantly aware of the potential and limitations of her offspring."

"You said Veda is different from you," he said, remembering their earlier incomplete conversation.

"Yes."

"How? I mean, what makes Veda so special if all of you have the ability to sync with your planet?"

"Veda evolved after Favadan's awakening. When a planet is young, evolution is guided by natural selection. The strong and the intelligent survive at the cost of the weak. But once a planet is awake, evolution takes on a new purpose. It becomes a means for expansion rather than survival. Only when a planet is fully awake and has found perfect harmony can she create a being like Veda."

"So, that's why he's more evolved than you?"

"Veda is not a *he*," Isha corrected.

"She, then."

"Veda is not a she. Veda is all things."

"O-kay. So… how do you refer to him? Her? What?"

"We have a special word for beings like Veda on my planet. *Kouri*. The being who is all beings. The closest words you might use are 'they' or 'all.' But even those are very inadequate."

"Are all those other elders Kouris?"

"No," she said. "In our universe, Kouri belongs to Favadan still. No other planet has created such a being."

"The Elder of Elders," Nathan remembered.

"Yes. Precisely." Isha smiled.

The sun rose into the sky with the irrefutable confidence of one who had announced more new days than could be counted. Everything filled with a golden promise of new life. Nathan saw this promise in the gentle rustle of leaves against the morning breeze. He dared to relax his grasp on the tightly bound mess of his emotions and felt the terror of letting go of the pain he knew so well. He took a deep breath and decided he didn't have to let his guard down quite just yet. For now, it was enough to spend time with these aliens. He did not have to commit to anything beyond this.

I can walk away at any moment, he thought, and the thought was a comfort.

"What now?" he asked.

Isha turned in her seat. She was smiling as though the answer contained a surprise meant only for him.

"Now, your training begins."

"What exactly does that mean?"

"You'll see."

"Should I be worried?"

"No, not at all," she said reassuringly.

"What? Why are you so happy?"

She bit her lip.

"The Moli-orath, they're quite marvelous creatures," she said. "You'll get to experience them for the first time, feel their collective gravity for the first time, listen to their disjointed yet perfectly synchronized chatter. I remember my first experience with them in this form. It was like looking into the entire universe through a peephole. All of consciousness expressed in one cohesive whole split into millions of isolated voices." She smiled. "I'm looking forward to you experiencing this."

8
not telepathy

"So, how far away is your planet anyway?" Nathan asked as Kiras pulled the car into a gas station.

"You planning a trip?" Isha asked.

Nathan followed her out of the car and across several rows of pumps toward the minimart attached to the station. Kiras stayed behind to fill up the tank.

"Depends," Nathan said. "Can I hitch a ride?"

They entered the brightly lit store through its sliding glass doors. On any other day, Nathan would not have noticed the pot-bellied erstwhile cowboy pouring coffee into a large paper cup, or the family of four standing in line at the bathroom door, each teenager slumped over a phone. But now, people were all he noticed. It felt oddly exhilarating to walk through the short aisles of the mart with an actual interplanetary alien. He watched the faces of these people in their mundane setting and was amazed that no-one suspected Isha of being anything other than ordinary. He wanted to walk up to them and shake them. *Really?* He wanted to ask. *You really don't see anything unusual about her?* It was as though they existed on some other plane of reality.

"Do people just ignore what you are?" He caught up to her at the back of the store, where there was a discount clothing rack.

"What do you mean?"

"Well, that you're not from here. Doesn't anyone suspect?"

"Did you suspect?"

"No."

"I guess not then."

"But you're so… different."

"Now that you know," she said, lifting up a pair of hideous stretchy jeans. "People see what they want to see."

"Who is that for?" Nathan's face twisted in disapproval.

"You think it'll fit you?"

"Oh, hell no. I'm not wearing any jeans with a rubber band at the waist."

"Don't you need some clean clothes?"

"Yes, clothes. Not *that* — whatever that is. Just put it back."

"At least get a few shirts," she said.

Nathan knew he should have grabbed more from his car than a dirty t-shirt, a sweater, and a pair of tennis shoes. These shirts were as dreadful as the pants: oversized with some of the most unappealing designs Nathan had ever seen.

"Oh why? Why?" He held up a crew-neck sweatshirt with the picture of a cat wearing a red, white, and blue sweater. Behind the cat, an American flag waved in the wind. "Why would anyone wear this?"

"Just get some of these." She handed him a bag of white undershirts.

"Fine." He dropped the bag into his basket. She tossed him three more.

"How long is this thing going to take?" he asked. "I don't have this many shirts in my closet."

She signaled for him to hurry up and walked away. On his way to the check-out counter, Nathan grabbed some water and snacks, a toothbrush and toothpaste. He placed the basked on the counter in front of a middle-aged man with leathery sun-blotched skin. The bored disinterest in the man's demeanor dissipated the moment he looked up at Isha. He was on his feet then, fully alert and a bit flustered. Without a single word, he started scanning the items, glancing at Isha every few scans, his mouth slightly agape. Nathan sympathized with the old man. He was all too familiar with the surge of desire and fear that accompanied noticing her for the first time. He, too, had found it impossible to not stare at her, as though he beheld in front of him a creature as mystical and as deadly as a sphinx.

He's probably asking himself: why am I so drawn to this perfectly ordinary girl? Nathan thought, because that was precisely the question he'd asked himself a thousand times during those lonely weeks when he couldn't get himself to stop following her. He reached out in front of him and palmed a pack of mints in direct view of the man, and smiled when this act went undetected. Isha threw a sharp glance in his direction. Nathan laughed and walked out of the sliding double doors, still holding the mints. He wondered if the old man would remember him taking them at a later time. Somehow, he doubted it.

Nathan strutted toward Kiras, who leaned against the car, waiting.

"It seems I spend half my life waiting on women," Nathan said. There was no reaction from Kiras, so he continued. "You know, I could get used to this walking around with aliens business. I bet we could have just walked out with all that stuff and the old fart wouldn't even have noticed." How far did he have to go to get a reaction out of this guy? "He might have a heart attack from excitement though if she stays in there much longer." The way Kiras ignored him, it was as though Nathan was a ghost talking to himself. "Do women react to you the way men react to her? No. Don't answer that. I'll just ask that girl over there. Hold on a sec, will ya?"

Kiras grabbed his arm. "Don't," he said.

"Oh, he speaks." When Kiras went back to ignoring him, Nathan added, "So, I've been meaning to ask you, what kind of name is Kiras anyway? Does it mean, like, asshole or something literal like that?"

"You shouldn't have taken the mints," Kiras said.

"Did she tell you about that? You know how women can twist the truth."

"I saw you take them."

"From here? That's impossible."

Kiras looked toward the minimart. The glass doors parted, and Isha emerged carrying several bags.

"You tattling on me?" Nathan said as Isha pushed past him and opened the door to the back seat. Without a word, she tossed the bags into the car and got in the front passenger seat.

"Let's go," she said.

"How does that work?" Nathan asked as he crawled into the back. He moved the bags to the floor next to him and rummaged through them for a box of breakfast bar. "The whole mind reading thing. How does it work?"

Kiras glanced at Isha before turning the key in the ignition.

"See? That!" Nathan exclaimed. "What did he just say to you? Are you like, reading each other's minds?"

Isha twisted in her seat to look at him.

"It's not the way you think of information exchange," she said. "We don't read minds or thoughts. Thoughts are the way you translate information. Knowledge is information in its purest form."

"So, when he says he saw me take the mints…"

"He saw you through my eyes."

"Ah," said Nathan, "that's much more creepy."

Isha turned back around. With her eyes on the narrow road ahead, she said, "The same will happen to you if Thaia awakens."

Nathan's chest tightened, and he found it difficult to swallow the large bite he had just taken from his snack. He dug out a bottle of water from one of the bags and downed it in one long gulp, feeling the strange sense of worry that her words produced in him. Yet it was not the prospect of losing his individuality that scared him, he realized. It wasn't even the notion of having to share his deepest desires, memories, and secrets with countless strangers. It was Isha's choice of words that rattled him. That instead of saying *when*, she had chosen to say *if*.

9
a government experiment

The dusty road stretched endlessly in front of them. Nathan leaned against the door, feeling the stiffness of inertia in his muscles. The lush green forest outside his window was replaced with a vast barren desert, sprinkled with chalky shrubs too parched to peel themselves off the ground. Even the scattered cacti that managed to stretch upward toward the blazing sun slumped in its smothering heat.

In Nathan's mind flashed images of destruction from his nightmare. Even with his eyes open, Nathan dropped into the familiar scene, trapped by the screams of a world ablaze. *If Thaia awakens,* Isha had said. *If.*

The car slowed to a near halt and bounced onto an unmarked dirt path that, as far as Nathan could see, led nowhere but into the heart of the desert. He wanted to ask why they had left the paved road, but kept the question to himself, feeling too weary for the condescension of the response.

Soon, the main road behind them was swallowed by skeletal bushes and short rocky hills. There was no sign of life in any direction. Still, Nathan had the eerie feeling of being watched.

Though forced to slow down by the uneven terrain, Kiras drove a bit too fast on the bumpy road. Nathan had to press one hand against the roof of the car to keep his head from bouncing into it. Soon, they passed threatening warnings confirming that they were under surveillance. Nathan slid to the middle seat, his heart pounding inside his throat. They drove past two large "Restricted Area" signs that threatened trespassers with criminal charges.

"No talking from now on," Isha said as though he had not already lost all ability to produce sound.

They pulled up to a guarded gate, cameras and two armed men in military uniforms stationed in plain view. A lanky guard with an angular pale face and a crooked nose stepped up to the car, scanning them with alert eyes. Kiras produced a short stack of documents, which the guard studied intently. One hand resting on the semi-automatic rifle on his side, he looked once more into the car, lingering on Isha and then on Nathan.

"You know where you're headed?" he asked, handing the papers back to Kiras.

"Yes," Kiras answered.

Wordlessly, the guard opened the gate, granting them entry.

Nathan leaned forward, his senses on full alert like a cat preparing to pounce. Once inside the gate, they turned behind a wooden office trailer and came to a halt next to a digital keypad that looked strangely out of place without a gate for it to open. In front of them, the desert had been stripped of its plant-life, leaving behind an arid sandbox.

Kiras got out of the car, and leaving the door ajar, he moved quickly to the keypad.

"You okay?" Nathan heard Isha's voice somewhere beyond his pounding heart. He nodded.

The desert floor in front of them began to shift and the

ground rose like the lid of a box, sand raining from its edges. Nathan's breath got stuck in his chest and remained suspend like the ground above his head. A paved road stretched ahead of them and lead into a well-lit tunnel beneath the desert.

"What's wrong with you?" Kiras asked as he climbed back into the driver seat.

"He's fine," Isha replied.

Am I fine? Nathan thought as they drove into the underground tunnel and came to a stop in front of an unmanned checkpoint. The scan of Kiras's badge gained them further entry into an ordinary-looking underground parking garage. Kiras parked the car between a black SUV with dark tinted windows and a black Lincoln. Nathan closed his eyes and swallowed his fear. *I am fine,* he consoled himself silently. *Nothing's fucked,* he added as a private homage to his brother, Pic, and forced a smile. *No*, he thought, *Nothing is fucked… not yet, anyway.*

"Don't forget your stuff," Isha said as she opened her door.

"We're staying here?" he asked.

"For now." When he hesitated, she added, "You know, there's nothing to be scared of."

"I'm not scared."

"Okay, but if you are—"

"I'm not."

The hot air that assaulted Nathan the moment he opened the door felt stale. They moved intently toward a solid metal door in the corner of the parking garage, which Kiras unlocked with his keycard. The door opened into a short gray entry with concrete walls and an identical metal door six feet in front of them. This door, too, had to be unlocked with Kiras's card — a redundancy that made no sense to Nathan.

They entered a long gray hallway lined with more metal

doors. Nathan wiped the sweat from his upper lip, glad this area was at least air conditioned. Two men in gray flight suits passed them and walked briskly down the corridor. One of them looked over his shoulder at them, and finding nothing particularly interesting, continued on his way.

For being in such a desolate place, this underground base was bustling with people. Uniformed officers came out of doors and entered others, talking in hushed voices. People carried stacks of papers, equipment, and weapons that were rarely concealed. No one seemed to pay any attention to them.

This must be a huge base, Nathan thought, *if no one is suspicious of unfamiliar faces.*

It was easy for Nathan to detect the non-humans. There was no mistaking them, and Nathan wondered how he had been fooled by them his entire life.

A petite alien with hair the color of fire eyed him curiously as she approached them. She kept her eyes on Nathan as she walked past him, a subtle private smile flashing across her parted lips. He twisted his head and looked behind him. Within the few seconds it had taken him to turn his head, she had already reached the far end of the long corridor and disappeared around the bend. Nathan jogged to Isha's side as she walked through a door into an even narrower hallway. He took advantage of the momentary privacy of the empty corridor and whispered, "Does she know why we're here?"

"Who?" Isha asked.

"The redhead who just passed us."

"No. She was probably wondering why you're with us."

"So, she can't read your mind?"

"Of course not," Isha said as though he had missed something terribly obvious. "She's a Chelis, I'm a Favadani, you're a

Human. Different planets."

At the end of the hall, Kiras's keycard gained them entry into a large service elevator. Another scan of his card took them three levels down.

"Heavy security, huh?" Nathan said under his breath.

No one acknowledged his words, which hung suspended in the air until the elevator doors opened and let them out. The corridor that stretched in front of them was narrow and dimly lit, with a low ceiling that was made even lower with exposed wires and tubes. The concrete that covered the floor and the walls was dark and rough. Dusty pipes and thick black wires ran the length of the hallway and were secured to the ceiling with bands of steel and oversized bolts.

Kiras stopped in front of a door halfway down the hall and placed his hand on its chrome handle.

"What? No security scan?" Nathan asked.

Kiras pressed down on the handle and pushed open the door.

"Well, hello there," said a female voice, far too sultry, far too flirtatious to fit in with the gray clutter of cables and coils that filled the small room they entered. It was as though dozens of computerized devices had vomited their guts after an all-night rager. Everywhere Nathan looked, he saw the mangled remains of devices, some he recognized, others he didn't, both large and minuscule. Half-finished Frankenstein-esque experiments were assembled in every corner, except instead of human limbs, it was severed parts of electronics that were fused together into unrecognizable monstrosities.

"Oh, honey," said the bemused voice, "don't look so stunned, will ya'?"

Nathan couldn't tell where the severed voice was coming

from.

"Hi Celeste," said Isha. "Thanks for making time for us."

"Time is all I got, darling. Sweetheart, stop fidgeting, will ya? You're gonna knock my babies over if you keep that up."

"Relax," Isha said to Nathan, who was turning around a bit too aggressively in search of the voice's source.

Nathan froze in place; only his head continued to scan the room. "Where is she?" he asked, to which Celeste responded with a genuine, booming laugh.

"You didn't tell him?" Celeste giggled.

"Tell me what?"

"Celeste is a computer," said Kiras impatiently. "There. Can we get on with it now?"

"What do you mean, she's a computer?"

"Oh. Baby," Celeste said. "You don't know what a computer is?"

"I do, it's just—"

"Celeste, did Veda tell you why we're here?" Isha broke in.

"Of course, darling. Personally, I can't wait to get in there and just, mmm," Celeste moaned, "I bet he's just *delicious*."

"What's she talking about?" Nathan asked.

"Oh, there he goes again being all nervous," Celeste said with exaggerated pouty displeasure. "It's okay, baby. It's just a bit of fun, that's all. No one's harming you on my watch."

There was the click of a lock and the metallic shelf against the back wall swung open, revealing a secret entrance into a brightly lit room.

"Here," Celeste said. "Why don't we just get started?" As they moved toward the hidden entrance, she added, "No foreplay, no fun."

Nathan was immediately struck by the disembodied sterility

of the bright room they entered. Every surface — ground, walls, and ceiling — was made of the same white polished material that had covered the walls and ground of the recovery chamber inside Veda's cabin. Despite the brilliant radiance of the room, Nathan could not find a source of light. No lamps or bulbs were visible anywhere. The walls at once seemed to emit light and swallow it, creating a disorienting sensation of being suspended inside a white abyss. Once the entrance through which they entered slid shut behind them, Nathan could not see any seams to indicate outlines of walls, ground, ceiling or even the door. The only evidence that there was a floor he was standing on were the dozens of discarded robotic arms that lay in front of him.

"Excuse my babies, darling," Celeste said. "It was just too short of a notice. I simply didn't have a chance to tidy up properly."

Something moved in Nathan's periphery: a humanoid robotic arm flew out of a mangled pile and floated toward him. Once it hovered a few feet in front of him, it reached toward Nathan, palm facing upward, as though inviting him to dance.

"Shall we get started?" Celeste asked.

Nathan looked to Isha for an explanation.

"Well?" said Celeste. "When a lady offers you her hand, what is there to do other than to take it?"

"Just go with her," said Isha.

Reluctantly, Nathan stepped forward.

"That's more like it!" Celeste's excitement was apparent in her voice and in the way her robot arm spun around itself once, swung around him, and then came to rest, palm on his lower back, gently pushing him forward into the middle of the room.

"And where are those little unruly imbeciles?" Celeste asked, with motherly disapproval.

Isha placed the heavy box a few feet away from him, un-buckled it carefully, and opened its lid, revealing the strange stone inside it.

"Oh honey," Celeste said, and Nathan thought he detected tension in the strain of her voice. "*Who* made these?"

"We're hoping you can answer that," Isha said.

"Oh, no. I… This is so peculiar. I have to… I need to take a closer look."

The rock inside the box started to glow a radioactive green that rapidly turned lighter and brighter, until Nathan had to close his eyes. A high-pitched metallic scream filled the inside of Nathan's head. He pressed the heels of his hands to his temples, shielding his ears, and averted his eyes. Then the heavy lid of the chest slammed shut, and the scream turned into the shrill shriek of a person who must have endured a sudden and painful blow. Except this human cry did not belong to a human at all. Nathan recognized it as belonging to Celeste and wondered how a computer could simulate such a perfect rendition of pain.

Celeste went silent just as the room went dark. It was a complete kind of a darkness, undisturbed by even the slightest ray of light. Nathan moved his hands to his face and held open his eyelids manually. Still, he saw nothing but a deep black void around him. The sound of his heavy, irregular breath was the only thing he heard.

"Hello?" he whispered into the void.

"Don't move," said Isha. "Celeste, are you okay?" For the first time since they'd met, there was anxiety in Isha's voice. "Don't move," she said again. "We'll be right back."

"Where are you going?" Nathan could feel the panic rising inside his chest.

"We're not going anywhere. Not physically. We need to find

out how to get out. We'll be right back."

He felt her familiar energy being sucked out of the room.

"You're okay," Nathan whispered to himself as he forced a deep breath. Then, not knowing what else to do, he started counting. "One… Two… Three… Four… Five… Six…"

In the silence of the room, Nathan could hear his own heartbeat and the swish of blood flowing through his veins. He also heard his panic-stricken internal voice screaming expletives into his hollow bones, as his external voice kept counting somewhere far in the distance. He stood frozen in the middle of an endless black nothingness and tried not to collapse. "Fifteen… Sixteen… Seventeen…"

He felt Isha's familiar energy flood the room and breathed a sigh of relief. "Oh, thank god."

"Keep counting," she said.

"Eighteen… Nineteen… Twenty… Twenty-one…"

A lock clicked and a crack of white appeared to Nathan's right. The invisible door slid open, and Nathan felt relief ripple through both aliens.

"Thank you." He heard Kiras say under his breath.

The front room felt oddly lifeless without Celeste's sultry voice to fill it. They hurried out of the door, and back down the hallway into the elevator.

"Where did you go?" Nathan asked Isha when they stood in the elevator.

"What?"

"In there. When you disappeared. Where did you go?"

"We needed to figure out how to get out."

"And?"

"We figured it out."

The elevator doors opened into a narrow hallway with sterile gray walls. Nathan had to almost jog to keep up with the fast pace of Kiras's steps. Kiras turned a sharp corner and increased his pace as he hastened to its end. At the end of the hallway, he scanned his keycard on a rectangular strip next to a set of metallic double doors. The lock clicked and the doors retreated, allowing them passage.

They emerged into a large hanger with a faraway domed ceiling. More than half a dozen military helicopters perched like giant insects in the open space in front of them. Directly above, a large circle marked the center of the ceiling. It was hard to believe they were still underneath the desert.

"What happened to Celeste?" Nathan asked, no longer able to keep the question inside him.

Isha stopped and turned toward him. When she didn't offer an explanation, he added, "I need to know."

"I know," she said.

"Is she going to be okay?"

"I think so."

"You *think* so?"

"Yes."

"But you're not sure."

"Come on," she said, walking into the massive hanger.

"Isha." Nathan didn't move. There was something that deeply disturbed him. When she turned to look at him, he asked, "Is the same thing going to happen to me?"

She stared into him, her silence more unnerving than any answer she could have given.

"Well?" he said, even though the answer he suspected terrified him.

"No," she said at last.

"Are you sure?"

"No."

She turned and walked toward Kiras, who stood at the far end of the hanger, inspecting a tar-colored, sleek helicopter. Groups of two or three men, wearing the same gray flight suits that Nathan had seen on several people earlier, worked in clusters around various aircraft. Kiras was on his knees, scrutinizing the underbelly of his chopper. Two men — both human — walked up behind Nathan and stopped on either side of him. Nathan crossed his arms, feeling uneasy and outnumbered. He wanted to walk forward the five or so steps that separated him from Isha. He wondered if that would attract undue attention to him — if it would make it plain that he did not belong here in this secret underground base.

"What? You think you can just waltz in here and take it?" said the man on Nathan's right. The question was directed at Kiras, though the alien didn't acknowledge it.

Kiras ran his hand along the body of the mechanical beast as he walked around it, prodding, poking, and peering into it. He inspected the thing as though he was inspecting an animal, checking its teeth and examining its pelt. When he was done, Kiras's hands were spotted with oil and dirt.

"We'll need a second one," he said.

"The nerve of this guy," said the man on Nathan's left as the other scuffed.

Kiras looked in the direction of the door through which they had entered. For a moment he seemed to be thinking.

"I'll take the Cyclone," he said, nodding his head toward a massive white aircraft that was more a camper than a helicopter. The man on Nathan's right scoffed again as though to say, *Who the hell does this guy think he is?*

"Good luck with that," he said. "No one takes The Clone."

"It's done," said Kiras. There was no humor in his voice. "Be ready for take off in five." He walked across with hurried steps to the opposite end of the hangar toward the Cyclone.

"Hey!" yelled the man on Nathan's right. "Who's gonna fly that thing?"

"I am," Kiras yelled back without turning around or slowing down.

"You and who else?"

Kiras ignored the question. He reached the massive chopper — Nathan thought it could carry a dozen soldiers with ease — swung open the cockpit door and climbed inside.

"What's he doin'?" asked the guy on Nathan's left. "How's he gonna fly it alone?"

"What a freak," said the other.

Shaking their heads and whispering to each other in hushed voices, the two men got into the cockpit of the black helicopter. Nathan noticed how small it looked in comparison to the Clone.

He sat next to Isha in the back of the smaller aircraft and fastened the harness around his chest. The engine roared to life. Nathan felt the rattle of the rotors inside his body. As the chopper floated upward, he wished he could have been on the ground to see the dome retreat to reveal the sky beyond it.

Sunlight blinded him when they rose above the desert floor. Nathan squinted behind the cover of his hands. When his eyes adjusted to the light, he looked out of his window and found two wrinkled shadows crawling across the spotted desert far below.

"What were they mumbling about?" Nathan asked, curious about the whispers that the pilots had exchanged before take off.

"They think Kiras is some sort of government experiment," Isha filled him in.

"What? Like a super soldier?" An amused grin spreading on

Nathan's face.

"Like a cyborg," she said, and for the first time since they met, they laughed.

10

nooritan and lanorien

"**C**onrad thinks he can fix Celeste." Isha had to almost shout, but Nathan knew the pilots could not hear them over the patter of the rotors, because he could barely hear her, and their faces were only inches apart.

"Conrad?" He shouted back.

"He helped us get out. He built her."

"When the chest closed…" he said, asking a question that was still bothering him. "Why did the lights go out?"

"There were no lights in that room. It was all her."

"That makes no sense."

"Celeste is a single unifying consciousness, operating through millions of microscopic organisms. She's Moli-orath."

"Kiras called her a computer."

"It was the easiest explanation."

"So, if Conrad made her, does that mean she's linked to him? Her consciousness, I mean?"

"Now you're getting it."

"What was she trying to do?"

"Understand the device," she said. "Figure out why it responded to you."

"But it didn't respond to me."

"It did. The Moli-orath moved toward you. That's them responding to you."

"I don't understand." Nathan said. "So what that they moved toward me? They're robots, right? So, what's the big deal?"

"There are two types of sentient races in the universe," Isha explained. "Nooritan and LaNorien. Those who can communicate with the Moli-orath and those who can't. Humans are LaNorien. It's as though your communications take place on two completely different radio stations. Not only can you not hear each other, you probably don't even know the other exists. This makes it impossible for the Moli-orath to respond to you in any way, let alone move toward you when you reached to them."

"Because to them, I don't exist."

"Precisely."

"Well, how many races are — you know, the ones that can communicate with them?"

"Nooritan. Three."

"Oh."

"Exactly," she said as though making a point.

"Your planet is one of the three?" He asked.

"Yes."

"So, why don't you just confront the other two?"

"Nooritan races are ancient and powerful. If we confront them, and we are right about their intentions—"

"You could push their hand."

"Correct. It could accelerate their plan. If their plan is to harm Thaia, that could create a great disadvantage for us."

"So, go to the others," said Nathan. "The La… what?"

"LaNorien. What if they're co-conspirators?" she asked. "We

don't know who else is involved."

"You said that."

"Yes, I did."

"I still don't understand. Aren't they supposed to protect Earth? I thought awakened planets are supposed to be peaceful."

"Our mission here is… complicated. When we arrived, we were hopeful that we could succeed in helping Thaia awaken. Now, it seems, there are some who doubt it's possible."

"So what if Earth doesn't awaken? We live our lives as savages, kill each other for resources, and build bigger mansions. What's the big deal?"

There was a deep sadness in the way Isha looked at him then, as though she did not have the heart to tell him the part of the story she was omitting. Shifting her attention to the scene outside the window, she said, "We've arrived."

The view was breathtakingly beautiful. Nathan was so engrossed in their conversion that he had missed it entirely. A sea of green covered the peaks of the mountain range below. The forest stretched in every direction, poking the jagged tips of its countless trees into the belly of the blue sky, whose serene calm seemed undisturbed by it. The Cyclone looked like a toy version of itself as it hovered above the thick mantle of trees, against a backdrop of fading crests, rendered translucent with distance. Their steady approach revealed a fissure in the woods with a glassy lake at its pit, framed by a messy display of bush and rock.

The Clone remained suspended in mid-air as the chopper that carried Nathan and Isha began to lower over the lake. Nathan watched the dance of leaves against the beating of the helicopter's propellers and was wondering why they had come here when his eyes plucked from the landscape the bright colors of a tent just beyond the tree line. There were, in fact, five tents nearly identical in shape and size sprinkled within view of the lake, their thin material threatening to lift off against the force of the chopper's wind. Nathan wondered if they were meeting someone here, and if they were going to land on water.

He looked at Isha, wordlessly asking her his questions, wishing he, too, could know what went on inside her head. She slid out of her harness, opened the helicopter's side door, and leaned out. A black-haired alien with porcelain skin whom Nathan had not noticed previously stared back at her from the edge of the lake.

This must be Conrad, he thought and decided that this tall, muscular creature with his angular jaw and piercing eyes did not look like someone who could have created something as playful and likable as Celeste.

Behind the alien, ordinary-looking humans crawled out of their tents.

Nathan saw two rosy-cheeked girls wearing shorts and thermal tops, their toes pressed into unlaced hiking boots. They hugged themselves tightly as they stared wide-eyed at the strange sight of a helicopter hovering above the lake. A pale, spindly man with greasy hair and dressed entirely in black, marched angrily toward the frozen alien, yelling and flailing his bony arms comically into the air.

Put him in a pair of tight leather pants and he's in a rock band, Nathan thought. *Even without talent.*

A chubby blond boy who stood behind the Rocker began giggling and was elbowed in the chest by an equally blond taller boy who, Nathan assumed, was his older brother. An older, grayer version of the boys stood at the entry of a different tent and looked directly at Nathan with worried eyes.

Isha poked her head into the cockpit, said something to the

pilots, and returned to her seat. The helicopter lifted over the tree line and followed the Cyclone to a large clearing a few minutes away where they set down, one after the other. It was such a relief the moment the engines shut down and the incessant pounding of the propellers faded into the silence of the forest.

"Now what?" Nathan asked.

"Now, we wait," Isha answered.

11
three-headed monster

Nathan sat on the bottom step of the helicopter with his feet dangling off the side, feeling utterly miserable in his boredom. As though being stranded in the middle of nowhere with nothing to do wasn't bad enough, no one would give him any information about why they were here, what they were waiting for, and how long it would be before whatever they were waiting for was going to happen. This uncertainty, he decided, was terrible and unfair.

After they set down, Isha had joined Kiras in the Cyclone — the wordless conversation between them was especially charged. Nathan didn't need to be told to leave them alone, the uncomfortable intensity of their combined energies had done that. The pilots, too, had distanced themselves from him by stationing themselves on a couple of tree trunks at the edge of the clearing, chain smoking and sharing animated stories in hushed voices.

He was seriously considering marching into the Clone and demanding answers when Conrad finally stepped into view, trailed closely by the black-clad Rocker, who had been so animated in his objections earlier.

Instead of walking over to them, the tall alien stopped at the edge of the glade and waited. The Rocker stood a few steps behind him, glaring at him disapprovingly. Nathan sensed the many questions he must have asked which, by the look of it, had gone unanswered, probably even unacknowledged. Next to arrive were the two girls. They emerged through the trees and came to a noisy stop next to the two men.

"Oh, bejeesus!" one of the girls exclaimed, throwing her pack on the ground in front of her and plopping herself on top of it as though it was a sofa.

"I thought we'd never get there!" said the other, dropping her pack to the ground and fishing out of it a dented pink water canister. She leaned against a tree as she took a long swallow. The first girl craned her neck and checked out the helicopters.

"Are we going somewhere?" she asked. "Is that why we're here? Are those taking us off the mountain?"

The girls waited for a response. When, instead, the alien turned to look at the forest behind him, the second girl said, "They're way back there. We might have to wait a while."

Great, thought Nathan, as he looked to the Cyclone and watched Isha and Kiras descend its tall steps.

"Is everything okay?" Nathan heard the first girl ask. "Is there some kind of emergency? How'd these people find us anyway? Do you have a tracking device on you? Is that how they knew where to look for us?"

"So, where are we going?" asked the second girl.

"Dunno," said the first. "He won't answer."

"I could really go for a snack."

"Or lunch," said the first. "I could go for lunch."

Nathan felt exhausted listening to their incessant chatter.

"They're here," said the second girl, and pushed herself off the tree she was leaning on.

The older of the brothers came into view first. He walked past the line of trees and threw his pack down as the first girl had done. He dropped onto the ground next to it, lying on his back on the rough bed of wild grass and dirt. The younger boy's wheezing breath announced his approach a moment later. He stumbled into view like a delirious, wounded soldier fueled by nothing but his will. With the relief of rest within grasp, fatigue descended on the boy. He nearly collapsed when he fell to his knees, then toppled over and dry-heaved. His swollen red face looked like an oversized tomato, comically big atop a man-sized body that had stubbornly held on to its baby fat and childlike proportions.

The boys' father entered the clearing shortly after, his steps heavy under the weight of the two packs that he carried — one on his back and the other strapped to the front of him. He threw one of the packs onto the ground next to his older son and dropped onto his knees. He, too, looked spent.

At last, the alien trekker came alive. Addressing the weary group, he said, "There's been an emergency of a nature I cannot discuss. I hope you will understand. That aircraft," he pointed at the Cyclone, "will take you back to town. Of course, all will be explained and your fares will be reimbursed." In response to the barrage of questions that descended upon him, he calmly added, "Please, take your seats on the aircraft, and all will be explained to you. I promise."

Tentatively, the hikers shuffled toward the Cyclone, glancing at Nathan on their way. When Nathan caught the blue eyes of the first girl staring at him, she blushed and looked away, whispering something to her friend, who giggled as she stole a glance to survey him.

How innocent they are, Nathan thought, and inside his mind flashed an image of their distorted corpses trapped beneath mounds of rubble. A sadness gripped his chest, and he felt the urge to run after them — to warn them of the coming doom.

Is this how serial killers get started? he thought, forcing the disturbing vision out of his mind. *By making up images of death and destruction where there is none.*

Kiras stood at the open door of the Cyclone, a warm smile on his normally tense lips, and his hand stretched toward them. Noticing the handsome extraterrestrial, the girls forgot all about Nathan and readily took his hand, smiling at each other as he lifted them into the Clone's belly one by one.

Suppressing a tinge of jealousy, Nathan pulled himself into the smaller chopper and strapped himself to his seat. He could still hear the sound of muffled voices outside, but Nathan was no longer interested in what they said. He looked at the pilots who seemed equally eager to take off.

"Conrad," Nathan heard a soft high-pitched male voice call out. It was the father of the boys addressing their guide. The gentleness in the burly man's tone took Nathan by surprise. The two men stood only a few feet outside of the helicopter's open door. All Nathan had to do was lean forward just a few inches to witness the entire exchange.

"What is going on?" the man asked and waited for a response.

Conrad smiled such an authentic, perfect smile that Nathan had a momentary realization. Here was a life form that could mimic another with such exactness that even the human it mimicked was fooled. Nathan remembered seeing a video of a bird who could replicate sounds it heard with equal precision. The sound of a man's cough or the click of a camera's shutter that came out of the bird were just as out of place as the smile on Conrad's face.

"Nothing too serious," the alien answered, his tone now kind and human, "It's a… private matter. Kiras — that young man in your aircraft — will take good care of you."

"Okay," the man said and lingered a moment before walking toward the Cyclone.

The scrawny black-haired Rocker, who had been standing a few feet behind the father, remained planted, his humorless eyes fixed on Conrad.

"You too, sir," Conrad said. "The aircraft is waiting for you."

For a long moment the two men stood with their eyes fixed on one another. Nathan stiffened in his seat, sensing a growing tension.

"No," said the Rocker defiantly. "I deserve an explanation." The Rocker's thick British accent added to Nathan's image of him as someone arrogant and self-righteous.

"As I said, you will receive a full refun—"

"It's not about the bloody money!"

"Whatever it is you want, I'm sure Kiras will—"

"No! *You* are supposed to take us up there."

"Believe me, if this wasn't of utmost importance—"

"I don't think you understand! I *sold* my life to be here. I quit my job. There is nothing for me to go back to! All because you promised me enlightenment!"

"I never promise anything on—"

"Your reputation suggests it. Why do you think we flock to you? Do you think we enjoy being cold and hungry and exhausted? No! We are here because you are supposed to have the answers!"

Conrad's face was unreadable. "The answers have never

been with me," he said.

"Not good enough," said the British man as he grabbed his pack from where it rested on the ground and threw it over his shoulder. Instead of approaching the Cyclone, however, he walked straight toward Nathan's helicopter. For a split second, Nathan feared that Conrad would pounce on the man and physically carry him to the Cyclone. But Conrad stood, his eyes fixed on Isha's. The Brit scanned the helicopter, his eyes flashing from Nathan to Isha to the two pilots. Without a greeting or an apology, he threw his pack into its belly and pulled himself on board.

He took a seat next to the window, facing Isha. Nathan noted how steady the Brit's hands were as he fastened the harness around his chest. What did he think he was doing? Didn't he know these aliens would not let him stay here? Was he not afraid of what might happen to him?

He must feel the danger he's in, Nathan thought. *His instincts must be telling him he's made the wrong choice.*

But if the man felt any trepidation about his decision to defy Conrad, he didn't show it. Meanwhile, Conrad walked up to the helicopter. Only his eyes betrayed the rage inside him.

"I'm not leaving," said the Brit in that posh accent. "You'll have to peel me off this seat."

Nathan felt the intensity of Conrad's energy.

"What do you want?" Conrad asked.

"I told you," said the Brit. "I want to know what in the bloody hell's going on. What's so important that I have to cancel my trip entirely. If I'm being buggered, I want to know why."

Conrad shot a sharp glance toward Isha, his look one of surprise mixed with disapproval. Nathan also looked at her, wondering what she'd said to him just then.

"You can fly with us," Conrad said as he climbed on board,

his words a shock to Nathan. Isha nodded once. *Why would she allow this?* Nathan wanted to ask her. How was this not a terrible idea?

"What you learn on this flight may or may not interest you," Conrad went on. "It may or may not answer your questions. When we reach Hailey, you will leave this aircraft willingly and without any more demands. Your money will be refunded to you, and if I return to work after this private ordeal, you may sign up for another trekking expedition where you may or may not find enlightenment. Do you understand?"

"Yes."

"You will not speak during this flight. And if you learn anything strange or interesting, you will not speak of it with anyone. As far as you're concerned, anything that is said here is classified and was never said at all."

"Ah," said the Brit, "now we are getting somewhere."

Conrad sat in the seat across from Nathan and fastened his harness. The Cyclone took to the sky first, climbing up far above the line of trees before starting to move across them.

Nathan sat with his arms crossed, staring out of the window and listening to the engine come to life. He ignored that there was a silent conversation going on between Isha and Conrad. Instead, he focused on the gray tips of the mountains that poked through the cover of trees. Despite his annoyance, he had to admit that this was a beautiful planet. Then, in an unexpected flash, he imagined everything below them, from horizon to horizon, engulfed by fire. In that moment, the desperate screams of an entire forest and its millions of inhabitants cut through him. He forced the image out of his mind, and closing his eyes, he tried to keep his body from trembling.

"Nathan?" he heard her say his name before he felt the calming warmth of her energy seep into him through his hands. "You okay?"

He allowed her energy to spread inside him, and felt calmness return to him. He sucked a deep breath into his chest and let go of the last of the disturbing image as he pushed the air out.

"Thanks," he said when he opened his eyes.

"Tell me about the dream," Conrad's voice took him by surprise.

"You don't want to wait until we land?" Nathan asked.

"No."

Nathan looked at the Brit then at Isha.

"He won't care," said Conrad.

"I've told it to her already. Can't you just get the details from her?"

"I need to hear it again from you. In case we missed something."

"Okay." Nathan rubbed the mark on his palm with the thumb of the other — a recent habit. The Brit's narrowed eyes were now fixed on him.

"I'm on a ship," Nathan began. "An old military-like ship. And I'm somewhere in the past. The ship is new for that time. Like I'm in the sixties or something. Anyway, I am on this ship, and there are all these soldiers around me. All in a panic because we're about to get attacked. All of a sudden this monster comes out of the water. It has three heads. The wave it creates when it rises out of the ocean is so big — it's enormous. Everyone's running this way and that way. Just terrified. But I'm not scared, because I'm an observer. Like I'm watching a movie. Except that I'm in the middle of it. So, all three heads are just towering over us — rows of teeth exposed — and everyone's panicking except for me. And there's something odd about the heads. I mean. It's a monster, all scaly and dark like a dragon but the faces… they look sort of like human faces, you know?"

He paused for a moment to gauge interest. The Brit's face was pulled into a scowl of doubt and disgust.

"Yes," Isha said, "continue."

"The heads — they dive into the water creating another huge wave. It's always the same three faces, one woman and two men. I run to the railing to look over the side, and I see these massive eyes staring directly at me. They're deep under the sea. And somehow, I'm the only person who can see the eyes. I see one of the heads rushing up — it's the woman! — her mouth is wide open, and she looks like a strange cross between a dragon and a person. She hits the ship, and the impact jolts everyone. At this point, I realize she's going to bite the ship in half — because that's what she always does — and I fly off. Then the other heads notice me, too, and they start to bite at me, but I'm too fast, and I start to fly all around them, dodging their open mouths."

"Did you see the ship from above?" asked Conrad.

"Yes."

"Did you notice anything about it? A name maybe?"

"I don't remember a name. I think… there was a number. When it breaks in half, one of the ends comes up straight into the air, and there's a number on it. Something 115. A letter then 115."

Conrad looked at Isha, and it was she who spoke next.

"What letter?" she asked.

"I'm not sure."

"Just focus. What's the letter?"

Nathan closed his eyes and visualized the ship. He saw the numbers clearly. 115. The letter was blurry in his memory. *An "A" maybe?* No. That didn't look right. *An "H?"*

"K!" he exclaimed, his eyes popping open. "K 115."

The Brit snorted. When Nathan looked in his direction, he cocked his head, a smug smile on his lips.

"K 115," Isha said, looking at Conrad.

"Does that mean anything?" Nathan asked.

"Is there more?"

"Well, there isn't much else. At this point everything is happening really fast. In the distance I see this bridge. It's not like a normal bridge. It's curved, and it has this other asymmetrical thing coming off one side of it. It's hard to explain. I can draw it if you want. I just know that I need to be there. But when I try to fly toward it, the monster gets my leg. I look back, and I see it explode into a million balls of fire. Then I look down, and I see the bridge I'd seen in the distance is right under me. Fire is raining from the sky. People are screaming. I see a woman get hit by a fireball. Her entire body catches on fire, and she screams and keeps screaming until she collapses, completely scorched. That's how she dies *every time*. It's horrible. Men, women, children — everyone's screaming and crying and running around. There is so much chaos. And I have this overwhelming feeling… Like I *know* that it's over. I *know* that we will all die. And there's just nothing I can do about it."

Nathan's voice trailed off. No one spoke. Nathan wondered what they were wordlessly saying to each other about the meaning of his dream. It was the Brit who broke the silence.

"Are you bloody kidding me?" He spoke slowly, accentuating every word. His thick accent punctuating his words with condescension. "You show up out of nowhere, unannounced, in military helicopters, and you sit here telling us this rubbish? Who gives a toss about your fantasies?"

"That's enough," Conrad scowled. His voice commanded

obedience. The Brit was silent for a moment, then he straightened in his seat and went on, his eyes piercing defiantly into Conrad's as though announcing he would not be intimidated.

"Three-headed monsters sinking a World War II ship?" the Brit scoffed. "A ship that was shot down by torpedoes seventy years ago, *not* bitten in half by some sea creature in the '60s. You tell me that's not rubbish. You're a bloody guide, for God's sakes, not this moron's psychiatrist."

Nathan shifted uncomfortably in his seat. He should have insisted on waiting until they had more privacy to tell his dream.

"What did you just say?" Isha leaned forward.

"You heard what I said, love. What is it with you and this idiot? You are far too pretty to be his date. You can't be his sister."

"What did you say about the ship?"

"What ship?"

"The ship from the idiot's dream."

Nathan shot a sharp glance at her.

"Ah, that ship. K 115, the *Levis*. It was a Canadian escort built in the early '40s. Not the bloody sixties. It was torpedoed on its first mission and sank a few hours later."

"Where did it sink?" Conrad asked.

"Why? Are you thinking of inspecting the wreckage for monster bites?" The Brit's tone became serious as he continued. "Somewhere south of Greenland. It was towed by the Mayflower – you know the Mayflower right? Yeah. It was towed for some ten hours after it got hit. The exact location may be a bit tricky to find."

"How can you know all this?" Nathan asked. The thought crossed his mind that the man was deranged and was fabricating facts for his own amusement. Something inside him, however, told him that the Brit was speaking the truth and that his being here was not a coincidence.

"I know ships." The Brit shrugged.

"Three heads, three devices," Isha said. "The dream is a map. The ship, the bridge. That's where we'll find the other two. Nathan, can you draw a picture of the bridge you saw?"

Conrad rummaged through his pack and handed him a notebook and a pen. Nathan opened it to a blank page and drew the bridge from his dream in three quick strokes.

"I know this bridge," Conrad said. "I know exactly where it is."

"I want in." The Brit leaned forward, a serious determination in his excited eyes. When he did not receive a response, he pressed his hand down on Conrad's notebook. "I want in," he said again, his face only inches from Conrad's.

"You are forgetting our deal."

"You need me," said the Brit. "No one knows more about ships than I do. Especially sunken ships."

"We don't need your help," said Conrad.

"Without me, you wouldn't even know what to look for," the Brit said smugly. "I have no doubt I can find the Levis. I can find it for you."

As the Brit spoke, a feeling Nathan had been fighting throughout their entire encounter solidified into an idea he could no longer ignore.

"Oh, shit!" Nathan exclaimed, looking at Conrad. Everyone fell silent around Nathan as three sets of eyes fixed on him.

Where the hell is my free will? Nathan thought.

"He has to come with us," he said. "Think about it. Why is this guy here? Does he look like the kind of guy who would go hiking, let alone sign up for a trekking expedition? And why is he *here*? So far from his home. Were there no other walks he could have gone on in England? Or wherever the hell he's from? And why is he sitting *here* in this helicopter when the rest of them are in the Cyclone? Something brought him here. Maybe the same something that brought me to you." Looking at Isha, he added, "The same something that's giving me this crazy dream, and is making me feel like I need to say these words that I really don't want to say. We need him. That's the only explanation."

12

left out

The first class flight from New York to Amsterdam, the limo ride to Rotterdam, the many impassive human and alien faces that stared at him as he walked past them — they were all a blur now. All that Nathan remembered of the trip was the feeling of being swept away, passed from one vehicle into another, being told what to do by strangers who seemed to know his alien companions. He felt like he was trapped inside a wave that forcefully dragged him along regardless of his will. When they finally boarded the eight-cabin charter boat that would be their home for the foreseeable future, he felt he could finally relax.

Laying on the narrow bed that was slightly too short for him, he listened to the steady crash of waves against the boat as they set sail toward Greenland. Even before their helicopter had set down, they had abandoned the original plan of returning to the military base to fix Celeste. Conrad had taken charge of the whole operation. Given all the new information about sunken ships and hidden bombs, he'd decided that before they did anything else, they had to find all three devices. They needed to know what they were up against. Then they could return to the base where he'd repair Celeste, and with her help, they would figure out a way for Nathan to control the mechanics that he should not be able to control. Everything seemed like a long shot to Nathan, but what else could he do other than just go along?

In a strange way, Nathan felt they had already arrived. The relaxed pace of life on this luxury liner suited him. After spending several nights in cars, it was refreshing to have a room of his own and a bed in which to sleep. Not to mention, a shower. Rolling himself into a ball beneath the covers, he closed his eyes and drifted into unconsciousness.

With the constant sway of the boat, his dream had now taken on a strange sort of lucidity. The ocean bridged the gap between the real world of his consciousness and the subconscious world of his nightmare. These days, while he dreamt, he was often aware of the three-headed monster as a physical manifestation of the three bombs that were meant to destroy his planet. His dream-self knew, beyond any doubt, that the destruction they brought about would be complete — that nothing would survive. The detonation of these bombs meant certain death to all things.

How? Nathan often thought in his dream, as he dodged the snapping mouths of the beast. *How can everything be destroyed? How will nothing survive? Life survived even as the dinosaurs went extinct. How is this different?*

Nathan was sweating underneath the wool blanket when he opened his eyes. Sunlight filtered into the cabin through a single round window above his bed. His stomach growled. Peeling himself from the covers, he dressed in a pair of jeans and his gray hoody, which was the only long-sleeve shirt he possessed and really could use a wash. Instead of all those t-shirts, he often thought, they should have bought him sweaters. He rummaged through a plastic bag for a travel-sized packet of trail mix and poured half of it into his mouth.

The ship had four decks. His room was on the main level where a hallway connected the stern to the bridge. Along this hallway, four doors on either side marked entrances to small, cozy cabins. Nathan, Isha, Conrad, and the Brit were each given one of these rooms when they first boarded three days ago. Despite their proximity to each other, Nathan had seldom run into the others.

He walked down this hallway into the saloon at the back of the boat. To his right, two large tables were set up as a dining hall, to his left was a living room with a large L-shaped sofa, a loveseat, a coffee table, and a large flatscreen television mounted to the wall. Nathan walked through the double doors at the far end of the common area and stood at the rear of the boat, studying the long trail of white foam that it left behind like the path of a snail. Nathan was struck by how still everything was. Despite the rapid roll of waves produced by the boat's speed, the two nearly identical blues of the ocean and the sky were flattened into complete stillness at the point of their meeting. A large bird dropped from where it must have been hovering several yards above the boat and floated next to Nathan, suspended inside a timeless bubble that seemed to exist outside of reality. The bird turned its head and looked directly at him. Then, as suddenly as it had appeared, the bird took to the air and disappeared from view.

Nathan climbed the wooden stairs to the promenade deck where tables and chairs were set up in front of an unstaffed bar. He stopped at the bottom of the stairs that led to the sundeck, listening. There was nothing much up there other than a scarcely-furnished terrace, populated with a row of reclining beach chairs set atop faux grass. It was an area created for the sole purpose of sunbathing and stargazing, but it had quickly become the Brit's go-to spot to hunch over his leather-bound notebook, alternating between jotting down notes and crossing them out. Nathan was almost certain that the Brit was up there now, but he didn't know if the others were with him. He listened for voices and considered climbing the stairs just to confirm that the Brit was alone.

It seemed that these days Nathan was forever arriving late, entering rooms after something important had already been decided. It was not a coincidence, Nathan suspected, that the Brit was always at the center of these secret, inconspicuous meetings, using terms like "reconnaissance" and "pressure density" — words that meant nothing to Nathan but twisted the faces of the Brit, the aliens, and the captain into knowing frowns.

Nathan decided that he didn't feel like being patronized by the Brit, and climbed back down to the main deck. He walked through the dining area and entered a door that led to the lower deck. He was always taken aback by how different this part of the boat, which was meant to be seen only by its crew, looked and felt in comparison to the rest of it. The already-narrow hallways, corridors and staircases, became claustrophobically so down here. Even the walls, which were made of soothing wood panels in the common areas were replaced with sterile white vinyl, scratched and stained with use. He climbed down the tight stairway and followed the gloomy hallway to the galley where a dark-skinned Pakistani in his twenties was picking onions out of a box with his back turned to the door.

"Hi… Farhad," Nathan announced himself. It always took him a moment to remember the cook's name.

The man looked over his shoulder at him. "As-salamu alayka. I make some food for you?"

"Ah… Yes. Anything, really. I'm… uh… very hungry."

Farhad smiled. "Samosa okay?"

"That would be perfect. Thanks."

"Okay. I bring up. Ten minutes."

Ten minutes, Nathan knew, would be twenty at the very least. He also knew the reason for the delay. Every time he asked Farhad for food, the man prepared two meals: one for him and one for the Brit. Nathan resented it.

He sat at the dining room table where he could see down the hallway to Isha's door. Bitterness rose inside him when he considered how sincere she had been when she told him that he was the key they were looking for, and how casually she had replaced him the moment someone more capable had shown up.

Nathan felt ignored, used, manipulated — an emotional concoction that was all too familiar in his dealings with the opposite sex. How many times had he experienced this? How many times had he felt this same confusion, this same resentment, this same anger bubbling up inside his chest? He felt invisible — utterly worthless. Replaceable. *Why bring me here?* he thought, *Why drag me all the way across the globe just to toss me aside?*

He looked away from her door, feeling as helpless as he had once felt, sitting in his car outside of her window.

Since that day in the helicopter, Conrad had not said more than five sentences to him, and most of those sentences were to order him around. *Come here. Go there. Get the door. Call the captain.* Nathan considered the possibility that his role was nothing more than to bring the Brit to the aliens. That this would be the extent of his involvement in this plot.

No, he said to himself, rubbing the imprint on his palm. *Those mechanics reacted to me.*

He thought about Isha keeping the device in its chest, hidden from him. When Nathan tried to ask her about it, she told him there was no sense in taking unnecessary risks. Kiras had gone to Taiwan to retrieve the device that, they assumed, was hidden somewhere near the bridge from his dream.

"He shouldn't be long," Isha had said. "It will be easier to study them once all three are in one place and Celeste is back to help."

To Nathan, it felt like she was having second thoughts.

The Pakistani emerged carrying two identical trays of food. Despite his irritation, all it took was one glance at the tray Farhad had placed in front of him for Nathan to evict the thought of the Brit out his mind entirely.

Meals were never simple when Farhad prepared them. He had a way of complicating even the simplest dishes, turning otherwise mundane fares into restaurant-quality meals whose photographs and recipes should appear in magazines under captions like *Not Your Grandma's Curry* or *A Scramble with a Tamarind Twist*.

Nathan's mouth watered as he pulled the tray closer. The main course consisted of two golden-brown samosas filled with chicken, potato, peas, and spices, served on top of both mint and tamarind chutney, garnished with two stems of fresh parsley. Surrounding the main dish were a steaming bowl of lentil soup sprinkled with green onions, a green salad topped with dried apricots, red onions, and almond shavings, a large glass of tomato juice, and a bottle of water.

Nathan devoured every morsel, shoveling it into his mouth like a man who hadn't eaten in days. When he was done, he climbed the stairs to the promenade deck, sat at one of the empty tables, and stared into the horizon. He kept an eye on the stairs that led to the sundeck where the Brit was still camped out.

What is he writing? Nathan wondered. More than a handful of times, he had tried to sneak a glimpse of the Brit's journal, but the endless rows of scribble were impossible to decipher.

Time seemed to stand still on the boat. Each elongated day felt like an eternity as it slowly faded into the next one. The longer they sailed, the longer the sky seemed to stay light. Nathan could no longer tell apart three in the afternoon from seven in the evening. All he knew was that the sun was finally on its descent. The chill had settled in his bones when he decided to return to his cabin.

As he pushed his chair back, he saw the Brit's dark shape climb down the sundeck stairs with his book of secrets under his arm, his food tray in hand, and his thin greasy hair tucked behind his ears. There was conviction in the man's steps as he marched past Nathan, ignoring him altogether. Nathan followed him down the stairs to the main deck. Instead of leaving the tray on the table and returning to his room, the Brit opened the door that led to the lower deck and disappeared inside.

Nathan stood in the middle of the saloon, contemplating whether or not he should follow. What was down there for him, other than watch the Brit return his tray to the galley and awkwardly squeeze past him as he made his way back up the stairs? On the other hand, what if the Brit was on his way to another secret rendezvous? Still, was it worth incurring that condescending look on the foreigner's face if he was wrong about this potential secret meeting?

"What else do you have to do?" Nathan said to himself as he walked to the door and swung it open.

At the bottom of the stairs, he turned and made his way intently to the galley at the end. There was no sign of the Brit anywhere. There was no sign of anyone. He turned on his heels and walked back to the stairs. He had taken two steps up when he heard muffled familiar voices from down the hall. Nathan jumped back down and followed the voices to a door halfway down the corridor. Without even considering to knock, he threw open the door.

A mess of maps and papers covered a small table in the far corner of a crammed room. Conrad stood at the edge of the table with his arms crossed, looking at an open page of the black notebook the Brit held out to him. The Brit's visible annoyance did not discourage Nathan from entering. Casually, he strolled to the table, leaning in closely to study the tiny scribbles of undecipherable gibberish that adorned the edges of various maps. He walked to Conrad's side, and looked over his shoulder.

"In any case," the Brit continued, "according to this, we have three more days."

The unlined page he held out to Conrad was covered with combinations of letters and numbers, held together with mathematical symbols, Greek letterings, and arrows. Small areas of explanation were scribbled in the margins in an illegible cursive that looked more like lines of ants crawling across the page than text. A few numbers here and there were circled, and on some areas of the page, entire blocks of marching ants had been eradicated with a pen. Nathan's eyes shifted to the expressionless face of the Guardian studying the page. Then Conrad placed a finger underneath one number in the middle of a long equation and said, "Is this right?"

"Oh," the Brit said, as though seeing something for the first time. He flipped through a series of loose papers, jotting down numbers, and reworking an equation that had been reworked many times before.

"Aaah!" he said, as though he suddenly understood something obvious. Rows of fresh ants spilled out of the nib of his fountain pen. When he was done, he handed the notebook back to Conrad. "Here."

"So, not three days?"

"No."

"Tomorrow then?"

"Yes. Most likely late afternoon."

———————

That night, the ship rocked violently as it charged through the sea. Clutching the edge of his mattress, Nathan fought the urge to throw up. The nausea got worse when he closed his eyes. Even sitting up provided only minimal reprieve. Grasping the closet door for stability, he pulled himself onto his feet and was immediately slammed against the wall. As he stumbled to the entrance of his cabin, Nathan viscerally understood why every piece of furniture needed to be bolted down, and why sailors had the reputation of being perpetually drunk. He opened his cabin door and slid out of his room before a jolt swung the door shut behind him.

For once, he was grateful for the narrowness of the hallway and for how quickly the walls caught him as he tried to make his way to the back of the boat. He had heard somewhere that the stern provided refuge from rough seas, and he hoped this wasn't some baseless myth. At the end of the hallway, he let go of the wall and wobbled to the L-shaped sofa in the saloon. Once on the sofa, he crawled his way to its far end where only a few feet separated him from the back wall. This was as close as he would get to the back of the boat. Even so, Nathan felt little relief, if any. His stomach continued to twist dangerously.

"It's choppy tonight." Isha's voice caught him by surprise. He could barely make out the dark outline of her silhouette sitting in the love seat next to him.

"Oh. I didn't see…" Nathan swallowed the rest of his sentence along with the heave that threatened to rise.

She moved to his side and sat down.

"Here." She held out something to him. He reached toward her hand, and Isha placed two small oval pills into it.

"I gave Gregory a couple of these an hour ago. He couldn't sleep either."

"Who's Gregory?"

"The other guy."

"Oh." Nathan had only thought of the other guy as the Brit. It hadn't occurred to him that the man also had a name. He dropped the pills into this mouth and swallowed them without water.

"Will they make me sleepy?" he asked, thinking he should have asked her what they were before swallowing.

"No. They'll just help with the sea sickness. Although, you really should have taken them *before* you got sick. Now it'll be a while for them to take effect."

Great, he thought and sunk back in his seat.

"I can help, if you like?" she offered.

Nathan had experienced the healing effects of her energy before, but since that day in the helicopter, she had kept her distance from him. He realized now how much he missed being close to her, and more than anything else, how much he missed her touch. He nodded once and was glad to see her smile.

Turning her body to face him, Isha held his face in her hands — the warmth of her touch instantly soothed him. Nathan's eyes flickered shut as he relaxed into the current of her energy, which flowed into him like a gentle stream that dissolved the pressure behind his eyes, soothed the burning in his chest, and settled the twisting in his gut. All was replaced by a gentle pulse that spread through his entire body and made him feel weightless and alive. The turmoil of the sea, too, slipped away into the distance and gave way to a sensation of complete contentment — as though he was exactly where he needed to be and everything was going to be alright. How had he made it through the last few days without being this close to her?

"Thank you," he whispered, opening his eyes, feeling euphoric.

How beautiful she is, he thought.

He grabbed her face and pulled it toward his and pressed his lips against hers, feeling them part as his tongue slid into her. Nathan tasted the sweetness of her mouth. As he held her energy in him and pressed his lips to hers, he felt something crack deep inside of him, and he knew nothing would be the same, ever again.

13
the light of thaia

In her three thousand years on Thaia, Isha had been kissed by humans more times than she cared to count. It was always a repugnant experience akin to ingesting raw meat, if that meat was still attached to a living being and was determined to fight for its life. Perhaps to the carnivore races of Magira or Ulum-tukay such a sensation would be enjoyable, but to the plant-eating race of Favadan, a simple human kiss was nothing short of a vile act that seemed to have little justification. She could and did, with varying degrees of comfort, tolerate any manner of human touch — for the most part, the particles that lived on human skin were benign — yet, a kiss, especially one that exposed her to the bacteria-rich saliva of its human host, was uncomfortable beyond description. After every such exposure, she would have to isolate and expel the large quantities of intrusive microscopic particles that attempted to penetrate her extraterrestrial shell.

Because she found kissing humans so appalling, during her first two millennia on Thaia, she had protected herself from the unwanted advances of aggressive human males by alternating between the male form and one of a haggard old female who had fallen out of favor long ago. In her current physical form, she had mastered the art of guiding her human companions out of any possibility of romance and into a safe platonic space where activities that encouraged the exchange of bodily fluids were deemed ghastly out of line. Still, every few hundred years, some-one came along who was more difficult to ward off than the rest. This person, despite Isha's efforts, persisted until a situation like this arose, and he found an unavoidable opportunity to suction his lips onto hers, making her think, *Shit! Not again.*

This kiss, however, was different. This kiss was not an in-trusion on Isha's much-protected personal space. It was not an attack. When she relaxed into it, Isha had to admit that this kiss was not even unpleasant.

It was a gentle hum, at first — the faintest of vibrations that she felt buzzing through his form. Had it not been for her acute sensitivity to energy frequencies, she would not have noticed it at all. But this hum was definitely different — somehow more crisp — than the hum of Nathan's often-chaotic energy.

Isha took his tongue into her mouth, feeling his intensifying excitement. The strange, new current within him also intensi-fied. Gradually, it quickened within Nathan. Closing her eyes, Isha entered the space in the center of his chest, where this new energy was most concentrated. Subtle as it was, there was no mistaking the clarity of it — the utter perfection of it.

Thaia, she thought, smiling. *But how?*

She climbed onto his lap, his hands guiding her hips, press-ing her into himself. Isha felt Nathan's internal expansion as Thaia's unmistakable light flooded into him and entered her from every point of contact between their forms. She received Thaia willingly, feeling a weightlessness she associated with being home. Was Nathan feeling this as well? Was he aware of what was happening to him? Did he know what a spectacular miracle this communication was?

In her extreme excitement, Isha released her mental wards and yanked Veda into her form with such force that it snapped the attention of all of her kin. It was a careless act and rash. She pushed Nathan away and watched him with awe as he tried to steady his breath.

"Wow," he said, the disbelief on his face making him look even more stupid than usual. "Just, wow."

"I know," she said, feeling Veda's presence inside her.

One by one, the Favadani entered her form, relived the kiss, and gazed silently through Isha's eyes at the ordinary human who regarded them through a swirling mixture of desire and disbelief. Soon, they were all with her, and they all started speaking at once.

Isha heard "impossible" whispered in a hundred and eighty-eight different voices. There was confusion among them. They pulled wordless answers to their wordless questions from her memory banks and from wherever it was she kept her unexpressed fears.

On Favadan, fear was an ancient, outdated notion that belonged to the still-asleep and had become obsolete when the awakening of the planet rendered it useless. Experiencing fear, for Isha, was a sort of regression. As her Favadani kin prodded through her mind and uncovered the experiences that had brought her to this moment, Isha felt within her yet another human emotion that had no place or purpose among The Awakened — an emotion she wished she could keep hidden now. In this moment, Isha felt a deep sense of shame.

But it was too late. They were inside her, digging through

the recesses of her mind, and there was nothing she could do to stop them.

"Is something wrong?" Nathan asked, his voice just another in a sea of voices.

Now, her kin knew what she knew, and even though they were hesitant to accept the conclusions she had drawn, Isha felt a sense of relief ripple through her. She was no longer alone.

As the chatter inside her turned practical, the questions emerged. How did she know there were three devices? She didn't seem to have concrete proof. The devices could be harmless. She could be overreacting. The hardest questions surrounded Isha's assumption that Thaia was communicating with her through Thaian beings. This was impossible, they all agreed. Whatever she had considered as proof could not be proof at all. At best, her assumptions were based on guesses, at worst, they were distortions created by this primitive emotion she had picked up — this *fear*.

All Isha could offer in response were the memories that had helped her in reaching the conclusions she had. *But were they the right conclusions?* the voices inquired as they relived her experiences. Were there other ways she could have seen and interpreted these events?

For the past several centuries, Isha had felt the presence of Favadan fading within her. The connection that was once as constant as her breath had begun to dim. She no longer felt complete. She felt like a piece of her, a vital organ or a limb, had been yanked out of her. In its stead, a growing hollow had opened up that seemed, despite her efforts, impossible to fill.

Perhaps if this had happened overnight, she would have been better equipped to address its cause. She would have crawled into her recovery pod the very next day and allowed her Moli-orath to remake her form and reconnect her to Favadan in the process. But the void inside her had appeared too gradually. She hadn't seen it as a problem until, several centuries later, when the very idea of being remade meant death more than it meant rebirth — another primitive notion, but one she found difficult to shake. Now, with the incessant chatter of her kin inside her mind, Isha wondered if she had become too human, and if it was her desire to belong that had caused her to fabricate this story — this emergency that would put her in the role of a savior.

Isha had assumed the device was meant for destruction. She'd based this assumption on the words of a homeless man who had looked into her eyes and declared all would burn unless she did something about it. Yet how could she be certain the man had spoken with Thaia's voice? She'd assumed this man sitting in front of her, with this stupid grin on his face, was the key because he had followed her around for a month at precisely the time when she was asking Thaia for help. She had assumed there were three devices because this man had had a dream about a three-headed monster.

She'd made too many assumptions, too many decisions based on those assumptions. Could she have been wrong? Had she misunderstood or misinterpreted the signs? Was Thaia really trying to communicate with her? Or had she been so terrified — so frustrated by her own growing inability to connect with her own planet — that she had fabricated a non-existing connection to this one?

Scrutinizing her memories through the eyes of her kin, Isha questioned even the smallest of her decisions. She was overtaken by doubt.

Nathan brushed a strand of Isha's hair out of her face and tucked it behind her ear.

"What was that?" he whispered. "It was so intense."

The voices inside Isha fell silent.

"Is it always like that when you... uh... kiss one of us?"

"No," she said.

"It was amazing, right? I mean, I feel — I feel so *powerful*."

Isha looked away.

"I feel like I can do *anything*," Nathan said. "So, what is it I'm supposed to do? I'm ready."

In the moment of her hesitation, his expression shifted and became serious.

"I'm here for a reason, right?" he asked. "You didn't just bring me here for nothing. I mean, I had the dream, I can see the rock glow. I'm supposed to be here. Right?"

"Well, you're here..."

"Why are you acting like this?"

"I think... that maybe I've made too many assumptions."

"Assumptions?"

"Yes. Maybe I'm... This whole thing with the devices — I was so sure about it, but..."

"No. No, you don't get to do this right now. You don't get to drag me out here, give me a tattoo on my hand, tell me I'm special, and then take back everything you've said. It doesn't work that way."

"What if I'm wrong?"

"What if you're right?"

"Yes," she said. "What if I am right?"

The minds inside of her shifted uncomfortably as the question spread amongst them. Could she be right? They could see it now, how she had gotten to where she was. The coincidences that weren't coincidences. Thaia had left her a trail of clues, each insignificant on its own, but taken as a whole, they created a rich tapestry of information.

If you're right, the voices now interjected, *why hasn't he started his training yet?*

It's too dangerous, she said. *You saw what it did to Celeste.*

It's too dangerous to wait, they admonished.

We don't have enough information, she fought back, and they understood that she feared he might die.

There are things he can do to prepare.

On Favadan, gifted newforms began their Moli-orath training before they were able to articulate words, and that was with the thoughts and memories of an entire planet surging through them. Here was a man in his adulthood who had never lucidly experienced any consciousness beyond his own. How could he possibly become one with the infinite mind of a planet when he hadn't yet learned to be one with himself? And how could he become one with the countless minds of the Moli-orath if he hadn't yet learned to be one with the mind of his own creator? There was a chance the training alone would destroy him, and she had a deep suspicion that losing him meant losing Thaia. Yet, what was their alternative? They could wait, but would it not be worse to send him into battle unprepared, if battle was indeed on the horizon?

Without the human, Thaia's demise is inevitable, Veda's voice boomed inside her. *He must learn to control the Moli-orath if he is to prevent the events that have been set in motion. We must trust that Thaia has chosen wisely. Tomorrow, his training begins.*

It was the final word. One by one, the Favadani left Isha until she was once again alone within the confines of her form.

"If I'm right," she said, "you need to start your training as soon as possible."

"What exactly does that mean?"

"It means you need to get some rest. Tomorrow's going to be a long day."

"Every day is long," Nathan said.

"Yes," she agreed.

"Can we just sit here for a bit."

"It's late. And you need your beauty sleep."

Isha stood up, her body stable despite the violent rocking of the boat. She extended a hand to Nathan, which he took as he pulled himself onto his feet. Wrapping her arm around his waist the way she had done once before, she stabilized his steps as they walked back to his cabin. Nathan hesitated in front of his door, one hand on the knob and the other pressing her shoulder into his chest. He lingered.

"Do you remember when you helped me walk back to my car?" he asked.

"Yes."

"That feels like so long ago now."

"Yes."

"I'm glad I jumped."

She slid out of his embrace. Placing one hand gently on the side of his face, she said, "I'll see you tomorrow," and returned to the saloon.

14
reinforcements

The aliens appeared unannounced and seemingly out of nowhere, scaling the luxury liner like an army of porcelain mannequins. Some looked like they had swum impossible distances to get here, but others dropped into the ocean from the sky like man-sized bullets. Their soundless movements gave them a ghost-like presence. If Nathan hadn't already been on the second deck, watching the suspended sun of the early morning which seemed to hang for hours just above the horizon, he would not have been aware of them at all.

He hadn't slept much that night. Instead he laid in bed, thinking about Isha and the kiss that had felt like an explosion inside of him. Something within him had been irreversibly altered in that moment, but in what way, he could not say. All night, he had tried to recreate the kiss and the feeling of weightlessness and power that had accompanied it. He remembered having the distinct realization that his body was not real, that it somehow did not exist. But how he had come to such a strange conclusion, he no longer knew. In fact, the very notion seemed absurd to him now.

It was after she had climbed on top of him that he had felt his body disappear. With his eyes closed, he had suddenly seen her as a human-sized ball of light, dissolving into him. He, too, became a pulsating formless mass then, and he made a mental note of how counter-intuitive this bodiless experience was. He would have thought that without a body, he would cease to feel physical sensations, when in fact the opposite was true. Every sensation, every touch, was amplified by his seeming disembodiment. The lightest stroke against his skin sent tsunamis of pleasure through him that continued to reverberate endlessly inside the mass of energy that he felt was now the reality of what he was. The compounding effect of this ceaseless piling on of pleasure was dizzying. He remembered thinking that he couldn't possibly feel more, that he would explode. But then, his bodiless self had become somehow larger and swallowed the new waves of ecstasy, and he had felt even more weightless, more powerful.

All of these sensations now existed only in his memory. The more he tried to access them, the more they seemed to slip out of his reach, like a dream. From the corner of his eye, Nathan glimpsed a taller, thicker version of Isha and felt the exact opposite of how he had felt last night. His heavy body, which shifted uncomfortably in its seat, could not have been more real in this moment. The unquestionable closeness he had felt with Isha had also completely dissipated and given way to insecurity and doubt. Nathan could not understand why Isha hadn't told him about the arrival of all these aliens — why she hadn't prepared him for this. He interpreted her silence as indifference toward him. With it, he thought, she was making a statement about how little he mattered to her. The disinterest he encountered from the aliens only confirmed his assessment. It was as though he was invisible — to them and to her.

Nathan wondered what the Brit — Gregory — would think about this sight. How would that pompous know-it-all handle the news that their strange companions were strange for a very good reason: they were not human. Nathan could not deny himself the flash of satisfaction that accompanied the thought of the Brit walking up the stairs to the promenade deck. He imagined the look of shock in his eyes, the wordless terror that would render him mute. The momentary enjoyment Nathan experienced, however, was short-lived. Pompous ass or not, the Brit didn't deserve to be ambushed like this. What if he had a heart attack, or worse, a complete mental breakdown? At least, if Nathan prepared him in private, he would not only save the Brit from public humiliation, but would also gain the added advantage of watching fear spread on the arrogant prick's face.

Nathan practically skipped his way down the stairs to the main deck and jogged the short distance to the Brit's door, which he found ajar. He pushed open the door and entered.

The Brit was sitting up in bed, gaping open-mouthed at Conrad and Isha. From the heavy silence in the room, Nathan guessed they had just told him the news, and were waiting for him to process the information. Nathan took a step into the tense room. No one acknowledged him.

"Magnificent," the Brit said at long last, "simply magnificent."

Where was the rage? The disbelief? The anger? The *fear*? Nathan could not wrap his mind around the words coming out of the man's mouth or the large ear to ear grin that spread across his face.

"I've so many questions," the Brit continued, excitement building in his voice, his accent grating on Nathan with its atrocious smugness. "I don't even know where to begin. Why are you here? Where is your planet? Is your planet similar to ours? How are you able to breathe our air? What do you eat? Gracious! You don't eat! Of course! I never see you eating anything! But you *must* eat *something*, right? And… you…" he pointed at Conrad, "*The greatest trekker who ever lived*! Isn't that cheating?"

"Gregory," Isha interrupted. "I promise that we will answer all of your question. But not right now. Now, we have company."

"You mean Nathan?" the Brit asked. Looking at Nathan, he added, "You knew all this, and you never said a word?"

"No," Isha said. "Not Nathan. More of us."

"Where?"

"Up there. On the top deck. They're still arriving. We're… really sorry for springing this on you. We hadn't planned on them showing up. It was sort of a… last minute thing."

Last minute thing? Nathan repeated in his head, wondering if she had known about this last night. Did she really find out about their arrival *after* he had gone to bed? Was this why she hadn't said anything to him? Then another thought: could the arrival of those aliens have something to do with what happened between him and Isha? Had she told them about it with her thoughts?

It's not telepathy. He remembered her saying so many times. So, what then? Had they actually seen them kiss, or worse, experienced it through her? Nathan cringed, feeling exposed and humiliated.

"This is the greatest day of my life!" The Brit climbed out of bed, naked, beaming with excitement. "I can't tell you how utterly thrilled I am right this moment." He was seemingly in no hurry to cover himself. Nathan averted his eyes as the Brit grabbed a t-shirt from a chair and put it on, his manhood bobbing to the sway of the boat. "I knew we were not alone. I just knew. I was always so sad that we are so bloody primitive — that we can't explore out there. Why do you think I'm obsessed with the sea? Because the stars are too far away. This is brilliant. Now, you've come here. You've brought the stars here. Brilliant! I can't believe you weren't going to tell me."

The Brit was still rummaging through a drawer for his underwear when Nathan rolled his eyes and walked out. He attributed this odd order of dressing to the man's arrogance.

Back in his room, Nathan lay on his bed. Why had it been so difficult for him to accept the other-worldly nature of these beings? Why had he felt such fear? Why had he been so surprised to learn that humans were not the only intelligent beings in the universe?

I am the chosen one, Nathan thought defensively, as though trying to convince himself of an idea he did not fully believe. *I was the one who was compelled by a will greater than my own to follow a path that brought me here. I made an alien shudder by simply kissing her. I have the mark on **my** palm that proves that I am an important part of whatever it is that's happening here. The mechanics in that device react to **me**.*

There was a gentle knock at his door. Before he could decide whether or not he wanted company, the door opened and Isha entered, holding the chest that housed the mechanic-filled rock.

"You okay?"

"I can't stand that guy."

A strange expression passed across her face as she placed the chest on the table. He sat up.

"What? What was that look?"

"It's nothing," she said, unbuckling the belt.

"It was something. What? You have a thing for him?"

"Don't be absurd. It's just… human stuff that I never quite understand."

"Like what?"

"Like the amount of dislike you feel toward Gregory. It's strange. He's… a part of you."

"He's another person. I have a right not to like him."

"That's where you're wrong. Not liking him is the same as not liking yourself."

"Are you even hearing how ridiculous you sound?"

"He might be in a different body and you might even think that you dislike him, but he is still you."

"We'll just have to agree to disagree on this, because beyond being male, I have *nothing* in common with that jerk!"

He sat on the edge of the bed, staring at her, wishing she'd get on with his training. He had an idea about what would come next. She would open the chest and talk about the device, and he would be instructed to do something with the mechanics that reacted to him and to no one else. She might even ask him to hold the thing — carefully, of course. It frightened him to think about what the mechanics could do to him. He had meant to ask her if it hurts when her mechanics took her apart. He was afraid of the answer.

"Are you gonna open that or what?" he asked. She seemed to be contemplating something. Then reaching an internal decision, she said, "You're not ready."

"I'm as ready as I was last night."

"No. As long as you see Gregory as a separate entity, you will not be ready."

"What's that got anything to do with anything?"

"It's got everything to do with what we're doing here. What we're trying to accomplish. You're one arm of a body, Gregory is the other. The body needs both to function properly."

"Okay, fine! But it doesn't mean I have to like it. Or that I have to like him for that matter."

"You really don't get it. The very concept of like and dislike creates separation. It prevents you from seeing the whole. How can you find a cohesive thought among a million voices if you can't find it among two?"

"I guess we won't know until you start doing your part."

She re-buckled the belt.

"No. Not until you can see him as a part of yourself."

"Well, that's never going to happen! He's a smug son of a bitch. Honestly, I wish I'd never spoken up in that helicopter. I don't even know why he's here."

She grabbed the handle and raised the heavy chest in one effortless motion. In her eyes, he detected disappointment. At the door, she turned to face him.

"We really don't have time for this," she said and walked out.

He grabbed a shoe from the ground, hurled it, and regretted doing so even before it hit the wall next to the door. He felt angry and hurt and betrayed. He stared at the door, expecting it to open at every moment, expecting her to return with the chest and tell him that she had been wrong, that, of course, she would train him. He was, after all, the chosen one. When it was clear she would not return, he lay down in his bed, trembling with anger and feeling the rejection in her last words.

We really don't have time for this, she had said and beneath the words, behind the disappointment in her eyes, Nathan had seen doubt — real, genuine doubt.

15

gregory walsh

Every time a new alien arrived, Gregory Walsh was there to welcome him or her on board, as though he was their designated human greeter. Their wordless method of communication fascinated him. Not only did every new arrival know exactly who Gregory was, but every piece of information attained through an encounter with any one of the aliens seemed to ripple out into the rest of them instantaneously. Was this an automatic transfer of information, he wondered, or did it require conscious effort on the part of the sharer or the receiver?

Once, he slipped and a raven-haired boy who looked no older than fifteen years old caught him, breaking his fall. The boy helped him to his feet saying, "There's no need for such excitement, Gregory." A few minutes later, a muscular woman with the face of a sixty-year-old and the body of someone half that age climbed out of the water directly in front of him. When she saw him, she smiled and said, "Is your arm okay?" He had banged his elbow on the edge of a table when he fell. He told her he was alright, but several minutes later, a lanky middle-aged man walked up to him, put a hand on his aching arm and asked, "Is the pain not going away?" Gregory shook his head, and just as the man held his arm, the pain faded until nothing of it remained.

Gregory had read Orson Scott Card's *Ender's Game*. He understood the concept of hive beings that was presented in the book — how they moved as one because they shared one consciousness. But these aliens seemed different. Despite sharing memories and perhaps even thoughts, each of the aliens in this cluster looked and acted like an individual. Gregory doubted that there existed a queen whose demise would cause the instant destruction of this entire race.

What do I know? he thought. *All my knowledge about extraterrestrials comes from books written by humans.*

He observed that despite their advanced telepathic connection which allowed for instant communication, the aliens also engaged in verbal dialogue. Many stood in groups of twos and threes, and spoke in hushed strange tongues. The scene did not look much different from any human gathering. Gregory wonderedwhy they chose to speak at all when they could exchange thoughts.

The boat had not slowed its rapid pace, yet the aliens continued to swim to it effortlessly. Scaling its walls with superhuman dexterity, they looked like fallen angels, returning to the surface of earth. As their numbers grew, so did Gregory's excitement, which he unsuccessfully tried to corral. Since boarding this boat, he had often reflected on that day when his quest to find himself had turned into the possible attainment of one of his life's greatest ambitions: to be the first person to discover a sunken ship. Still, never in his wildest dreams could he have imagined the perfection of this moment: That the sunken ship they looked for had played a role in history was splendid enough, but working so closely with a race of actual extraterrestrials from a different planet in order to find this sunken treasure was fantastic beyond his imagination.

Wasn't this how life often worked out? Gregory had witnessed on so many occasions that it was in the complete hopelessness of having given up on a dream that the very thing he desired most in life somehow materialized into being. Wasn't that how he had received his professorship position at the University of Cambridge? Just as he had given up on the dream of becoming a lecturer, he had received the phone call that would — at that time — change his life. And before that, had it not been in a moment of complete despair that he had found Isabella — the honey-eyed Spaniard who, over the course of six beautifully chaotic years, had allowed him to experience a type of fierce passionate love that he had longed for since he was a boy.

Life was a mystery that solved itself once you stopped looking for the answers. Why, he wondered, try at all, when your dreams were delivered to you only *after* you've given up trying?

Gregory cringed whenever he remembered the impolite manner in which he had addressed Conrad on the morning that those strange helicopters had arrived and changed his fate once more. What had possessed him? Even as the words tumbled out of him, he had trembled internally, imagining his mother's disapproving stare descending upon him. He was acting entitled like a posh English boy. Looking back, he could see that a general sense of unease had seeped into his life long before that morning. It was this unease that had crescendoed into the compulsion to vacate his flat, leave his secure post at the university, halt every aspect of his life, and embark on a quest to find — what? What had he been searching for? Perhaps, what had made the few months leading to that fateful morning so incredibly infuriating was that, despite the immediate urgency he felt to find that thing which occupied him so completely, he had no idea what it was he was actually searching for. It was not until Nathan's speech in the helicopter that all the events of the previous months crystalized into a full image that somehow made sense.

Everything in Gregory's life had led him to that precise moment.

And now, standing on the top deck of a boat in the middle of the ocean, surrounded by dozens of extraterrestrials, hours away from fulfilling his greatest childhood dream, Gregory felt it was actually *this* precise moment toward which he had worked his entire life. He felt comfortable among these beings — as though he understood them on some deep primal level, even though he knew almost nothing about them.

Nathan had made himself scarce for most of the morning — not that Gregory cared much about what the man-child did. Nathan's passive aggressive behavior, his unpredictable mood changes, the arrogant way in which he thought the world did and should revolve around him, and the way he was actually irritated when it did not, reminded Gregory of a five-year-old child who had not been taught proper manners.

Before learning the truth about the aliens, Gregory had been slightly confused by how the American fit into the picture. The man-child did not seem to have any particular skills and spent most of his time sulking or staring blankly into space. Since the revelations of this morning, Gregory's confusion was heightened. He felt perplexed that these advanced beings would choose such an average, moody companion. Surely, they could have chosen better.

Gregory wasn't certain what prompted him to turn his head, but when he did, he saw the most beautiful creature he had ever beheld. Even his ex-wife Isabella, whose striking beauty had riled up much talk in their small English village, paled in comparison to the exquisite being who stood against the railing, ringing the water out of her glistening raven hair. He leapt forward at the sight of her, almost involuntarily, grabbed a towel from a pile next to him, and jogged to her side.

"Here," he said, handing her the towel. She was as tall as he was, with golden brown skin and large, knowing eyes.

"Thanks, Gregory." She smiled. "I'm Margot."

"Pleasure."

Margot grabbed the towel and walked away.

By now, Gregory knew she didn't actually need to dry herself — none of them did. He had seen them go from sopping wet to dry within seconds by puffing air out of their pores. Still, he had wanted an excuse to talk to her, and she had humored him. As she walked away, he studied the dip of her lower back, the subtle sway of her hips as she walked, and the perfect roundness of her bottom. When he caught a glimpse of someone looking at him, he became suddenly aware that, even though her back was turned to him, she could probably see him through the eyes of the aliens surrounding him, and his face reddened with embarrassment. Gregory sat down, and resting his forehead on the table in front of him, he concentrated on keeping his eyes and thoughts as far away from Margot as he could, wishing the pounding inside his chest and the throbbing in his loins would subside.

———————

After lunch, the ship slowed and the engines were cut. They had arrived. Gregory felt an actual flutter in his stomach. If someone were to be watching them, if they stood far enough away, they would perceive a moment as ordinary as any other.

But standing in this specific location, at this specific moment, with these specific beings by his side, Gregory knew there was nothing ordinary about this scene. People waited their entire lives for a moment like this, and most would never attain it. Gregory imagined the sunken HMCS Levis waiting patiently some 2,500 meters below his feet, and his heart skipped a beat.

The aliens gathered on the second deck. Gregory had counted forty-four earlier, including Isha and Conrad. They waited, their smooth olive skin sparkling in the sun, their deep green eyes wild with anticipation. Each of these beings on his own would be considered an exotic beauty. Standing in a cluster, unblinking and barely moving, they resembled an assortment of high-end mannequins to be used in posh displays at overpriced shops.

Isha emerged with Nathan in tow.

"All of you know why we are here," Conrad said, standing in a corner. Everyone turned to face him. "We have one of three devices in our possession. The second device should be in the wreckage below. We think the third will be near the Lover's Bridge." Turning to Gregory, he added, "Some of our kin are now in Taiwan looking for this device."

How many of them are on this planet? Gregory wondered.

"You were all with Isha last night," Conrad continued. "So, you understand the urgency of this situation. If Isha is right, and at this point we must assume she is, Thaia's very survival may be at stake."

As Conrad spoke, Gregory detected no surprise on any of the faces surrounding him. Everyone knew what Conrad was sharing. They knew it even before the words were spoken. This meeting was for his benefit alone. He wondered who Thaia was and what her demise might mean to the humans living on Earth.

He glanced over at the American and saw him standing next to Isha with his arms crossed tightly across his chest, his back stooped, and his eyes fixed on a spot on the ground right in front of him. There was such discomfort in his posture that Gregory actually felt pity for the man-child. He also began to consider a new possibility. What if, he wondered, Nathan wasn't so terrible after all? What if he was just a young person, in over his head? Gregory had also been young once, and so he knew that pride and insecurity made for lousy personality traits.

"Based on the evidence that Isha has gathered, it is highly probable that these devices have been programmed to harm Thaia," Conrad went on. "We all know what this means, but, there is something more. Something I discovered in my conference with Veda moments ago. There is news of stirrings at Viliov: secret meetings held in the cover of the forest. For three thousand years we have known no secrets among the Awakened. Such activity during this sensitive time does not bode well."

There was a rustling among the aliens as they straightened and turned into stone statues, as though they had all simultaneously looked into the eyes of Medusa. Gregory had never seen anything like this. He took a step back, and was startled when he bumped into the stone figure of a man — cold, hard, and immovable. The blood drained from him. When he turned around, he caught Nathan's unimpressed eyes staring back at him. An amused smile passed over the man-child's face.

"It's okay, Gregory," said Isha. "Don't be frightened."

Only Isha and Conrad had retained their human facades.

"Oh, I am not frightened. Just surprised is all. What's happened to them?"

"They have hardened," said Conrad. "They didn't know about the meetings at Viliov — the Camp of our Elders. They have left briefly to join our Elder, Veda, and learn the details."

"They've left?"

"Yes," said Conrad, "their consciousness is no longer here. It is easier for them to receive this information from Veda's mind than through my word."

It makes sense, Gregory thought. *It's not a hive. They actually **leave** their bodies and enter someone else's. They **share** their minds.*

"Are you all right?" asked Conrad. Gregory nodded.

"This… this is a remarkable ability," he said, nodding as he looked around. "Such an efficient form of communication."

The statue of a young man next to him softened as he stared at it. The sight brought a smile to Gregory's face, and made him wish he could touch one of these statues and *feel* it transform. He decided he would make at least one friend who'd allow him to feel the change.

"Thoma and Ma'ona," said the young man next to Gregory, "the cunning and the survivalist. We should have guessed."

"Nothing is certain," said Conrad. One by one, the statues around them came to life. "If this plan belongs to them, we must proceed with extreme caution."

"Ma'ona is the only Nooritan who would plot against the Awakened," said a voice behind Gregory.

"But she cannot be the mastermind. She is not imaginative enough to deceive us for so long," said another.

"We must alert the others."

"No," said Isha. "There is a reason Pa'arians have penetrated Thaian politics so easily. One of their greatest gifts is their ability to collect allies. If Thoma is behind this betrayal, we do not know whose alliances he has secured."

"We cannot sit idly by and wait for the execution of their

plan," said a woman.

"We are not idle," said Conrad. "We are not alone either. Thaia has chosen these humans to help us. You have all seen how Gregory's extensive knowledge of Thaian history led us to this location. Once we find the devices, Nathan will learn their purpose and disarm them."

All eyes shifted to Nathan. Gregory could almost feel the weight of their expectant stares. A phrase Conrad used replayed in his mind and started to solidify into a new realization. Conrad had praised his knowledge of *Thaian* history. Could it be that Thaia was what they called Earth? Could it be that it was his planet's fate that was in question?

"A planet does not make mistakes," Isha said, as though in response to Gregory's unasked questions. "Thaia has chosen him for a reason. He is more powerful than he knows."

Nathan dropped his gaze and shifted his weight uncomfortably. For a brief, fleeting moment, Gregory had the strange urge to step in and protect the man-child from further scrutiny. He ignored the impulse, and the moment passed.

16
doubt

Nathan wanted to scream, to punch something, to throw himself off the side of the ship. For a fraction of a second, he even wished for the three-headed monster of his nightmares to burst through the cover of the ocean and swallow him whole.

He couldn't even hear them any more over the shouts of his own racing mind. All of them — the aliens, the ship, the ocean, and even the threat of annihilation — drifted away somewhere beyond the cold emptiness of his existence. The only sound inside the chill that occupied him was the cacophony of vicious attacks of his own internal voice, which screamed its disapproval of his stupidity, pointing out what a fool he'd been, reasoning that his only saving grace would be to end his worthless life. And in the very center of the dizzying chaos inside him was a nauseating shame. He knew this feeling all too well. It was the emotional signature of his childhood. This shame enveloped every experience he wanted erased from his life. It told him of asthma attacks during birthday parties, of being betrayed by friends, of being ridiculed for the weak, small nothing that he was.

He had felt such relief last night when he saw her on the sofa. Even before she'd placed her hand on him and taken away the physical symptoms of his seasickness, he'd felt better just by her sheer proximity. Now, he saw what a fool he'd been.

You were all with Isha last night. Conrad had said, and the words continued to twist inside him on a loop, threatening to burn a hole through him.

The strange look in Isha's eyes, her hesitation, the piercing tension that had appeared out of nowhere — it all made sense now. They were all with her in that private, intimate moment. How naive he'd been to think that an encounter with him could mean anything at all to her. He wished he could go back and erase the evening, erase this week, erase the last two months, erase his whole life.

What the hell are you looking at? Nathan thought as his eyes caught the Brit's intrusive glare. *You know nothing about me!*

Everything, he decided, was the Brit's fault. The arrogant prick had showed up with his fancy degrees and technical jargon and swayed them against him.

I am the chosen one! Nathan wanted to scream. *I have the mark on my hand. I am the one who had the dream that brought us here! You should believe in ME — not him!*

Even in the midst of his silent declarations, Nathan doubted the soundness of his claims. The dream, the mark on his hand, the mechanics — what if none of it meant anything? What if everything that had happened to him was an elaborate ruse to make sure the Brit — their true hero — made it onto this ship?

With his eyes fixed on Isha's, Nathan thought about how she had failed him, how she had rejected him, worse, how she had sided with the Brit against him. She had humiliated him, and even now, she continued to humiliate him with her empty words, which no one, including Isha, believed.

Isha placed a hand on his arm, which Nathan shrugged off.

"Empty words," Nathan said under his breath.

"Nathan—" Isha began.

"Come on," Nathan interrupted. He could not bear hearing more lies. "Be real for just one moment. Even you don't believe the bullshit coming out of your mouth."

"It's not—"

"I can see it in your face. I can see it in all your faces. Not a single one of you believes I can do whatever the hell it is I'm supposed to do. Not a one. And you know something? You're right. I don't think I can do it. I really, truly don't think I can do it, because I don't know what the hell it is I'm supposed to do. You'd think that, at some point, someone would clue me in on why I'm even here."

It was the disappointment in Isha's eyes that made him back up until he found the railing behind him. She had no right to be disappointed. Not after all she'd put him through. He turned and walked down the stairs, his chest about to explode from his shame.

"Nathan," she called after him. "Nathan, stop!"

Despite his urge to run back to his cave and lock himself into his room, Nathan froze at the bottom of the stairs, his back turned to her.

"You say that we haven't been training you?"

"You haven't." Nathan turned to face her.

"Your training began the moment Thaia chose you. The moment you started having that nightmare. All you have to do is close your eyes and see with—"

"Stop with the damn riddles."

"It's not a riddle."

"Close your eyes and see? That's your answer?"

"Nathan." She descended the stairs toward him. "To control the Moli-orath you must become one with them."

"What the hell does that even mean?"

"It's a dangerous process. We train for it all our lives."

"So, shouldn't you be showing me what I'm supposed to do instead of ignoring me?"

"Ignoring you?"

"I guess on your planet you show affection by leaving someone alone all day after you've rejected them?"

"Rejected you?"

"Don't play coy, Isha."

"I was giving you space to meditate. To reflect. You must learn to be one within yourself before you can be one with the Moli-orath."

"Stop! Just stop with the damn Yoda talk. I'm tired of all your games — of this… bullshit."

"I assure you, this is not a game."

There was nothing more to say. He saw pity in her eyes as he turned away from her, and felt angry at the audacity of this emotion. All he could do now was to rush back to his room before he screamed or punched a hole into a wall or threw himself off the side of the boat.

He entered his room and slammed the door behind him, instantly regretting every word he'd spoken. Had he overreacted? His mother often accused him of being too proud to admit when he's wrong and too stubborn to apologize. With his back pressed to the door, he slid to the ground, wondering if his mother's words held true in this situation.

Could it be that there was room for both him and the Brit in this plot? And if that was the case, and if the fate of Earth was truly on the line, should he not return to the upper deck and make peace with the aliens? Make peace with the Brit?

Nathan lay down on his side, and collected himself into a tight ball. The pressure of the hard floor that pressed heavily against his arm and hip bone, the scratch of the rough carpet against the smooth skin of his cheek, the piercing cold of the metal at the bottom of the door against his back — it all felt oddly appropriate in this moment. Why was it so difficult to walk out of this door and up those stairs? The thought of admitting that he may have acted rashly felt like a mountain crushing down on him. He compressed himself into as small a thing as possible. Then, he closed his eyes, hoping sleep and his nightmare would take him.

17

alive and unfulfilled

Typical, Gregory thought.

He'd had students like Nathan. Young adults who lacked the ability to sit with problems long enough to discover solutions. Students who, with their lack of patience, perpetuated a sense of confusion and helplessness that followed them around like a stink.

As Nathan spoke with Isha at the bottom of the stairs, Gregory had felt Nathan's frustration, his utter powerlessness, and he had thought, *Just shut your mouth for one bloody moment and listen!*

"He will come around," said Conrad, addressing the group. "There is much to do. We must dive. Do we have the blueprints?"

From inside of his black notebook, Gregory produced a number of papers that he unfolded onto a table.

"The *Levis* is reported to have been torpedoed in 1941," he said. "Before it sank, it was towed for several hours, so its exact location is unknown. But no one knows mathematics and the history of the ship and this part of the ocean as well as I do. And based on my calculations, my knowledge of protocol at the time, and of course of human behavior during crisis, I believe the ship should be half a click southwest of precisely where we are standing." He paused more for effect than to gather his thoughts. It was strange not receiving any response. To perform these calculations required a unique set of interests and an acute technical prowess that Gregory happened to possess. And yet, if these extraterrestrials were impressed, their impassive faces did not reveal this.

"Now, I understand that you are anxious to dive," he went on.

"We don't get anxious," a voice interrupted.

"Right. All I'm saying is, I suggest taking a look at these blueprints before you dive, even though you might be feeling — I'm sorry, if you are not anxious, what are you feeling?"

"It's not important," Conrad said.

"I mean, you look anxious. You're certainly acting like people who might be anxious. So, what? You don't actually feel it?"

"We don't feel the way you feel," Conrad said. "We're able to receive the information that a feeling would communicate without actually experiencing it as a sensation within our bodies."

"So, a feeling without a physical response?"

"More like information without a feeling," Isha said. "Feelings, to us, are a rudimentary form of communication."

"None of that is relevant right now," Conrad cut in. "So, if you would, please."

"Right." Gregory tried to gather his thoughts. "The ship itself should be mostly intact despite imaginary monster bites." He forced a smile ignoring the large portion of his attention that was still preoccupied by the idea of emotions that did not feel like anything, but rather provided information. "Personally," he went on, "I would start the search in the underbelly and work outward. But I don't want to tell you how to do your job."

The aliens gazed at him impassively, wordlessly. He continued, without looking at them. "There should be a chamber in this area — it's not in the blueprints but, based on my research, I have reason to believe that it exists. My guess is that it was built to hide sensitive information. Most of these old ships have hidden chambers. My bet is that your device is hidden somewhere inside this room."

"*If* the room exists," someone said.

"It exists," Gregory said defensively. "Also, there should be at least one cavity inside one of the walls that could fit a chest. The second place I would look is here, in the captain's chamber. I would look for something — a desk, a chest, a shelf — something that you can push aside to reveal a secret opening. If someone wanted to hide a time bomb on the ship, this would be the perfect spot for it. Most of the sailors wouldn't even know about it, so hardly anyone would ever look here."

"The device would not need to be hidden from human eyes," said one of the aliens with a deep voice. "Its shape is its disguise."

"From what I understand," said Gregory, "it is not being hidden from human eyes alone."

"In which case placing it in a hidden chamber would do little," said a short man with a long angular face.

"So, what are you saying?"

"That the most obvious location may not be the right one."

"I'm merely outlining a plan."

"We are, Mr. Walsh, the most efficient beings on this primitive planet," said a tall, lean man. "If the device is anywhere within a ten-click radius, we will find it in less than a Thaian hour — with or without your plan."

Conrad stepped in just as Gregory's lips parted for a reply.

"Gregory is right," Conrad said. "We may be fast swimmers, and our senses may be more sophisticated than anything this planet has produced, but even we need a starting point for our search. If we're done here, please, let's dive."

Without any more objections, the aliens walked to the edge of the balcony, on their way glancing at the blueprint of the WWII ship and the map of the ocean that Gregory had laid out. Silently, they removed all their clothes and dove into the ocean stark naked, without any scuba gear.

The water was calm. It rose and fell like the gentle rapid breath of a sleeping child. One by one, it swallowed the bodies that passed into it, erasing all traces of them almost immediately.

Gregory had observed that they did not need to breathe under water, but it was still strange for him to see that, once submerged, they never returned to the surface for air. As the number of the aliens on deck diminished, Gregory felt his heart sink into sadness. He wished he could simply take off his clothes, and dive in alongside them. Soon, he, Isha and Conrad were the only three people remaining on the deck. The rest of the ship was occupied by Nathan and the crew, none of whom seemed to care about the treasure hidden deep below them.

Conrad slipped his feet out of his shoes, and stood barefoot looking out into the horizon. "I understand you'd like to see the ship," he said.

"More than anything."

"We won't be down there long, and as soon as we find the device, we will need to come back up. But, I can persuade them to wait until you have seen what you've come to see."

Gregory turned to face Conrad. He could barely process what was being said to him. He knew that without special equipment, which they did not have on board, it was impossible for him to reach the ocean floor.

"The obvious problem with this suggestion — if indeed you are suggesting what I think you are," Gregory said, "is that the ship is at more than two thousand five hundred meters below sea level — it's an impossible depth."

"True. And if you were diving on your own, you'd never be able to make it that far down. But the advantage of diving with one of us, Mr. Walsh, is that we can use our bodies to protect yours."

"How?" Gregory's heart nearly stopped beating. Could this proposition be real? Was there a way for him to dive that far below sea level without risking his life?

"When it stops being safe for you, I will connect my body to yours," Conrad explained. "To be more precise, I will wrap my body around yours and will absorb the pressure to protect you from it. Think of me as a personal submarine."

"Wrap your body around mine?"

"Yes."

"How?"

Conrad smiled. "You'll have to see to find out."

Gregory realized he had never seen Conrad smile before. In fact, he had only seen a few smiles among the dozens of aliens he had encountered. The smile Conrad shared with him was warm but also coy. Whatever this technique was that they had developed, he was proud of it, and perhaps even excited to share it.

"And that will allow me to dive as deep as the sea floor?" he asked again.

"Yes. We have only tried this once before. We lost only one human among more than a dozen. But that's because his Guardian did not monitor his vitals closely enough. Our advantage is that we were able to learn from her mistake. If I sense your body might be in danger, I will turn back to the surface. Do you understand?"

"Yes. Alive and unfulfilled dreams is better than dead and at the bottom of the sea."

"Precisely."

Without another word, Gregory ran down the stairs to a small closet that housed the scuba gear, feeling within him a joy he had not experienced since his childhood — the joy of Christmas mornings and of hot cocoa, the joy of seeing Roger, his first golden retriever, for the first time, the joy of fresh baked cookies and finding an extra bonbon when he thought them gone. He was a child again as he hurriedly shed his clothes and replaced them with the rubbery second skin of a scuba suit.

18

sunken treasure

G regory was no stranger to diving. From the time he remembered, the beautiful, eerie scenes that existed just a few meters below the surface of the sea had beckoned him. In his twenties, he had spent every holiday and every last quid that he had painstakingly earned on exploring majestic, silent worlds that only a handful of humans would ever see.

He loved the feeling of floating inside an infinite sapphire abyss, where his own breath was all he could hear. He often imagined himself on a different planet when he dove — an intergalactic explorer, suited up in his special garb, carrying his precious oxygen, descending onto uncharted lands with strange creatures and their stranger ways of life. And in his fantasies, when he encountered the native inhabitants of the planets he visited, Gregory would often suspend his breath, even for just a brief moment, and float weightlessly among them, listening and watching with awe.

He had seen many incredible sights over the years, some he would never forget or be able to describe in any meaningful way. It was impossible to describe, for example, the feeling of utter wonder when the call of a humpback whale vibrated through his entire body moments before the whale and its calf passed just a few meters above him. He thought he had learned the meaning of life in that fleeting moment. He could have died right there, in that expanded, frozen instance, and his life would have been complete.

In all his years diving, however, Gregory had not encountered an animal as strange — as so completely otherworldly — as Conrad, swimming along his side. There was nothing *human* or even *earthly* about the being that took shape in front of his eyes. The creature that Conrad became only a few meters below the surface of the sea would fascinate any scientist in any field of study. Illuminated by some internal source, Conrad's entire body pulsed with a faint golden glow that made him look almost translucent. On the surface, Gregory had witnessed the transformation of the aliens' skin from flesh into stone and back to flesh again. Down here, Conrad's entire body took on a strange new consistency.

In the way that Conrad's body flattened and elongated in response to the pressure of the sea, Gregory saw the incredible amount of control it must have taken these beings to assimilate to life on Earth. The alien, who had resembled a humanoid just moments before, with his distinguishable limbs and seemingly solid outer membrane, now melted into a directionless mass that danced its way through the darkening sea almost aimlessly. Even his face had disappeared — smoothed into a luminous flatness that could only be told apart from the rest of it by the blotch of hair still attached to its head.

Gregory realized how little he knew about the true nature of these beings and wondered what conditions needed to be present on Conrad's home planet to demand such flexibility of form from its most evolved species.

At forty meters, the glowing mass that had once been Conrad came to hover directly above him. Gregory felt his heart rate accelerate and had to consciously slow his breathing — he did not want to run out of oxygen, not on this dive, not with so much at stake. Conrad's body expanded above him as it flattened into an imposing canvas. Then the elastic mass descended onto him like a blanket, wrapping itself around Gregory's body until nothing of Gregory remained exposed aside from the few centimeters of his mask through which he could still witness the wonders beyond.

The physical relief he felt was immediate. All at once, the familiar pressure of the sea faded away. With no gravity and no sea pressure to work on his body, Gregory experienced an entirely new kind of weightlessness.

This is what a child must feel inside its mother's womb, he thought, not without a private sense of glee.

He felt safe inside this cocoon of alien flesh. Gregory did not resist the descent into the dark abyss below them, which was happening at a frightening acceleration. He focused on his breath and closed his eyes. Only when he opened his eyes for brief moments did he realize the fantastic speed of their drop. He noted that despite the increasing depth, his body continued to be protected from the bone-crushing pressure that would have otherwise claimed his life.

At the bottom of the ocean, they were surrounded by an endless impenetrable blackness — a complete and utter absence of light. He remembered the light mounted to the top of his mask, but when he tried to reach for it, the resistance he encountered reminded him that his limbs were no longer his own. But Conrad realized what he was trying to do, and Gregory's arm floated up on its own to switch on the light, revealing a desolate world just beyond. Gregory consciously registered the utter incredibility of the fantastical experiment in which he was participating.

The seabed was empty and eerily uninviting. He had only seen such an underwater desert in nature documentaries, and had found it fascinating that even at this impossible depth with its harsh conditions, if one looked hard enough, life could be found. But not here, apparently — he saw no signs of life as they floated a few meters above the barren floor.

Like a giant emerging from an all-encompassing fog, the HMCS Levis came into view. Gregory's heart nearly stopped for a moment as he took in the magnificent sight. The massive, exceptionally well-preserved, silt-covered ship lay on its side like a sleeping beast. Strange blobs of alien flesh dove in and out of its many cavities like translucent ghosts — their elongated limbs whipping through the heavy water effortlessly. Observing the incredible efficiency of their movements, Gregory understood their frustration when he was attempting to educate them. He felt embarrassed for assuming there was anything at all he could teach them. These beings were far more advanced than what he, with his limited human imagination, could have fathomed. He remembered now, too, what Isha had shared with him earlier — that they had arrived on Earth a little over three thousand years ago. Now, witnessing a completely alien side of these extraterrestrials, Gregory thought about how incredibly long three thousand years was and how casually Isha had talked about this massive block of time as though it was no more than an afternoon.

He marveled at how relative everything was — his notion of time, their similarities and differences, the very depth of the ocean. Every idea he formulated in his mind was dependent on everything else he knew and understood about the world.

Change one tiny detail, and all that precious knowledge fell apart.

It was as though Conrad could read his mind. All Gregory had to do was to think an act and it would be completed on its own. The whole thing was a dance, simple and effortless. Their conjoined bodies floated toward an opening that Gregory noticed on the side of the ship. He wondered how Conrad was doing this. Was the alien actually reading his mind? Was this even possible? Or was there a far simpler explanation?

The answer came to him.

Of course, he thought, *micro-movements.*

It made perfect sense. Whenever he thought of doing something, his body responded with movements that would, above water, prepare his body for the action and therefore precede it. It was these micro-movements that Conrad must be responding to, Gregory decided, and once again, he felt completely in awe about the complexity of the being that literally carried him.

Gregory had visited many shipwrecks in his dives. Every ship that was within a diving depth, Gregory had made an effort to explore. So, he was familiar with the strange feeling of drifting through abandoned hallways, trying to reconstruct a life that had been cut short by tragedy. He was fascinated by how time and environment changed an object, sometimes beyond recognition. A shipwreck — especially one close enough to the surface to support ample life — was the most beautiful analogy he had ever found for how all things, even objects, wanted to live beyond their intended lifespans and sometimes outside of their intended purpose. You never knew what a thing was meant for until it found its own place in the world. Like the ships he explored, Gregory longed to find his own true purpose, and often wondered what tragedy in his life would, at last, help him unlock this internal puzzle.

Now, as Conrad's body carried him into the HMCS Levis, he questioned even this deep-held belief that a thing could find its true purpose after its death. Never before had he seen a shipwreck so devoid of life, so desolate, so sad. What was the purpose of this ship, lying here at the bottom of this ocean, where no person, creature or plant could interact with it in any meaningful way? For what had all those soldiers who once roamed these corridors lost their lives?

The Captain's chamber was eerily intact, and Gregory found it curious that it remained undisturbed, wondering if the aliens had deliberately left this room untouched. Gregory decided they had most likely left this room alone because they knew he would enjoy exploring it. It was, after all, the first room to which Conrad had brought him.

The duo hovered at its entrance, giving Gregory time to process the sight. Gregory thought about tilting his head toward a cabinet in a corner, and without any more effort from him, his body floated to it. His and Conrad's conjoined hands drifted into view and with one swift, effortless motion, pulled away the large wardrobe from the wall. Gregory's heart nearly skipped a beat at the sight of a child-sized door revealed behind the cabinet. He had half expected to be wrong. The accounts that suggested a secret passage built into a ship like the Levis were few and often from unverifiable sources.

As Conrad carried him toward the small door, Gregory wondered how much oxygen he had already used up, and how much time he had left to explore. He had come to instinctively know these answers by always being aware of the weight of the oxygen he carried. But now, with Conrad assuming all of his weight, these details he often took for granted turned into mere guesses. His only option was to trust that Conrad was aware of the vital functions of his body. A sentence Conrad had casually brushed over earlier, now stood out in Gregory's mind. Hadn't he mentioned that someone had died doing precisely what he was doing now?

Their bodies pushed the door open and glided through its snug entry into a narrow passageway barely tall enough to stand in. They darted through the empty hallway a bit too fast for Gregory's comfort. After diving for decades, he had learned to move into dark, tight spaces slowly and deliberately. One never knew what dangers lurked in the hidden corners of the sea. At the end of the hall, the passage split into two. The accounts with which Gregory was familiar spoke only of one of these paths — the one on the right, which, would most likely lead to a small chamber behind the command room. Gregory looked to the left wondering why this second fork existed and where it led. Conrad moved them into the direction of his gaze. Near the end of the corridor, a dark, uneven heap caught the tail of his headlamp's rays and came into view. It was the first unusual thing they had encountered since they entered the ship.

It could have been anything — a creature, perhaps a nest of sorts. As his heart pounded inside him, Gregory tried to remember and categorize any creatures he knew about that lived at this intense depth. From sharks to squids to fish, it was always the most terrifying that survived inside this crushing void. He held his breath as Conrad accelerated toward the thing. This was not what he would have done.

They stopped directly above the pile, their backs pressed into the ceiling. The creature they encountered had been dead a long while, but it was not alien, nor of the sea. Lying beneath them, wide-eyed and open-mouthed, an eerily well-preserved corpse of a WWII soldier stared back at them. The soldier reminded Gregory of every frightening animatron he had encountered at theme parks and shops — strange, mechanical human-shaped things that moved just enough to terrify but not enough to inspire awe.

The soldier clutched a rectangular box to his collapsed chest.

Could it be? Gregory thought. Could this be what they had come here to find?

Their arm reached down and, with the precision of a surgeon, snapped the lock on the box. Gregory's body tensed with anticipation. He no longer had the will nor the self-awareness to control his rapid breath.

Though they were looking for something specific, Gregory did not know what it was they had come to find. Whatever it was, however, this dead soldier had no business carrying it. In fact, this alien contraption, which by Isha's own admission was more destructive than any bomb devised by human minds, did not have any place on this planet, let alone on this ship. Still, as Conrad flipped open the lid of the metallic box, Gregory hoped they would find the device for which they had come.

The alien device was not what they found. Instead, Gregory stared into a chest filled with golden coins. This was an actual treasure. His hand floated down and removed a single coin from the heap, which it squeezed into the small pouch on Gregory's utility belt before they hastened out of the narrow passage in the same direction they had come. His time, Gregory realized, had run out, but not before he'd found what every archeologist would have given up an arm or a first-born son to discover: a perfectly preserved body, aboard a long-lost WWII ship, clutching an actual treasure. The social, political, and historic implications of such a find could be groundbreaking. Later, when everything was settled and well, Gregory would have to return — this time with a crew — to excavate this marvelous site. He realized that the purpose of this sunken ship was intimately tied to his.

Conrad must have read his mind, because before exiting the Captain's chamber, he closed the door to the secret passage and blocked it once more with the cabinet. When they re-emerged out of the ship, Gregory took in the sight of the Levis one last time before Conrad began their ascent at a much slower pace. As he allowed his body to be pulled upward, Gregory hoped everything would go well, that Nathan would do his part to save Earth, and that he would be able to return one day with more time, funding, and proper equipment.

He had finally found the sense of purpose that he'd been looking for his entire life.

19
cracked open

The knock at Nathan's door was relentless. Three little taps at a time followed by another three little taps followed by another three little taps. It was enough to drive a person crazy. Nathan opened his eyes and tried to make sense of the sideways view of the cluttered floor. The sole of a shoe stared back at him from only a few feet away. Next to it, the edge of a discarded candy wrapper peeked out from beneath a white towel.

"Nathan?" Her voice pierced through the door. "Nathan, open the door."

Nathan's stiff neck cracked as he peeled himself off the ground and straightened himself into a seated position, leaning heavily against the door behind him.

"Nathan," she said. "Please."

"Hold on." Nathan's voice was coarse.

Once he was standing with his hand on the doorknob, he paused. What would happen if he didn't open the door? Would she eventually give up and walk away? He could feel her energy, just inches away, seeping into him through the solid door. He wished he was someone else. Someone more brave. Someone less plagued by anxiety.

"Nathan." Her voice was just above a whisper, but he heard it as though she was speaking inside his head. He twisted the knob and opened the door.

"Hi," she said.

"Hey."

"Can I come in?"

He shrugged, walked into the cabin, and sat down on his bed. She followed him into the room.

"I know you're upset," she said, "but we need to work together. We're on the same team."

"That's the problem," Nathan muttered under his breath. From basketball to debate, there was not a single team he had not let down with his incompetence. Perhaps if she had done her due diligence and interviewed some of his previous teammates, she would declare defeat now and save herself all the disappointment that awaited them in the future.

She sat down next to him. "What's going on with you?"

"Nothing, I just need some time alone."

"We don't have time."

Nathan scoffed.

"You don't have to take my word for it," she said. "You feel the urgency. I feel it growing in you."

"What's growing in me is frustration."

"And anger?"

"Yes! Anger. I'm just — I want to punch something all the time."

"And you feel you need to punch something now?"

"Yes."

"You feel an urgency."

"Yes. No — it's not what you're saying."

"Your emotions are communicating with you."

"Yes. They're saying that I shouldn't be here. All of this is a mistake."

"No. That's not it."

"How the hell do you know what my emotions are telling me?"

"What happened up there?"

Nathan shrugged.

"I'm confused by you, Nathan," she said. "To be perfectly honest, your behavior makes no sense."

"No offense, but you're not exactly the authority on human behavior."

"It's true that there are things I still don't understand about humans. But I am willing to learn."

"Is that why you're here, Isha? To study us? Am I a science experiment for you? Some kind of sick game?"

"You're not being serious."

"Maybe I am. Maybe I don't know anything about you or what you want. What exactly are your motives?"

"Do you really think that what's happening here is an experiment?"

Nathan did not have an answer.

"Well? Do you?"

"No," he admitted.

"Then, why are you doing this? What are you fighting?"

"I'm not... I'm not fighting anything."

"Are you sure?"

"I'm not," Nathan said, though he could feel the fight inside him. In reality, he was fighting everything and everyone. He was fighting her and her unrealistic expectations. He was fighting the idea that he was special and the knowledge that his life meant nothing at all. He was fighting his thoughts that told him all this was a mistake, that there was no future in which he didn't fail. Her question was too casual, and it had hit too close to the truth. He felt exposed.

She placed a hand on his knee, sending waves of her electricity into his thighs and up his spine. Nathan felt the lump in his throat tighten in response to her touch. Every part of him was drawn toward her. All he wanted was to melt into her until nothing of him remained.

"Last night," she said, "you allowed Thaia into your body. I felt her through you. Do you know how you did that?" There was genuine curiosity in her voice, yet Nathan could not think straight. Her touch occupied him. It possessed him.

"This is how it starts, you know? The Awakening. With small bursts of insight, maybe a general feeling of lightness. Losing awareness of time and space. Feeling like you are beyond your body."

"I…" Nathan swallowed, trying to concentrate. "I didn't feel any of that."

"You didn't?" She removed her hand from his knee, relieving him of the intensity of her touch. His eyes focused on her parted lips. The thought of kissing her was the only thing that made sense.

"It's natural to not understand what happened," she said. Her hand returned to his thigh and came to rest an inch above his knee. "Your body and your mind are not used to that level of awareness. An adjustment period is expected. But you need to stop fighting it." Leaning in slightly as though she was sharing a secret, she added, "You need to stop feeling sorry for yourself."

All Nathan could do in response was to shake his head. He

wasn't feeling sorry for himself. She was wrong. But he could not find the words to object. Did she not know what effect her touch had on him?

"This amazing thing has happened to you," she exhaled into his face, her voice stern like that of a school teacher, "and instead of trying to understand it, instead of trying to use it to get ready for the task you've been assigned, you choose to sit around and sulk in your room."

Unable to restrain himself any longer, he pounced on top of her, his hand grasping the back of her neck and pressing his lips into hers. Inside his chest, Nathan felt something tear open and through it, he saw a white infinity, expanding beyond the reaches of time and space. A bright, endless light flooded into him until it completely engulfed him. His body pulsated as an endless stream of the most vibrant glow rushed through him. He understood the true meaning behind the words *life force*. This was what it meant to be alive. This was what it felt to have the force of life flow through him.

Her body stiffened beneath his as he kissed her. The intense current inside him became unruly, uncontrollable as it rushed through him and into her. She twisted in his arms, her fingers digging into the flesh of his chest as her trembling hands attempted to press him away.

Forcing himself to pull away from her, he pried her hands from his body. The moment her fingers unfurled, she flung herself backward, her hardened body hitting and splintering the dresser at the end of the bed.

She remained there, frozen in time, her burning green eyes piercing through her cold, stone shell. The energy that had filled Nathan retreated into the crack inside his chest, and disappeared. Soon no trace of it remained except for a tingling lightness inside his head. The image of the stunned alien in front of him distracted Nathan from the pain in his own body. The thought that he had hurt her terrified him. He waited anxiously for her to soften, unable to look away from the pained expression on her frozen face.

"Oh, thank god," he breathed when she finally softened. "Are you okay? I'm so sorry. I didn't mean to —"

"I'm okay."

"I didn't mean to... I'm... I'm sorry... I didn't mean to hurt you. I'm so sorry."

"It wasn't your fault," she said. "Also, you can't hurt me that easily."

"But I saw you—"

"It was intense but not painful."

"But you looked —"

She laughed. "I don't experience pain the way you do. I was... struggling, because... I was trying not to hurt you."

"Hurt me?"

"Nathan, what I could do to you if I'm not careful... You might want to learn to control that energy — for your own sake. How're you feeling?"

"I'm not sure." This time, Nathan had felt the source of the energy deep inside himself. It tore through some invisible depth that he didn't know he had, and filled him with such unimaginable power.

"I see it now," she said, "the source of your resistance. I should have seen it all along... You're *afraid*."

"I'm not." Nathan shrugged, but in his heart he felt the truth of her words.

"Fear is good," she said.

"I'm not afraid."

"Fear means you know what it is you must do. And fear can be overcome. It's weak, and it becomes weaker with every step you take forward."

Nathan looked away.

"You're only paralyzed by fear if you're standing still," she said. "You just have to keep moving. That's all. I'm sorry I doubted you."

20

just sit

Nathan sat in the middle of the large sofa at the end of the saloon, waiting for Isha. She had decided that his room was not a safe place for his training, considering their recent encounters. He needed to keep his head clear, she said, to which he responded by pointing out that it was she who had instigated physical contact between them, and made it impossible for him to keep a clear head. Nathan wished he had kept that last bit to himself, because she had instantly put several feet of distance between their bodies and refrained from touching at all.

Whenever Isha carried the intricately carved wooden chest, Nathan had to remind himself how heavy it actually was. The effortlessness with which she swung it toward him as she walked into the saloon and lowered it ever-so-gently onto the coffee table in front of him made her look like an ordinary girl, sharing with him her recent acquisitions at the mall.

He tried to identify what the crooked smile on her face meant as she turned the chest toward him and unbuckled its belt. Was she actually excited about this? Was she eager to see him be destroyed? Or was there apprehension concealed beneath the subtle tension of her smile?

The faint buzz of the mechanics became audible to him the moment she lifted the heavy lid. Rubbing his hands on his knees, he scooted to the edge of his seat and peered into the box.

"So, what do I do? Just stare at it?"

"No. You don't just stare at it. That's why you're not making any progress."

"I've made plenty of progress. Or am I not the *only* human who can even see them?"

"Yes. And since the first time you saw them, you've made no progress at all."

"That's just not true."

They were interrupted by the click of a door. The Brit emerged from his room, carrying his black notebook, and actually smiled at Nathan as he strutted past them toward the double doors at the back of the saloon.

Why does he get to do whatever the hell he wants? Nathan thought. It was not fair. The Brit was here of his own free will. To him, this was probably an exciting adventure. Perhaps even a dream come true. Isha had told Nathan that the aliens had allowed the Brit to dive with them, and that he had spent some time onboard of the sunken ship. Clearly, whatever he encountered under the sea had put him in a particularly good mood.

For Nathan, on the other hand, this boat was a prison. He had been coaxed here against his will, drawn to it by a force he could not understand nor control. And yet, as much as he had come to despise being here, the thought of being separated from Isha made him physically ill. He had nowhere to go and no way to leave.

"When you kissed me," she said, pulling him back into their

conversation, "you were filled with an energy. Do you know what I'm referring to?"

"Of course."

"Where do you think that energy came from?"

"I don't know."

"Where did you feel it?"

"Here," Nathan said, rubbing his chest.

"Do you remember what you were thinking about right before?"

"Which time?"

"Either time."

Nathan closed his eyes, and drifted into those moments leading up to the kiss. He remembered the overwhelming longing he had felt for her. What had he thought about? The shape of her lips. The thin orange veins that spider-webbed through her forest green irises. The way her fingers moved almost in slow motion as they grazed his thigh. Every dizzying detail of her came into crystal focus as he recreated the moment before the kiss. He could see the part of her lips, feel her breath on his — what was she saying to him?

The kiss — both times — marked a moment of complete weakness. He had not decided to kiss her — not planned it. He had also not been prepared for the surge of heat that entered him as he pressed her into himself. He remembered her fingers digging into his body, her body twisting in response to what he had assumed was pain — the evidence of her struggle still remained visible on his chest in the shape of four purple bruises, tender to the touch. How close had she been to seriously hurting him? What had caused such a reaction in her? What had he thought about in that moment?

Nathan tried to isolate the moment in which he had found

himself at the mercy of the energy that filled him. This new energy was different than Isha's. It felt more chaotic, more intimate, more familiar. It made him feel invincible. But there was something else. His mind had gone completely blank, his closed eyes had adjusted and he had found himself staring into a vast blackness that spread into an infinity of space. Then, as his chest cracked open and his body flooded with the blinding brightness, for the briefest moment, he had seen the entire universe.

"I don't think I was thinking at all," he said. "It was like my mind went blank."

"What did it feel like?"

"Like nothing."

"Anything you can remember? Anything unusual?"

"There was one thing," Nathan said reluctantly. He wasn't sure if what he was about to share meant anything at all, but he went on. "It felt like... I was inside a place — but not like this." He grabbed the sofa to demonstrate its physicality.

"Not a physical place," she said.

"Yes! Not physical. And..." Nathan hesitated.

"And what?"

"Well, it's weird. Even though my eyes were closed, I *felt* like my eyes were open and what I saw was this pitch-black space that went on forever. Like the place itself was dark, does that make sense? And the other weird thing about it was that even though it *looked* empty and dark, I *knew* it wasn't empty."

"There was something there with you?"

"No. Not something. It was like... the emptiness was a thing. I know it sounds crazy. How can nothing be something? But that's what I felt."

"It's not crazy," she said. "What you experienced, we have a word for it. It roughly translates to *No Thing All Thing*. Humans have also called it by many names. I personally like *The Quantum Field* or simply *The Void*."

"It felt like some kind of a void, but... *alive*."

"That's a great way of explaining it. The Void is the space you must enter before you can hear Thaia. It's the gateway that connects your consciousness to hers."

"So other people have been there?"

"Yes, lots of them."

"And they can hear Earth?"

"In a way, yes. They can sense her, but the communication is very crude."

"So, why isn't one of those people here now?"

"I don't know. You must have something they don't have."

She twisted her body toward him. "You'll have to learn to enter The Void on your own," she said.

"How?"

"Just sit back. I'll guide you."

Nathan closed his eyes and tried to follow her instructions as she asked him to focus on the silence between sounds. Could he isolate the pauses between sounds, the pause between each breath? He couldn't. His mind flooded, almost immediately, with thoughts and images that entered him without his consent, and twisted around one another like ribbons in the wind. Images solidified behind his closed eyelids, each taking him down a winding path that led to another thought and another until he could no longer trace the chain of images to their source. There was no logical progression to where his thoughts began and where they ended up. He could start, as he now did, with the sound of the ocean and find himself a few moments later in a science class from his childhood. Somewhere in the distance, Isha's voice instructed him to focus on his breath, or on the stillness between breaths — what did that even mean? — or on letting go of his thoughts, as though that was even an option.

As frustratingly confusing as her instructions were, everything became worse when she stopped speaking. Isolated thoughts drifted into the front stage of his mind and multiplied into mounds of images, ideas and emotions that took over him entirely. He felt fundamentally incapable of not thinking. By the time he opened his eyes, his frustration was palpable. What she was asking him to do was humanly impossible.

"I can't do it." He jumped to his feet. "I don't know what you want. It's impossible. Humans are not meant to not think. We have brains so we can think."

"Plenty of humans meditate every day."

"Well, Earth should have picked one of them!" Nathan stormed away and turned to face her once he reached the hallway. He didn't know what to do. His impulse was to lock himself in his room until… *until when?* He thought. *Until the planet burns to the core?* He couldn't run away, but he also could no longer bear sitting here, forcing himself to do something so idiotic — something so completely unnatural.

"It would have made my job much easier," Isha admitted, "if Thaia had sent someone who is at least connected with himself."

Nathan stood with his back to the hallway, his arms crossed across his chest, and his face twisted into a hopeless scowl. Collecting himself, he walked back to the sofa, and sat down next to her. "Can we just make out instead?"

"You have to learn to do this on your own."

"But maybe if you just…"

"No. If you can't find The Void by yourself, you won't be able to access it when you need it."

"I'm just saying that it might help."

"It won't."

"You don't know that."

"Will you be able to focus better if I leave?"

"No. I don't think so."

"Okay," she said. Shifting her attention to the device, she added, "are you able to see them any better?"

Nathan looked into the chest. The glow of the device remained dim, although, he thought it may have been slightly brighter. Very slightly.

"I'm not sure. It might be a little brighter. Maybe."

"That's not enough."

"Actually, I think I do need to be alone. Your pessimism is holding me back."

"My pessimism?"

"You try learning something new when the person teaching you doesn't think you can do it."

"I don't—"

"Just, tell me what's supposed to happen. I enter The Void and then what?"

"You'll know when it happens."

"You wanna be a little more specific?"

"Ideally, you'll be able to hear them, and you'll see them."

"I already hear and see them."

"No. I mean, you'll *really* hear and see them. It'll be different."

Nathan opened his mouth to object, but she held up a hand, and his words remained in his throat.

"Don't worry about *them*," she said. "Just try to connect to that quiet space within yourself. Only when you become as you are can you experience them as they are." She got up, and hesitated. "Are you sure about this?"

"Yes."

"Just… don't touch them."

"Got it."

21
something missing

Nathan sat in front of the open chest and struggled to quieten his racing mind. He sat with his back flat against the sofa, his eyes closed. The more he tried to not think, the more his head flooded with images of the past and possible futures. His body, too, suddenly became filled with objections. He noted that he had sat through countless movies or epic video game marathons without any discomfort at all, yet sitting here with his eyes closed and his mind in shambles, his back felt utterly stiff, his hips ached, his head felt too heavy for his neck, and was a constant urge to stretch his shoulders. He wanted nothing more than to get up and move about. And more strange still was the feeling that there was something other than this he needed to be doing — that he was wasting his time, sitting here, doing nothing.

What do you have to do? he asked himself. *You literally have nothing else to do but to sit here.*

The seconds crawled by — each moment longer than the last. Nathan opened his eyes at every strange sound, of which there were now many. The creek of the walls, footsteps on the second deck, the constant splash of waves against the boat.

The saloon door slid open, and the Brit walked past him and retreated to his room. Glancing at the device, Nathan saw no difference. Its glow remained the muted speck he had first witnessed, the buzz still faint and distant, easily swallowed by the much more prominent sounds of the sea.

After a time, the Brit reemerged into the hallway and disappeared through the door that led to the lower deck. Nathan remembered that he, too, was hungry. Relaxing into the sofa, he allowed his neck to stretch across the cushion behind him until his head came to rest on the back wall. He did not hear Isha enter, did not notice her until she was sitting next to him.

"You're not trying."

"I honestly don't know how I can try any harder." Despite the inactivity of the day, he felt utterly spent. "I've been sitting here all day, doing exactly what you told me to do." Turning his head toward her, he added, "Maybe we should just take the shortcut."

"This isn't a joke," she said.

"Don't you think I know that?" He raised his marked hand towards it. "Maybe I can just—"

"Stop. Seriously, stop."

He stopped.

"Do you not see them move toward your hand?"

Nathan looked. He could see subtle changes in the moss-like pattern that covered the surface of the rock, but he saw nothing moving toward him.

"No."

"If you can't see them, if you can't hear them, if you can't even tell them apart from yourself, how do you expect to control them? There's nothing I can do for you if they ingest you. Do you understand that?"

Nathan dropped his hand to his lap. "I know," he said, "for the hundredth time, I know. What you fail to understand is that I am trying really hard here, and it's not my fault that it's not working. It's not like I wanted to be here in the first place. I'm doing what you wanted me to do, and nothing, absolutely nothing is happening. You think you're frustrated? Try being me!"

"Your dream," Conrad's booming voice startled Nathan, "there is something not right."

Nathan sat up. Conrad stood at the back entrance of the saloon, against a backdrop of a dozen aliens.

"The device is not here," Isha said.

The knot inside Nathan's stomach twisted. "What do you mean it's not here?"

"We need to re-examine the dream," said Conrad.

"I've told you everything," Nathan said. "If something is missing, it's on you. Maybe they didn't look for it hard enough."

"The chance that we missed the device is slim," said Conrad, "but it's one possibility we must consider."

The aliens turned their back to Nathan and began moving toward the edge of the deck, this time much slower than the last. None looked toward him as they dropped into the sea below.

Nathan looked at Isha for an explanation.

"They will dive again," she said, her voice calm and intimate, "but they will not find it, because it is not here."

"Then why look for it?"

"They're giving you space, so you can learn where it is actually hidden."

"I don't understand."

Once the last of the aliens had vacated the deck, Conrad turned to face him.

"When the Moli-orath enter you," he said, "you have to give

yourself to them. Completely."

"What is he talking about?" Nathan asked Isha.

"We're running out of time, Nathan," Isha said. "You must ask the Moli-orath."

"Won't they tear me apart in seconds?"

"Don't think in terms of time," Conrad said. "Every second contains within it an eternity."

What does that even mean? Nathan thought.

"Time is capricious," Isha said in response to his unspoken question. "A lot can happen in a second."

"I don't care about how *long* it takes them to take me apart."

"The only way to control them," Conrad went on, "is to give yourself to them. When you become them, they become you. That's how you'll know everything they know."

"There could be another way," Isha said.

"Do you see another way?" Conrad asked her.

"Even if he knows what they know, he may not be able to tell us."

"You are the Channel," Conrad said. "It will be upon you to extract this information before it's too late."

"There *has to* be another way," she said.

"Then find it." Conrad turned and stepped off the ledge, disappearing instantly into the ocean.

"Why don't you take a break," she said when they were once again alone. "Eat something."

"What did he mean?" All the blood had drained from Nathan's face. He felt cold and nauseous. "Isha, what did he mean?"

The Brit entered the saloon carrying a tray of food. Behind him, Farhad carried a second tray. Nathan could not even think about food. He was shivering.

"I won't let it happen," she said. "Not until you're ready."

"It doesn't sound like it's your call." Nathan trembled as he allowed himself to sink deeper into the fear that gripped him. His body was shaking as his vision became blurred. She cradled his face in her palms, flooding him with the gentle calm of her energy. Nathan's eyes rolled up in his head, and he collapsed into a dreamless sleep.

22
the conduit

Gregory placed his tray on the dining room table and walked to the sofa where Isha sat with the unconscious man-child sprawled next to her. He didn't need to be told the details of what was happening. He could sense the disappointment in Conrad's voice, the urgency of their situation, and even the threat to Nathan's life. Isha did not turn toward him. She sat at the edge of her seat with her body curled slightly toward the sleeping man, looking more like a bird than a person.

Isha often reminded Gregory of a bird with the way she glided soundlessly from one room to the next, or the way she seemed to always be perched in a corner — observing — even when he didn't initially realize she was in the room. She was always present and had a way of blending into the background. Unless he specifically looked for her in the shadows, she remained hidden from him. This was perplexing because her presence seemed to fill an entire room. When he did notice her, he often wondered how he could have ever been unaware of her.

Gregory felt connected to Isha even though he hardly knew anything about her. After learning about her extraterrestrial origin, his feelings toward her had deepened and developed an intimate quality. There was a sense of nostalgia that he could not quite pinpoint. He knew, too, that he trusted her with his life.

It's more than that, he thought as he studied her expressionless face. *It's as though she's here for me.*

Gregory sat down on the far end of the of L-shaped sofa, feeling both a desire to observe and an urge to speak with her. He wanted to know everything about her, not just as a friend and travel companion but also as a scientist interested in distant worlds. He allowed his body to sink into the cushions, and without consciously intending to mimic her, he stacked his legs and curled his body toward her, his eyes never leaving her face. She looked far away. He wondered if she had left her body to join those who were looking for the device far below them, or if she was with some others of her kind whom he had not yet met.

He leaned forward, curious about this rock — this device — that was at the center of such tension. He reached into the chest, and touched the dark, rough-looking surface, and was surprised to find it smooth to his touch. Spreading his fingers around it, he looked up at her one last time before lifting the thing out of the chest.

The rock was lighter than Gregory thought it should be, weighing nearly nothing. Although the green and black moss that covered it looked rough, the thing felt silken underneath his fingers, as though he was touching the surface of water. It was neither cold nor warm. If he closed his eyes, he would not know he was holding anything at all. When he decided to put this theory to the test, however, an internal resistance kept his eyes fixed on the thing.

How strange, he thought.

She was staring at him when he looked up. When their eyes

met, the expression on her face shifted into curiosity. There was a familiar quality to the way she looked then. Her eyes oscillated between two shades of green as they dropped from a rich forest green into a lighter shade, and he knew, in that instance, that this was not the first time they had met.

She reached out, and Gregory deposited the device into her open palm, his fingers grazing her hand. An electric charge flooded into him through his fingertips and sent a familiar shockwave up his arm and into his body. He remembered then who she was and what she had done for him so many years ago. He stared at her in disbelief.

"Have you ever been to Ipswich, England?" he asked.

"Of course. Many times. "

"Thirty-four years ago?"

"Sure. Why do you ask?"

"Something happened to me at that time. I was with my grandmother. I thought I had dreamt the whole thing… But now, I remember. *You* were there."

Isha was silent as she stared at him, her gaze distant. Then her expression morphed into one of surprise then recognition then unfiltered kindness. She was by his side in a flash, her body turned toward his.

"You're Evelyn's child."

"Grandchild, actually."

Her confirmation was enough to open the gates to his childhood. Memories rushed to him like a swarm of bees. Isha curled her fingers around his hands. Her electricity surged into him as that magical, mysterious night came to life inside his mind. Looking at Isha now, Gregory noticed that she looked exactly as she had so many years ago when she sat, holding his much smaller hands in hers, telling him that everything was alright and he needed to go to sleep now.

He was seven years old and had only met his grandmother a few months prior. Yet somehow, Evelyn had convinced his mother to let him accompany her to Ipswitch.

"I'm not exactly sure what happened that night," Gregory said. "For a long time, when I spoke of the Sky People, people told me I had imagined it. When I grew older, I started believing them. I thought maybe I'd dreamed it all."

"When children notice us," Isha said, "they know instinctively that we're different. And when they feel curious about us, they learn the truth simply by wanting to know. You met many of us that night, and you were curious. You wanted to know why we were different, and the knowledge came to you as another fact of life."

"Yes. You were… standing in a corner, in the shadows — like you do now actually."

She smiled.

"I remember the house was quite large," he went on. "It was dark. I don't know what woke me, but I just knew where to go, and I walked into this room with no furniture, only people sitting on the ground in a circle. Someone was singing this beautiful, hypnotic song. I think I can still hear it."

"Evelyn did have a wonderful voice, didn't she?"

"Yes. I remember being so surprised when I saw it was my grandmother singing. She smiled at me when she saw me. Then she glanced at something behind me. I wanted to see what she was looking at, and when I turned around I saw you, standing in the shadows next to a bunch of strange Sky People. You know that's the word that came into my head? Sky People."

"It is quite accurate, don't you think?"

"Yes. It doesn't seem so strange now, talking about it. But at the time, everyone made such a fuss."

"People fear what they don't know. Your race has not yet learned the wisdom of your young."

"My grandmother — she didn't conform to that. I remember, I felt so smart talking to her. She asked me so many questions as though I had the answers she was looking for."

"In a way, you did."

"She was peculiar, wasn't she?"

"She was quite special."

"You know, I didn't even know I had a grandmother until she showed up at our doorstep just a few months before. My mum told me her mother was dead. Why would she do that?"

"Your mother had a hard time with all this."

"She knew?"

"As much as she could understand."

"Why then let me go with her on that trip?"

"Why do you think?"

Gregory remembered his tears, his tantrums — hours of begging, of chipping away at his poor mother's ironclad resolve. How he had screamed and cried for days.

"I didn't leave her a choice, did I?"

"No."

"She got what she wanted though. After that, I didn't have a grandmother again."

"I know it was very hard for Evelyn to lose you. She checked on you every chance she got."

"It was hard for us, too. Why didn't she return?"

"Evelyn was a wonderful Conduit — one of the most loving, most inspiring. She believed deeply in the work she did. She tried to explain her work to your mother, but—"

"My mum thought it was witchcraft. She was very superstitious."

"Your mother was afraid of what she did not understand."

"What was it that my grandmother did that made her sacrifice her own blood?"

"Our only purpose on this planet since the day we arrived has been to help Thaia awaken, and to do this, we needed people like your grandmother to teach others how to connect with Thaia. If you asked her what she did, she'd say, 'I'm ushering in The Great Becoming.' That's what she liked to call Thaia's awakening."

"The Great Becoming?"

"Yes. It's poetic, isn't it?"

"It is."

"Evelyn had a way with words. But she never took credit for them. She'd say, 'They're not my words, I'm nothing more than a pigeon delivering a message attached to my tongue.' There were many ways she helped people connect with Thaia."

"You speak of her as though she is no longer alive."

"She isn't."

Gregory felt the weight of those simple words inside his chest. A deep sadness filled him. He had spent most of his life looking forward to an unanticipated knock that would reveal a thin, white-haired Evelyn at his door.

"I'm sorry," said Isha.

"When?" Gregory struggled against the lump in his throat.

"Three years ago. She led Awakening Circles until the day of her transition."

Silent tears dislodged themselves from his eyes, and streaked down his cheeks.

"Would you have rather not known?" asked Isha. Gregory shook his head.

"I only met her — and you — that one time," she said, squeezing his hand. "I can't believe I didn't recognize you right away."

———

When the Guardians returned to the boat, they did not congregate on the second deck as they had become accustomed to doing. Instead, they puffed themselves dry on the small deck immediately outside the double doors of the saloon, made a minute effort to cover their nude bodies with a towel or a piece of clothing, and entered the living room area where Gregory and Isha sat on the sofa. Soon, the duo was surrounded by a dense ring of bodies as more continued to squeeze into the already-packed room.

Gregory looked to Isha for an explanation. Had something happened? He wondered. Had they found what they had come to find? In their steady, unblinking stares, he detected a warmth that revealed a deep affection. He leaned into Isha as he asked, "Is everything alright?"

It was not Isha who answered him. Instead, a middle-aged alien who had wedged herself directly next to him on the sofa, placed a gentle had on his shoulder and said, "Evelyn is missed by all who worked with her."

Evelyn. They were here because of his grandmother. His deduction was confirmed by the many nods of agreement that rippled through the crowd.

His mother had never forgiven Evelyn for her long unexplained absences. Did she know about this intimate partnership that his grandmother had forged with one of the oldest races in the universe? Would she feel less betrayed if she understood that it wasn't strangers or dark magic that had taken her mother away, but rather a sense of duty toward the planet that she loved?

Even with the room full of aliens, Gregory noticed Nathan shifting as he regained consciousness. The American sat up, puffy eyed and pale. The dread that occupied him intensified as he took in the large congregation. Gregory could almost taste Nathan's anxiety and felt a pang of sympathy for him.

"What's going on?" Nathan asked. "Did you find it?"

"No," said a voice from the crowd, and Gregory saw Nathan's face lose another shade of color.

"Maybe someone moved it?" Nathan's voice was faint and desperate.

The room was utterly silent. How strange it was to be surrounded by so many and hear one's own breath. Nathan's suggestion was not entirely implausible. If they had interpreted the dream correctly, then one logical explanation for the absence of the device was that someone had, in fact, moved it.

If, Gregory thought, *the interpretation is correct.*

He suddenly knew the answer.

"No," Gregory said. "No one moved it."

He looked around at the aliens, his eyes glistening with excitement. A smile spread on his lips.

"It was never here in the first place," he said. "In your dream, the head of the monster comes up from the depth of the sea and bites the ship in half. Well, the HMCS Levis was shot down by torpedoes. From a submarine." Nathan straightened. In Conrad's face, too, Gregory saw a realization. "The submarine, that's the monster. That's where the device is."

23
too loud too bright

Dinner was a seafood casserole, thick and moist with generous chunks of white fish, scallops, lobster, shrimp, and a mouthwatering aroma that filled the entire main deck. Every bite produced an explosion of flavors inside Nathan's mouth that he had to pause periodically to savor. He did not remember ever enjoying food as much as he did in this moment. In fact, in his previous life, he had seldom noticed what he put in his mouth. He had always seen food consumption as a necessity of life akin to using the restroom and trimming his toenails. Right now, however, he was grateful to be alive. He was grateful for Farhad and the meals he prepared for them. He was even grateful for the Brit, whose new interpretation of the nightmare had saved him from certain dismemberment by the Moli-orath.

The boat was, once again, sailing at full speed. Nathan sat at the dining room table, feeling a sort of satisfaction he had seldom experienced. Was he actually sad that this meal might come to an end? He washed every few bites down with gulps of sweet lemonade.

The Brit entered from the outside and sat down across from

Nathan, where a second tray awaited him. Only a few bites were missing from his meal.

"Hello," said the Brit.

"Hey." Nathan glanced up at him.

"Are you alright?" The Brit picked up a small piece of the casserole with the tip of his fork, and leaning in slightly, deposited the morsel into his mouth. His lips closed around the tip of the fork, and the utensil emerged clean.

As Nathan watched, he was glad he had not paid any attention to the way the foreigner ate until now. He would have been irritated by the exactness of his method — the blatant condescension of it.

"You really don't mean to do that, do you?" Nathan asked.

"Do what?"

"That. I mean, the way you talk, the way you eat. Like you're somehow better than everyone else."

"Better than everyone else? Surely, you're joking."

Shaw-ly yaw joe-keen, Nathan's internal voice mocked.

"You come across as very condescending."

"I come across as condescending?"

"But it's okay. I mean, I was bothered at first, but I get it now."

"You get *what* exactly?" The Brit — Gregory — had set his fork and knife on his tray, and was staring at Nathan. Deep frown lines appeared between his brows.

"Come on," Nathan said. "Don't be offended. It's alright. I get it now. I get why you're supposed to be here. You're important. We're on the same *team.*" Nathan filled his fork, then placed it down on his plate. He had used the T word, and he had meant it. He understood now what Isha had tried to tell him. They *were* on the same team, and they *each* played unique but complementary roles. "I'm sorry I said anything. Your food's getting cold."

"It's already cold."

"Listen, I really didn't mean to upset you."

"No? Calling a person condescending is not upsetting at all."

"I didn't mean it that way."

"How exactly did you mean it?"

"Only that I *thought* you were condescending. Before. But I realize now that this is just the way you are." No. That wasn't it. "Not that you *are* condescending. I only mean that you come across a bit… I don't know. I only mean that I didn't like you before, and now I think you're alright. I get it now. I get why you're here. That's all I'm trying to say."

Gregory stared at him, then picked up his fork and knife, and resumed eating in that very particular manner that reminded Nathan of high-class villains in James Bond movies.

There was still a good amount of food left on Gregory's plate when Nathan cleared his and leaned back in his chair, feeling stuffed and satisfied. Nathan watched as his companion deposited bird-sized bites into his mouth and chewed thoroughly before swallowing, his rhythm only broken by the tiniest sips of juice.

"So, where's this submarine we're looking for?" asked Nathan.

"South of Spain."

"We're sailing there?"

"No."

Nathan waited for more information. When it was apparent that Gregory would not volunteer it, he asked. "How're we getting there then? Flying?"

"Yes."

"Flying from where?"

Gregory pricked a shrimp with the tip of his fork, cut it in half with his knife, and placed it carefully in his mouth. Then he chewed longer than any piece of shrimp had a right to be chewed.

"From Iceland," he said at last.

Nathan pushed his tray to the side, and leaned forward, placing his elbows where his tray had been.

"Listen, I'm sorry. I really didn't mean to offend you. I don't know what else to say."

Gregory ate two more small bites, chewing methodically. When he was done, he drank the rest of his juice in one big gulp, got up, and disappeared through the galley door.

Great! Nathan thought, *not only does he eat like a girl, he has to give me the silent treatment like one, too.*

The sun had finally dipped into the horizon and the sky had begun its slow fade into darkness by the time Nathan returned to his room. This long stretch of dusk always reminded him of how very tired he was. Every day on this boat felt like two or three days. Sometimes, ten minutes felt like an hour, while an hour seemed to drag on for so long he could barely stand it. Most of the time, it felt like time stood still all together. Even so, no matter how slowly time crawled by, it was nearly impossible to get any rest. The tireless rocking back and forth, the incessant slap of the sea, the lack of complete darkness even at night, and the growing anxiety inside his chest kept him in a constant state of agitation. Sleep, when he did drift into it, was restless at best and brought with it chaos and exhaustion.

Nathan did not need to turn on the lights in his cabin to see, even though it must have been close to midnight. Leaning against the wall for stability, he waddled to his bed. He could easily make out the dark shapes of table, chair, and dresser. Atop the table, the rounded silhouette of the chest looked somehow different. He squinted, and eventually realized that the lid was left open. She must have thought he would work some more tonight.

He pulled his t-shirt over his head and dropped it to the ground. Lying down, he slid off his pants and pushed them off his feet. Then he crawled under the thin, wool blanket. His body sank into the firm mattress, and he drifted from one ship onto another where soldiers were already running about the deck, their faces coated with terror.

This is why I'm so tired all the time, he thought inside his dream. *How am I supposed to get any rest when the world ends every time I close my eyes?*

Nathan sat up in bed, startled. Inside his head a dizzying throbbing made it impossible to think. Pressing his palms into his temples, he curled himself into a tight ball, squeezing every muscle as he tried desperately to contain the unbearable pressure inside his head. He buried his head beneath his pillow and pressed into his ears with all his might, but the deafening noise inside him only seemed to get louder.

The chest. The word was the first conscious thought he could muster. Had the mechanics entered him while he slept? Were they taking him apart?

He groaned in agony. The mechanics must have entered him. They must be devouring his brain. Soon, the entirety of him would be dispersed among millions of microscopic machines, and he would be lost forever, unable to will himself back into existence. How stupid he'd been to think he could control them. How utterly naive.

Do it already! He screamed at them inside his head. *Do it and get it over with!*

"Shhhhhh." It was her familiar current that entered him. The relief was instant. The ear-piercing ringing inside his head dropped to a low hum as though someone had turned down the volume. Slowly, he opened his eyes. Never had he been more grateful by another person's presence. She sat next to him, her hand on his head, looking like an ancient statue in the gray moonlight.

"I'm going to let go," she said. "Don't fight them. Just listen."

"Are they going to take me apart?"

"Not unless they enter you."

"They *are* in me. I can feel them."

"No. That's only their sound. Listen."

She relaxed her hand, and Nathan grabbed her wrist.

"Wait. What do you mean by that? It feels like my head's going to explode. They're *inside* my head."

"Yes. I know."

"Is that how you hear them?"

"Yes."

"It's too loud. I can't hear my own thoughts. Is that what you're hearing *now*?"

"Yes."

"How can you stand it?"

"You can't fight them. You have to relax into it. When I let go, try to listen. I'm here if you need help."

The instant she removed her hand, the buzzing amplified.

"Relax," she whispered, and he exhaled the air he had been holding.

Don't fight, Nathan thought, *just listen.*

And he did.

At first, all he heard was the overwhelming thunderous screech that seemed to attack his ears from the inside of his head. The sound seemed to occupy *physical* space inside of him — a growing mass that pressed against his skull. Then, when the pressure became so great that he could no longer stand it, the sound split. Like a camera that zooms into a snowstorm and focuses on individual snowflakes, his mind separated the buzz into thousands of individual tracks, each slightly different from the rest.

There was a unique clicking that each mechanic produced. For some of them this was a slow repetitive thump, like a tiny drum being struck at steady intervals. Others produced a rhythmic rattle. Most of the mechanics produced sounds that were steady and ranged from low-pitched gongs to high pitched swishes. Aside from the individual clicks of the mechanics, Nathan heard the delicate strikes of their endless collisions as they bumped into each other, producing scratching and crashing noises that were so subtle he wondered how he was able to hear them at all.

Nathan opened his eyes. The brightness of the room took him by surprise. Isha must have turned on the light.

Squinting, he covered his eyes with his forearm, and waited for his vision to adjust. The light was brighter than it should be, and Nathan wondered if it was sunlight streaming into the cabin.

It can't be morning yet, he thought, *it was the middle of the night a moment ago. I couldn't have fallen asleep. Or did I?*

What he heard shifted back and forth between separate individual clicks and a collective buzz. Even though it was still loud, he heard everything else just as well, perhaps even more clearly than usual. The roll of endless individual waves created by the ship's speed, the creek of the wood beneath him, the gentle whistle of his breath through his subtly clogged nostrils. His mind seemed to catalog every sound with equal importance, bringing them all to the forefront of his attention.

Nathan rubbed his eyes. Every time he removed his hands from them, the light blinded him.

"That's a bit tougher," Isha said. "We may need to get you sunglasses, although I'm not sure if that'll help. Your eyes are just not made to see that frequency of light."

Then he understood. What he was experiencing was the brightness of the mechanics. The next time he attempted to open his eyes, he felt heat enter them. The brightness felt alive.

"Close it!" he said, fearing he might go blind.

She shut the lid of the chest. Instantly, the heat of the mechanics, their blinding light, and their ceaseless chatter, which he was beginning to get used to, dissolved into the silent blackness of the night.

The cold air that hugged his face felt comforting. His eyes adjusted, and he saw her statuesque body, turned towards him in the blue tint of the moon, eyes wide with wonder, looking like a goddess. The thought occurred to him that she might have been considered a god a few millennia ago. That, perhaps, Aphrodite or Venus were based on this beautiful immortal being sitting here by his side.

She was most likely Athena or maybe Wonder Woman. The thought made him smile. He would have to ask her about that someday. But now, there was something more important he needed to do.

He sat up in bed and leaned toward her, his face only inches from hers. This time, he lowered his lips onto hers gently as though asking for permission. When her lips parted and she invited his tongue into her mouth, he surrendered himself to her and sank into the infinite nothingness that expanded inside of him. This was bliss. She did not resist as he slowly lowered their bodies onto the bed. He relaxed into the void that he was able to access only in her proximity, and felt the tingling inside him before his chest popped open, flooding his body with a magnificent light that made him feel powerful and alive. Warmth streamed into him along with this light, and a sensation of complete peace.

You need to learn to control it, he heard her say in his mind. With his eyes closed and their bodies intertwined, he decided that she was right. He would need to become familiar with this energy intimately — for her sake and for his own. He'd need to learn to control it and to access it at will.

Her body relaxed under his. The light within him cocooned them both. She let him take her then, their distinct currents weaving together into a tangle of energy that pulsated with the rhythm of their thrusts. Her permission made him feel even more powerful — immortal even — as though he, too, was a god.

24
the calm before

Nathan did not notice falling asleep. One moment he was curled tightly around her petite body, stroking the silken skin of her forearm with the tips of his fingers, the next moment, sunlight flooded the cabin, its golden kiss caressing his closed eye lids, making him feel alive and in love.

Without stirring, he studied the way the sun hugged the contours of her porcelain features and made her raven hair glisten as it draped effortlessly across the white sheets. He inhaled the sweet scent of this new day, intoxicated by the memory of their passionate union. How intense their mingled energies had been as he plunged himself into her with a force that would have shattered any mortal. But neither of them was mortal last night. Nathan had felt himself transform from a helpless, insignificant human into a superhero of sorts. That brilliant light had entered him once again, and this time, instead of fighting it, he had surrendered to it. Reality shifted in that moment and suddenly everything had made sense, and he had felt a deep peace within himself.

Brushing her black hair gently aside to expose her delicate

collarbone, Nathan thought about the way his sweat had formed glistening pools in the base of her throat and in the dip between her breasts. When he entered her, her eyes had flashed yellow as though a steady flame burned inside them, and for just a brief moment when he climaxed, his mind, along with the rest of him, disappeared inside her. He saw her eyes transform into something entirely alien then as their whites disappeared into a golden blaze.

He had made love to an alien. No, it was much more than that. He had made love to a being so ancient, so entirely, incomprehensibly perfect that it would take him a thousand lives to fully know her.

Isha's smooth, hardened skin was cold to his touch, yet Nathan felt closer to her than to any other being. He wanted to protect her. He wanted to be everything she saw in him and more. He wanted desperately to live up to her expectations of him and to save everything. He wanted to become immortal and to live so many lifetimes beside her that he lost count.

The thought of his mortality pierced through him. If Earth truly did awaken, would *he*, too, overcome the plague of death? And if not, would she remember him after he was gone?

He kissed the top of her exposed shoulder and felt her skin soften beneath his lips. The warm rosy tint of youth spread across her pale skin and made her look beautifully alive. His breath got stuck in his chest when she looked at him with those wild gentle eyes that revealed genuine affection toward him. Nathan felt the pang of love inside his heart. Burying his face in the nape of her neck, he closed his eyes and sank deep into her as her fingers slid through the tangle of his hair. His body was instantly alive, pulsating with a dizzying desire that made him feel lightheaded.

Drunk with love, he thought as he pulled back to look at her again. He was glad to see her smile.

You don't love her, his brother responded in his head about every girl he had ever loved, *girls are good for two things: driving you crazy and breaking your heart.*

Nathan fought back against the memory.

Without disturbing his hand which rested on her waist, she rolled toward him and raised herself onto her elbow.

"Your training is going to be harder now that you can see and hear them," she said. "The sound is easier to manage. The light… That's another story. Human eyes are not meant to see the Moli-orath. I don't actually know if you can look at them directly without damaging your eyes."

He leaned in for a kiss, mostly to keep her from talking. It was too early for this level of seriousness. She pulled back before his lips reached hers.

"What? No kiss this morning?"

"We have work to do."

"And here I thought we were working."

"So, I am work to you then?" She smiled.

"Well, every woman is work." He pulled her on top of him as he turned onto his back. "But you are my dream job."

Placing her hands on either side of his face, she studied him as her hair created a secret cavern for the wordless communication of their eyes. Nathan loved everything about this moment. The weight of her body on top of his, the twitch of her lips as they parted into the subtlest of smiles, the way her eyes flashed between yellow and green, the drape of her soft hair that tickled the sides of his face.

He breathed her in, feeling the pressure of her weight on his chest as it expanded with her scent. She twisted his hair around her fingers as she began to lower her face onto his. A shiver ran down the length of Nathan's body in the anticipation of her lips.

Suddenly, with only inches separating their faces, Isha stopped. Her eyes widened with shock and burned with a dark intensity. She looked as though she was witnessing something terrifying. She was no longer looking at him. Despite their proximity, her eyes pierced through him into some faraway horror that rendered her catatonic.

"What's wrong?" Nathan tried to move, but was trapped beneath her forceful grasp. Her body became taut with tension, her elbow piercing into his collar and her tiny frame threatening to crush his ribcage and hips. Nathan groaned, struggling to free himself.

For the briefest moment her eyes focused on him and revealed a pain so deep that time seemed to slow down to yield to it. The instant her body turned inanimate, it was flung aside by the force of Nathan's resistance. It hit the wall and landed on its side next to him, its arms still bent at the elbows, its fingers still curled around an imaginary lock of hair.

"Isha. What's going on?" Nathan was faint with fear as he tried to squeeze her rigid shoulders. Even her eyes, which always betrayed life, turned into gray stone. "Isha. What's wrong? What can I do? Isha! Isha!"

She softened. When her wild, distracted eyes focused on him, Nathan saw no recognition in them. Something terrible was happening to her. She grabbed his arm in her anguish, her terror-filled eyes pleading for help. He felt her chaotic, desperate energy spread inside him as it took on a dangerous, homicidal quality. He was under attack by the violence of her reckless current. He needed to fight against it but could not conjure up the light inside him at will. By the time he pried himself out of her grasp, he was seething with pain and on the verge of collapse. He dropped out of bed.

"What the hell?!"

"They... Kiras..."

Kiras was in Taiwan, Nathan remembered, looking for the third device.

"They found it?" He asked as he dragged himself away from her toward the far end of the room.

She nodded once.

"That's good?"

The slow, painful shake of her head suggested a situation far from good.

"They... you don't mean Kiras."

A nod.

"Someone else found the device?"

A nod.

"And Kiras?"

Like a dying star before its final implosion, her energy swelled in the already dense room. From Isha's extreme reaction, Nathan gathered that wherever Kiras was, he was in great danger — or worse, the danger had culminated into something frightful. Even without physical contact, her expanding energy penetrated him. It churned inside him, twisting around his organs, stretching him apart.

Pressing himself into the wall behind him, Nathan groaned in agony as waves of unbearable pain pierced through his body. His vision blurred with the pressure inside his eyes. He clasped his head, trying desperately to keep it from cracking open. He wanted to tell her to stop, but his words along with all cohesive thoughts were lost inside his distress.

Their desperate eyes locked for the briefest moment. In the blink that it took for her to harden, Nathan registered the sorrow inside her. Then, she was gone. All the pressure of her destructive current was sucked out of the room as her consciousness disappeared, and her lifeless shell — suspended in her moment of despair — remained lying on its side, one hand still stretched toward him for help.

Nathan's body shook in the aftermath of her assault. His eyes darted around the room, his mind trying to think. His hand found his upper lip in response to an itch and returned moist with thick blood. Nathan's eyes focused on the blood, trying to make sense of it. As he studied his crimson fingertips, his eyes focused onto tiny dots of red sprinkled on the surface of his palm. He turned his hand and followed the dots across the back of his hand and to his elbow, his shoulders. Even his chest and stomach were covered in tiny red dots. He realized what they were when he touched his belly and his hand left behind a thin smear of red: They were tiny droplets of blood, pushed out of his pores by the force of Isha's charge.

Nathan stumbled into the bathroom and encountered a frightening sight staring back at him from the mirror. His body and face were splattered with red dots. Thick streaks of dark blood ran down his nose and out of his ears. She could have killed him, and there was nothing he could have done to stop her. Whatever had happened to Kiras, it had turned her into a threat. He trembled as fear settled inside his chest. He needed to get as far away from her as possible.

As his shaking hand tightened around the doorknob, Nathan remembered four dozen aliens still onboard. A cold shiver ran down his spine as he imagined what would happen to him and to the rest of the humans on this boat once they all softened.

25
loss of life

Private Detective Stanley Borden stood in front of the severed head of Kiras, contemplating their next move. The light in the Nooritan's eyes had dimmed and threatened to go out. Through Kiras's eyes, Borden knew, the entire Favadani race was watching them. Their secret was no longer a secret.

Borden was an imposing figure, though he stood no more than five feet tall. What Borden lacked in height, however, he made up in girth. Humans often used unimaginative words like "short," "fat," and "ugly" to describe him. They uttered these words under their breath when they thought he was out of their earshot, which he, of course, never was. Borden was a Magirian, after all, and Magirians' exceptional hearing was one of their greatest protections against the many threats that plagued them on the desolate planet of Magira. Threats that were far more deadly than banal words.

What humans did not know was that much of the mass hidden beneath Borden's oversized clothing was due to additional limbs that, if exposed, would offend the sensitive human sensibility. Painstaking effort went into disguising four extra arms while keeping them accessible enough to use for support whenever necessary — effort that no Magirian exerted without resentment.

In contrast to Borden, his Pa'arian accomplice looked and acted almost at home on this unbearable hell that was Thaia. Borden's accomplice was known among humans as the United States Senator Ian Gibson, the lanky, white-haired senator from Tennessee.

"We should have left him," Borden said. "In the ocean he was a distraction. Here, he's an informant."

"The risk is too great." Gibson's slow, drawn out manner of speaking always felt at odds with Borden, who much preferred communication of any sort to be as short and as concise as possible. "We are too far along to jeopardize everything."

Borden resented that this albino race of cowards was regarded as one of the most clever in the universe. Still, he had to acknowledge that the plan the Pa'arians had devised was smart, even if it did require them to partner with a Nooritan race to carry it out. Pari Pa'ari, the twin planets Gibson and his kin called home, were LaNorien. Such planets did not possess the organic technology needed to execute this plan. Only three of the Awakened Twelve used such technology. Favadan was one, but that was Veda's planet, and Veda would never have agreed to harm Thaia, let alone destroy her. The yellow-eyed, black-skinned race of Gron was also out of the question. Groniens were as rigid as a Magirian's shell and as duty-driven as the ancient warriors of Tumacq.

No. The Pa'arians had made the right choice recruiting Borden's kin. In all of the universe, there was no race more practical and more resourceful than the Magirians. And for good reason. Magira was a small, dreary rock which, by all laws of physics known to most advanced races, should not have been able to support life. Yet, it had given birth to some of the most resilient beings in its galaxy. All Magirians were hybrid beings, comprised partially of living machines that were carried to the remote rock on the back of an asteroid billions of years ago. For this reason, controlling Moli-orath was second nature to them.

But there was a second, more important reason that made Magirians a perfect accomplice for carrying out this act of betrayal. Even beyond morality and duty, Magirians valued survival. Unlike the races of Favadan and Gron, Magirians understood that the survival of their universe hinged on Thaia awakening. If Thaia were to not awaken, the universe would be lost. Even so, if Borden hadn't hated this miserable existence on this torturous planet as much as he did, he might have had second thoughts about a plan that was so terribly final.

Gibson's face was impassive as he bent down and lifted Kiras's head to his eye level, staring directly into its unblinking eyes.

"The cat is out of the bag, so to speak," Gibson said. "All we can do now is kill it and send a message. Your Moli-orath can see to it."

Borden dropped onto all eights, instantly feeling the relief of distributing his weight among all his limbs. He moved closer to the edge of the sea where his men had deposited the dismembered remains of Kiras.

"He's already dead," he said, shuffling Kiras's limbs into a pile.

It had taken Magirians exactly one step onto the surface of this planet to know they would be the race that would suffer the most. For three thousand years now, Borden cursed Thaia's intolerable gravity, which was almost twice that of Magira. Those first few Thaian days had felt like an eternity — every step a struggle. It had seemed impossible to stand erect on two limbs, let alone move about freely without collapsing. Even now, he could barely lift a severed arm without strain.

"He's not exactly *dead* now, is he?" Gibson said. "In this state, he is like a pile of shit, attracting those incessant flies that are bound to make our plans that much more complicated. We destroy the shit, the flies disperse, and maybe they're too distraught to come our way."

Borden wondered if Gibson talked this way to his council members at the White House. He sensed Gibson's frustration with how wrong everything had gone.

"Go on then," Gibson said, grabbing the device from one of Borden's men and handing it to him. "Blow up this pile of shit."

Borden took the device in his meaty hands. The Moli-orath inside it recognized him. He recognized in them the sixteen-year-old native girl he had sacrificed five centuries ago. He remembered the eager look in her eyes when he'd told her that she would one day save the entire universe. All that she needed to do was to relax, and let the light take her. She didn't know what the universe was, or what she would be saving it from, but she relaxed for him anyway. This was the first device he had modified with Thaian DNA. By stripping the Moli-orath of his cells and injecting them with Thaia's, he had done what the Awakened considered impossible: he had turned a LaNorien race into a Nooritan. And just like that, he had accelerated Thaia's evolution by a million years, and turned it from a primitive race without living technology into one that could, in theory, control the Moli-orath.

At first, even Borden had doubted it could be done, but Gibson had insisted on the experiment, and when it worked, Borden knew this could change the universe.

He now told the girl, who was dispersed inside millions of mechanical beings, to enter Kiras and consume him. The swarm of Moli-orath left the device like a cloud of light, and entered Kiras's dismantled limbs. Cell by cell Kiras disappeared inside the light until no trace of him remained.

When it was done, Gibson asked, "Will he be able to persuade her to remake him? Can he take over her?"

"Maybe. She's been Moli-orath for five centuries. He has been Nooritan all his life."

"We can't take that risk. Have her break each cell in two and dispel it."

This would be the end of Kiras. With each cell split, not even his own Moli-orath could reassemble him. This felt cruel even for Gibson. While Magirians were violent, they were never needlessly so. Their attacks were always justified by either survival or honor. Unnecessary violence was frowned upon.

"Is this necessary?" Borden asked.

"Yes. Of course."

Borden hesitated.

"I told you it's necessary. In fact, everything hinges on it."

Reluctantly, Borden told her to execute this horrid act. From the cloud of light that hung over where Kiras's severed limbs had once been, a rain of ash began to fall. Kiras's remains fell to the ground as a thin layer of invisible dust that was swept into the ocean by a sudden gust of wind. Borden felt the loss of life deep inside him. If ever he was committed to this plan, it was now.

Despite his disdain for this planet and its primitive race, he dreaded the inevitable steps necessary to see this plan through. He had stalled detonating the bombs all these centuries, hoping humans would show them that they were capable of awakening, and that Thaia did not need to be destroyed. But now, the time for waiting had passed. Now, there was no turning back.

When the Moli-orath returned to their device, he heard the girl tell him, as she had done so many times before, of the next solar flare.

"Two days' time," she said, her soft voice echoing through millions of clicks. "Is that the one?"

Borden looked up at the sky then at Gibson.

"Two days," he said.

"Great!" exclaimed Gibson.

"It will be a small storm. Hardly visible."

"Then we need to make sure the other devices are not locked up when the time comes. I should have taken that damned chest when I had the chance."

26

demons

Nathan took the stairs two at a time as he ran to the second deck. On some level, he hoped Isha had overreacted to whatever she witnessed when her consciousness left the intimate embrace of their physical bodies and landed somewhere in Asia where something terrible was presumably happening to Kiras. The sight he encountered on the top deck of the boat, however, told a chilling story. When he saw the horrid expressions on the hardened figures, he knew the situation was dire.

Fear took him then — the kind of palpable panic one might experience upon finding oneself trapped in a ditch surrounded by a pride of sleeping lions. He inched back down the stairs, cold sweat turning into a sticky mess as blood caked heavily on his forehead and oozed down the sides of his face. The threat on his life was imminent. Hands trembling, he grabbed the railing for stability as he fought the urge to vomit.

Nathan could barely see through the fog of his distress. Time lapsed and he found himself on the ground, leaning against a blood-smeared door. He had no recollection of how he had made it across the saloon and down the hallway, and no way of knowing how long he had been lying there unconscious. He didn't know whose door this was either.

He reached up, grabbed the knob and turned it. The door slid open and Nathan dropped into the room, shaking from the effort.

"Oh, bloody hell!" Never had Nathan been more glad to hear the high-pitched pierce of the Brit's voice. There were hands on him then. "What happened to you? Can you walk?"

All Nathan could do was nod. He draped himself over the Brit's shoulder as he pushed up onto his legs. Together they walked to the bed where the Brit sat him down on its edge.

"You're in shock. I need you to breathe. Just look at me, and breathe."

Nathan struggled to focus on the deep diagonal lines that formed on Gregory's forehead as he deliberately sucked in air through his nose and released it through his mouth. As his breathing normalized, he noticed that he was clutching the Brit's hands and loosened his grip.

"There you go. Do you want to lie down?"

Nathan nodded, and the Brit helped him onto his back.

Nathan sank into the bed and fought against the tears that threatened in the aftermath of this momentary relief. When he looked over, he saw the Brit sitting on the edge of a chair, elbows propped atop his knees, holding back questions.

"I…" Nathan began feeling a lump of gratitude in his throat.

Thankfully, the Brit knew exactly what to do to save him from further humiliation. He jumped to his feet, dispelling the emotion of the moment.

"Alright. Get washed up then. You're a bloody mess to look at."

With slow, deliberate movements, Nathan got up and walked to the bathroom.

He was a frightful mess, as the Brit had pointed out. His agitated skin felt like it was on fire. Nathan stepped into the shower and adjusted the water to a gentle cool flow that washed over him like a stream. He sat down beneath the chilling rain and breathed deeply as he watched the water turn from crimson to pink, and finally, to clear.

By the time he reemerged from the bathroom, he looked and felt, once more, alive. The Brit, too, had taken advantage of the moment and tidied up the room. The bloody sheets and the clothes the Brit was wearing earlier lay in a pile in a corner, along with several reddened white towels that Nathan guessed had been used to wipe the ground, the dresser and the table that Nathan had touched earlier.

"You look much better."

"Thank you. I feel better."

"There are trousers in that drawer. Shirts and a jumper, too. Grab what you need."

Wordlessly, Nathan pulled open the drawer and selected a pair of black pants and a navy sweatshirt. The Brit waited until Nathan pulled the sweatshirt over his head to ask, "Care to explain?"

"I'm not sure actually."

"Let's start with how—"

"Isha… she did that to me."

"Isha? Why? How?"

"She didn't mean to. I think… she saw something…"

"Saw what?"

"I'm not sure. But it had to do with Kiras. I think… from her reaction… I would guess…"

"Spit it out."

"I think something happened to Kiras. Something terrible. Maybe… I think maybe they killed him."

"They? Is that possible?"

"I don't know. But I can't think of anything else that could be so… devastating."

"Devastating?"

"You know those machines that make garbage really small?"

"A compactor?"

"Yes. A compactor. It felt like I was trapped in one of those. And she wasn't even touching me. She was all the way across the room. It's like she wasn't even there. She was… just— wherever she was, whatever she was seeing, it wasn't good."

"How did you get out?"

"She… realized what she was doing and hardened."

"Ah."

"There's more."

"What more?"

"We can't stay here. On this ship. We have to collect the crew and leave."

"Leave where? We are in middle of the ocean."

"As far from them as possible. We need to get in a life raft and…"

"You're thinking we are in danger?"

Nathan nodded.

"Because of Isha?"

"Yes. And also, the others."

It took the Brit a moment before he realized that by *the others* Nathan meant the other aliens perched on the boat. Understanding spread on his face.

"We… should not be too far from Iceland," the Brit said,

jumping into action. "I can speak with the captain. He might not want to abandon his ship — captains normally don't — but I can ask him to adjust his course further into the ocean — away from land."

"Okay," Nathan said. "I'll get the rest of the crew."

"Quietly."

"And fast."

———————

The crew consisted of Farhad, the young man responsible for all of their meals; Philippe, a large dark-skinned Haitian whom Nathan had seen pulling on ropes and buffing the sides of the ship; and Mohammad, a white-haired Syrian man with a round, hard belly who did anything that needed to get done from tending to the galley to relieving the captain when he needed a break.

Mohammad was the most difficult of the three to convince. Using Farhad as a translator, Nathan demanded they had to leave and they had to do it now, leaning more on the urgency of his request than any specific reason. The old man insisted, in a stream of percussive glottal sounds that he could not abandon the ship, that he was responsible for the crew and those people up there. He couldn't leave the captain. He had made a promise when he took on this job, and he had his honor to uphold.

It was Philippe who convinced the man in the end, placing one meaty hand on his shoulder and saying something to the man that seemed to soften his demeanor and his resolve.

The Brit was waiting in the lifeboat when they arrived, each carrying belongings and food. Wordlessly, they boarded and pushed away. They waited until a safe distance separated them before starting up the engine. The Brit looked at his compass and at the map in front of him, and adjusted their course. A chilling wind tousled their hair and puffed up their shirts. Nathan was glad that, at least for now, he did not share his mind with any of these people. That he was still an individual, separate from them and capable of having his own private thoughts. He wondered if the rest of those aliens had been there with him last night as he made love to Isha. He wondered if they had told her to come to him, if she was simply following orders when she let him enter her. The thought made him angry. Why had he not considered the possibility that he was making love not to a person but to an entire race?

He was glad he didn't have to share the ecstasy of that experience with these people, and for a moment, he wished Earth would never awaken.

The ship became toy-like in the distance, then it disappeared altogether. Nathan fought the urge to return to it. He had started feeling that old familiar tug when only a few yards separated him from her. The farther they pulled away, the stronger the tug became. When the ship disappeared completely from view, the urge to be close to her became unbearable. He slid to the floor of the lifeboat, curling himself into a tight ball in an attempt to smother his longing for her.

The imprint on his palm burned as though he was clutching hot coal. He clasped his hand to his chest, and wished he could just cut it off and toss it into the sea.

Nathan was too preoccupied with the discomfort he was experiencing to notice the effect his behavior had on his boatmates. It was the frantic murmuring of the Syrian that pulled Nathan out of his own misery. The pot-bellied man was rocking back and forth with his eyes closed, whispering under his breath a string of urgent words. He looked like he was casting a spell.

"What's he doing?" Nathan asked Farhad, who looked uncomfortable. Farhad shook his head nervously, and dropped his gaze.

"Hey." Nathan shook Mohammad's leg. "Buddy! What are you doing? Hey!"

Mohammad stopped his chant and opened his eyes. He looked at Nathan with contempt.

"What were you saying?"

Mohammad said something in Arabic.

"What did he say? What's he saying?"

"He say, he not fear you sir," Farhad answered.

"Why would he…"

Another string of words came out of Mohammad, this time faster and louder.

"He says you bring demons from the sea with black magic. They sleep for a thousand years. Even before his grandmother's grandmother. But you bring back the sleeping demons."

In his periphery, Nathan saw the Brit look up from his map, as surprised by what he was hearing as Nathan.

"We will pay for your lust," Farhad went on.

My lust? Nathan thought.

"His lust?" asked the Brit. "What does he mean by *his lust*?"

Farhad asked, and Mohammad answered, looking at the Brit.

"Last night," Farhad translated, "the magic man anger the demon lady when he try to steal her power."

"What does he mean by that?" The Brit asked Nathan. "What did you do?"

Nathan felt his face redden with embarrassment. How did this man know about last night?

"Nothing. He's talking nonsense."

Mohammad began to say something else but Nathan yelled:

"Stop!" and the white-haired man fell silent. "Just... stop!"

Nathan felt almost sorry for the fear that his words left behind on the old man's face.

They spent the rest of the boat ride in a heavy silence. Land was closer than they had anticipated. The Brit kept them on a steady course until they spotted the distant shoreline of what Nathan assumed was Iceland. Nathan felt the Brit's unspoken questions that he, thankfully, kept to himself. Mohammad spent the entire ride staring at Nathan. No one had ever looked at him with such hatred. Farhad never relaxed. The Haitian sat so still that Nathan forgot about him completely. Yet, when he did notice him, just as land became visible in the distance, the man's presence produced a strange sense of calm within Nathan.

The wind seemed to pick up as land expanded in front of them. Nathan felt a chill inside his bones. He wished now that he had taken a jacket or a blanket to wrap around himself. He got up and stood hugging himself tightly, his teeth chattering in the wind. The distant coast looked barren. He imagined himself as an explorer in search of distant shorelines.

No. He wasn't an explorer. He was a coward.

We should have stayed, he thought. Then, *If we'd stayed we'd all be dead. We did the right thing.* Then, *Did we do the right thing?*

He could still feel her energy surging through him, changing him into something more. He remembered the softness of her lips against his, the heat of a new current whose source lived deep inside his own chest — an energy that made itself known only in her presence.

The shoreline showed no sign of human life, and Nathan wondered what they would do once they arrived. The crew had brought some food, but Nathan doubted they would share their supplies with *him* — he who had brought back demons from the depths of the sea. And now, with the immediacy of danger gone, he began to feel his empty stomach twisting with hunger.

The boat curved around a bend, and Nathan spotted man-made structures, sprinkled sporadically on the elevated land. Gregory maneuvered the boat around another bend, keeping land to their right, and Nathan saw fishing boats docked a short distance from the shore where the cliffs had tapered to sea level. A few more seconds brought into view houses and roads, a harbor filled with colorful boats of all sizes, and rusty cars scattered about dirt patches that bordered brick buildings. For a moment Nathan thought they would pull into the harbor, but the Brit continued along as though he had not seen the village.

Their destination came into view when they cleared the next bend. Acknowledging privately that the Brit did seem to have things under control, Nathan tried to relax. A town stood in the hollow of the land, and was protected from the harsh wind that had plagued them the entire boat ride. A feeling of hope took root inside Nathan. They were now surrounded by sailboats that were occupied with rosy-cheeked people in thick parkas. The Brit slowed as they approached the harbor. Nathan was grateful for the reduced wind. His body was numb from the cold.

The Brit pulled the lifeboat into an empty slip in the harbor and shut off the engine. The Haitian jumped onto the pier, rope in hand, and fastened the boat to a large two-headed hook. Mohammad moved off the boat with the dexterity of a man half his age, murmured under his breath and shuffled away. As Farhad was leaving, he turned to Nathan and said, "You are not the devil like he thinks. But you have brought great evil."

"I didn't bring evil," Nathan said defensively. "It was here from the beginning."

"Maybe what you say is true. Then you cannot run away like a mouse."

"It's run or die. No offense, but I don't need a lesson from a galley rat."

Farhad stared at Nathan. He looked sad as he turned and walked away.

"Where are you going?" yelled the Brit behind him.

"I will go after them," boomed the Haitian's voice. Before he walked away, he added, "The boy is right. You must not run, and you must not fear."

Then they were out of sight, leaving Nathan alone on the lifeboat with the Brit who did not have to speak a single word to scream his disapproval.

"What?" Nathan snapped.

"You tell me," said the Brit in that condescending voice that got under Nathan's skin. "Explain to me your interactions with those people."

"There's nothing to explain. They're small minded, superstitious — honestly, now I see why the aliens have been in hiding for so long. If you're that different, you're either a witch or a demon or the devil or the son of God. There's no middle ground."

"What did you do last night?"

"Nothing."

"Why was Isha in your room this morning? Was she with you last night?"

Hot blood shot through Nathan like lava. In a heartbeat, he was on his feet, his face inches from the Brit's.

"What happened last night is none of your damn business," he growled. Staring into the Brit's eyes, he tightened his hands into fists, ready for a fight. All he needed was to give himself permission, and his fist would fly into the Brit's face.

This isn't me, Nathan thought, in a momentary flash of clarity, and took a step backward. *What the hell's happening to me?* He collapsed onto the bench that stretched across the width of the boat. The Brit was pale with shock. *I can't be close to anyone,* Nathan thought. *I'm... dangerous.*

Where had that surge of violence come from? He got up, and climbed out of the lifeboat.

"Stay the hell away from me," Nathan yelled as he walked briskly toward colorful rows of weather-worn buildings, trying not to think about what he might have done had he not come to his senses. The ground beneath him felt unstable. Soon, buildings and pedestrians surrounded him. What was he going to do out here, alone? He fought the impulse to run back. Instead, he trudged along, not certain of anything at all.

27
of friend and foe

He was barely out of the harbor's view when ominous clouds rolled over Nathan, hiding the sun and its warmth. It was tempting to take the hiss of the wind personally — to see it as a disapproval of sorts meant to scorn specifically *him*. Nathan distracted himself from such ridiculous thoughts by focusing on the rows of cramped buildings that reminded him of San Francisco and of the New York–New York Hotel in Las Vegas and of his trip to Denmark when he was a child and his mother's grandmother had died.

The temperature continued to drop as he hurried along. A growing anxiety took root inside his belly. Soon, an all-encompassing numbness spread within him, dulling his senses, and he had the distinct thought that maybe the chill he felt running down his spine had little to do with the cold breeze and was, in fact, a result of the sickening angst growing inside him.

Pink-faced strangers glided past him almost in slow-motion. Their animated gestures and percussive sounds added to Nathan's alienation. They were nothing more than blurred aberrations as he trudged through the thickening fog inside his mind. A fading voice within him still nudged him to return to the boat, yet his feet labored along into the cold unknown of the city.

A faint drizzle he had barely noticed turned into a violent downpour whose sodden drops exploded onto him like a barrage. Blinking through the water streaming down his face, and not quite noticing the chatter of his teeth, Nathan stopped in mid-step, feeling disoriented. His sopping clothes clung to his shivering body as he stood in the middle of a city he did not know, unable to continue moving forward and finding it impossible to turn back.

Nathan wanted to scream, but even that required a decision he wasn't able to make. Never had he felt so confused — so utterly paralyzed by the inability to decide. He did not notice a door opening only a few feet to his right, did not hear the distant bark of orders. It was not until something was tugging at his arm that Nathan came to himself enough to turn his head. He saw a white-haired woman hunched next to him in a nightgown and slippers, the edge of her umbrella poking his cheek.

For a moment, he did not understand what this meant. The woman had no humor about her. She slapped the back of his head, and dragged him by his collar to the door left ajar, the entire time murmuring under her breath. Once inside, she shut and bolted the door, ignoring Nathan as he stood in the entry, dripping and dumbfounded. He was always slightly uncomfortable around the elderly, especially ones who looked this ancient. The woman's loose, blotchy skin, cotton candy hair and pruny face reminded him of every excruciating hour he had spent in agonizing boredom at nursing homes against his will.

The woman continued to berate him in a raspy voice that revealed too many years of too many cigarettes. All Nathan could do was stare at her. Without hiding her disapproval, she gestured to him to wait and shuffled down a narrow corridor. She re-emerged, carrying a wool blanket folded into a gray square. Standing in front of him, she unleashed a string of undecipherable commands that bounced off him and fell expectantly to his feet. He was still trying to think of what the appropriate response might be when she grabbed the bottom of his shirt and yanked it upward.

"Oh," he said, "take this off?"

The woman sucked in air as though she swallowed a single hiccup. When he didn't move, she made the sound three more times, sucking in air in quick successions, and followed the strange hiccups with a string of percussive syllables that would have meant nothing if it weren't for her animated movements, gesturing for him to shed his clothes. Nathan eyed the blanket and knew she would not hand it to him until he did as she demanded. He pulled his drenched sweatshirt over his head. It wasn't until he started unbuttoning his pants that he remembered he wasn't wearing any underwear. She must have sensed his embarrassment because she shuffled away down the hallways and returned with a towel on top of the blanket.

Nathan wrapped himself in the towel before removing his sopping pants. He felt a slight relief when she dropped the blanket to the ground and made her way, in slow dragging steps, to the living room where she lowered herself onto a faded sofa that was covered by a flowery sheet. He stared at her white cotton candy hair peeking above the back of the sofa as he dried himself with swift movements. He dropped the towel next to the pile of his drenched clothes and wrapped himself tightly with the blanket, feeling instantly more alive.

Outside, the rain trickled to a stop, and he could see stray rays of sun filtering in through the living room window. The old woman laughed when he entered the living room and pointed to the window as she said something in that raspy voice.

"Yes," Nathan replied, "it stopped raining."

He sat down on the chair closest to the entrance of the living room, aware of his nakedness beneath the blanket. The small apartment was crammed with dust-covered trinkets and ancient furniture that should have been tossed or replaced decades ago. Across from the woman, a flat-screen TV looked oddly out of place against the faded floral wallpaper and the antique, chipped wooden shelf beneath it. Bright, high-definition images of a home improvement program played silently on the screen and reminded him that despite all appearances, they were still in the twenty-first century.

Everywhere Nathan looked, he found dust-covered snow globes sprinkled among yellowing photographs. Miniature worlds stared back at him from the mantle above the fireplace, from mismatched side tables, from shelves crammed with too many books, and from the weathered coffee table. He was only able to recognize a few of the cities and countries trapped in these globes. Had she really visited all these places, he wondered. For every locale he could name, there were a dozen worlds that were a mystery. On the mantle, a miniature Paris and its Eiffel Tower was surrounded by cityscapes whose locations Nathan couldn't even guess. The leaning tower of Pisa, the Statue of Liberty, The Taj Mahal were among the very few he could name.

When Nathan's eyes circled to the table next to him, his heart nearly stopped at the sight of the globe sitting only a foot away from his elbow. He raised it to his face, his heart racing and his hands shaking as he inspected it. Inside the glass sphere was a replica of the bridge from his nightmare. He turned the globe and gasped when pieces of silver and red glitter danced around the white bridge. The red confetti was shaped into tiny hearts, but to Nathan, it looked like a rain of flames, engulfing the tiny landscape in a tornado of destruction. Nathan read the inscription on the base of the globe: "Lover's Bridge of Tamsui, Taiwan."

Breathing heavily against the sudden tightness in his chest, Nathan inspected the asymmetrical bridge — the stretched wires that he had seen snap so many times, the concrete structure that he had flown through as he tried to escape the bite of the beast, and which he had seen crumble atop countless people. In his mind, he saw a stroller engulfed by fire and heard the screams of a mother as she tried desperately to save the burning child. Terrifying scenes from his nightmare were interrupted abruptly by a hand yanking the globe out of his grasp. All at once, he snapped back into this reality where, for a moment, he did not recognize the wrinkled face and the glass-blue eyes staring sternly at him. The old woman muttered something incomprehensible under her breath as she returned the globe to the side table and lowered herself carefully onto the sofa.

The sound of the front door slamming yanked Nathan's attention away from her. At the door stood a blond girl in her late teens — the expression on her face more annoyed than confused as she examined Nathan's wet pile of clothes. The old woman craned her neck to look at her. Nathan tightened the blanket around himself as the girl and the old woman exchanged several fast sentences. The old woman had the last word, and from the girl's expression, Nathan guessed the old woman *always* had the last word.

The girl marched to the small kitchen and placed her bags of groceries on the counter before returning to the foyer and retrieving Nathan's clothes. She disappeared with them into the hallway. Nathan heard the sound of running water in the distance. The girl returned carrying his wrung-out damp clothes, draped his shirt and pants on the backs of wooden chairs, which she put next to an electric heater in the corner. Without looking away from the TV, the old woman yelled her orders, and the girl, swallowing her irritation, disappeared into the kitchen.

Satisfied, the woman leaned close to Nathan, and through a frightful yellow smile and in a hushed confidential tone, shared with him a string of undecipherable sounds. All Nathan could do was return her smile. The girl yelled something out of the kitchen, seemingly in response to whatever the old woman had just entrusted to him. The woman threw her hands in the air and snapped back. A moment later, the girl stood in front of him, holding a sandwich on a plate.

"You hungry?" she said with a thick accent.

"Ah, yes. Very much." Nathan had surpassed *hungry* long ago.

She handed him the plate, and saying something to the old woman, returned to the kitchen. Nathan finished his sandwich in only a few bites, chewing as little as possible before swallowing. The dry, salty meat held together by thick slices of hearty rye bread was no competition for Farhad's masterpieces. Nathan felt a pang of regret at the thought of the kind, well-natured cook whom he had treated so harshly. When the girl brought him a glass of water, Nathan drained the drink in one long gulp, trying to wash down his guilt along with the dry food.

He handed her both the glass and his empty plate saying, "Thank you." When she returned to the kitchen, he heard the clatter of dishes, the turning on and off of the faucet, the crunch of vegetables being chopped on a wooden cutting board.

The sun peeked through the gaps in the curtain, brightening

the dusty room. Once again, Nathan felt that the cold rain had been directed at him, and that the sun was now mocking him.

Well what was I supposed to do? he addressed Earth in his mind. *That place wasn't safe anymore. You saw what she did to me!*

On the television screen, an over-grown, drab backyard transformed into a colorful garden oasis. The old woman seldom stirred as the girl busily flittered back and forth between the kitchen and the rooms. All the while, Nathan sat guard over his clothes, watching the painstakingly slow transition of colors that indicated they were drying. After a few hours, when his clothes were, at last, dry, he slid to the front of his chair and contemplated retrieving them. The keen, old woman read his intention, and speaking in that strange percussive tongue, she gestured for him to grab them already. When he held his clothes in his hands, she yelled, and the girl appeared at the entrance to the living room.

"You change in washroom," she said and ushered him down the narrow hallway to a small bathroom with chipping tile and frayed towels.

Standing naked in front of the oval mirror that was mounted too low for him to see his face, Nathan folded the blanket, placed it at the edge of the sink, and used the toilet before putting on the clothes he had borrowed from the Brit.

He stood at the entry of the kitchen and watched the girl dry dishes and put them away into crammed cupboards with splintered wood doors. She had a seriousness about her that revealed the weight of responsibility at a young age. She was pretty in an unconventional way. Her nose hooked slightly at the tip and veered to the left, yet it looked natural and *appropriate* on her face. She was attractive in person, but Nathan guessed she probably did not photograph well.

"You speak English," he said and watched the subtlest blush of color enter her cheeks before she answered.

"No." She brought two fingers together in a universal gesture that meant "only a little bit."

"You certainly fooled me," Nathan said. He was pleased to see her suppress a smile. "Thank you," he added.

"Why you thank?"

"For taking me in. For feeding me. I... I wish I could pay you, but..." He pulled out the insides of his pockets.

"No. No money. Always she do this. Bring stranger home. And she never leave. Where she find all stranger? I don't know."

"Well, she saved me."

The kitchen brightened, illuminated by a flood of warm sunlight. Nathan suddenly understood the significance of this girl and the old woman who sat in the living room. The brief storm that had left him soaked and shivering wasn't meant as punishment. It was Earth beckoning him to return to the boat. But he hadn't gone back. Instead, he had stubbornly plunged himself forward, farther away from where he needed to be. The idea occurred to Nathan that had he turned around then, the storm would have ceased as quickly as it had begun. But he had ignored Earth's pleas, and in turn she had sent him into a place where he could rest until he was able to see things more clearly. Looking at the rays of light filtering into the kitchen, a sense of deep gratitude expanded within him. He smiled.

"Thank you," he whispered to Earth. The girl turned her head toward him. He smiled at her, too. Looking into her sky-blue eyes, he said, "Thank you for everything."

Dashing into the living room, he squeezed the old woman's hands and kissed her on the forehead saying, "Thank you. Thank you so much." Then he returned to the kitchen and kissed the girl on the cheek, whispering his last "Thank you" into her ear and ran out the door.

A renewed sense of purpose spread inside Nathan as he sprinted down the street, retracing his steps.

We need to get back to the others, he thought. The danger of being inadvertently killed by whatever bad news had possessed the aliens had surely subsided by now. The Brit had proven himself a capable navigator. With his help, which Nathan was certain he could count on, they would find the rest of the crew in no time. There was plenty of daylight left. Even if they had to sail long into the night, there would be plenty of light for them to see. Could they be back, reunited with the aliens, before night fell?

Nathan slowed his pace when he reached the harbor, searching the stalls for the familiar boat and familiar faces. He was certain that they would all be there, and that in just a few moments, he'd be able to embrace them and apologize. For the first time in his life, Nathan looked forward to taking responsibility for his idiotic actions — the very thought of it excited him.

His heart seemed to stopped beating when he did not see them. This could not be. They could not have left without him. An outcome in which he would remain stranded alone in this strange town did not make any sense. They *had to* be here — somewhere.

Nathan scanned the sea in search of the boat as he ran up and down the harbor muttering, "No. This can't be. No…" In his distress, he frantically darted between nearby buildings and the harbor, repeatedly looking into the same storefronts and behind the same buildings, always returning to the harbor where he looked into the same empty stalls, as though at any given moment, the boat might materialize out of thin air.

By the time he stopped pacing, the sun hung heavily above the horizon and turned the sky into a menacing red. Defeated, Nathan sat down on a curb and stared at the bleeding clouds painted across the vast purple sky. Hope disappeared along with the last of the sun. Night fell upon him like a heavy shroud with all of its weight and none of its warmth.

Nathan's palm itched. He scratched at it absentmindedly, which seemed to aggravate rather than alleviate the discomfort. There was an urgency to the sensation, like a warning. The irritation intensified, and soon, Nathan's attention was turned completely to his marked hand. The feeling quickly escalated to pain, then turned into a burning that intensified until he felt his entire hand engulfed by fire.

He was so consumed by his aching hand that he did not see them approach; did not hear their footsteps. Suddenly, he found himself surrounded by dark figures. Two meaty musclemen stood only a few feet away on either side of him. When he first noticed them, for the briefest moment, he hoped they were *his* aliens, but he knew he was wrong. He considered running, but where would he run to? He had nowhere to go.

"What do you want from me?" he yelled as they closed in on him.

A thin figure separated from the shadow of a building and floated toward him like an apparition. His silver hair glistened in the streetlight. Nathan was certain he had seen this man before. No. He had seen someone *like* him before. He remembered the six elders who had confronted Veda in the woods. This man looked very much like the ghost-man whose words had dissolved the tension created by the hiss of the spider lady. He had called Veda wise and had suggested they go about their business without paying much heed to the *human*.

Did that mean that these aliens were allies? Were they working with Veda? Had they been sent here to collect him and return him home?

"I'm sorry. I didn't catch your name." The edge of condescension in the man's otherwise buttery voice gave Nathan pause. He felt his face go pale, and a shiver ran down his spine. Every cell in his body told him to run. He remembered that even despite the supportive words that he had spoken, the ghost-man in the woods, too, had given him an uneasy feeling.

The man put a hand on his shoulder and a strange sense of relief took hold of Nathan. He surrendered to the sensation and allowed his body to relax, feeling like he had just run into an old friend.

Why are you relieved? His own voice inside him asked. *He's manipulating you. You can't trust him.* Nathan pushed against the desire to melt into the man's strong hands, and his body tensed as the threat of danger returned to him.

"Impressive," said the ghost-man. Nathan *felt* the man's voice pushing against his emotional boundaries.

"Stop it!" Nathan yelled, pushing back.

"Very impressive."

"What do you want?"

These are not friends, Nathan thought.

"We want to know why you were at Viliov."

"I don't know what that is."

"Don't play dumb, human. You were at the Camp of the Elders. Why? What does Veda want with you?"

"I don't know what you're talking about."

"Wrong answer."

Nathan received a punch in his stomach that knocked the air out of him. He fell to his knees. Someone grabbed his hair and yanked his head back until he thought his neck would snap. The ghost-man looked down at him through an icy glare.

"Last chance," he said.

Definitely not friends, Nathan thought, fighting to breathe. Nathan wanted to tell them what they'd come to hear. He would tell them everything! Anything to stop what was happening to him. When he reached for the words, however, he found nothing but a chaos of images that he was unable to express. It was as though language had left him. Instead, panic filled him, and his entire body began to convulse.

The man released his head and slammed him into the ground. Nathan sucked air into his lungs as the ghost-man knelt in front of him.

"Please," Nathan choked. "Please."

"Talking *is* the wise choice," said the ghost-man, his menacing stare stirring up terror inside Nathan.

"I followed her around. I just… I couldn't understand why, but I followed her around."

"That's no reason for her to bring you to Viliov."

"She…" Nathan struggled against the man's control. He struggled to find the right words. "She didn't."

"It's very difficult to lie to me, isn't it?"

"No," Nathan said, deciding a new approach. "I stalked her. I'm telling you the truth. I stalked her for a long time. She didn't know. I hid, outside her apartment. I just sat there and watched. And I hid… I hid in her trunk. I didn't know where she was going. That's the truth."

"You're saying she didn't know you were in the trunk?"

Nathan nodded, not trusting his voice.

"Do you know what she is?"

"Crazy and beautiful."

"And beyond that?"

"Like… her job?"

The ghost-man stood up. "Is this all you'll tell us?"

Nathan nodded. Then, forcing himself to push against the man's manipulations, he lied one last time.

"It's all I know."

He didn't know how many punches he endured before everything went black. He didn't know that it was possible for him to receive so many blows to his face and torso and legs. Later, on those rare occasions when he retold the story, he did not dwell on the beating he had received that night. He simply summed up the event with one sentence: "The kicks were unnecessary."

28

buried alive

Darkness embraced Nathan. It was a complete black that made him wonder if his eyes were open or if the severe beating he had endured had left him blind. Was it yesterday? The day before? Last week?

Time no longer existed. It had slipped away and become a concept so abstract he was unsure it had ever made sense. Like a man trapped between two levels of hell, he drifted back and forth between a murky semi-conscious state of this darkness and a dreamless delirium.

He knew he was alive by the pain that continued to shoot through his body. Even the distant, muffled voices he heard during those rare moments when the throbbing in his head eased seemed too menacing to belong to the world of the living. More rare still were instances when he slipped into a blissful existence where he became both minuscule and massive at the same time — both insignificant and divine. He could spend an eternity in that formless, timeless state, but instead, he was always yanked back into the claustrophobic darkness that threatened to crush him.

Once, he woke screaming, but about what he did not know. Nothing remained from his nightmares but a silent terror deeply lodged in his core. He often noticed the sheen of sweat that covered him and shivered even as his body burned with fever, wondering if these were all new moments he was living or if he was stuck inside a never-ending loop of torment.

A semi-cohesive thought formed inside this delirium.

I'm buried alive, Nathan thought, and he let the darkness take him again and again.

29
channel

Gregory's eyes flashed between the thick black waves of Margot's silken hair, bouncing to the rhythm of her fluid steps and her mile-long legs. Gregory had been surprised and more than a tad pleased to learn he would be joining her on this search for Nathan while the rest traveled to Spain where they hoped to find the final device in the heart of a sunken submarine.

"You recon he walked this far?" asked Gregory. He was fatigued from the day's drudge through the town. The sun sat suspended above the horizon, giving Reykjavík a mysterious glow in its amber light.

Margot ignored him as she had ignored his last three objections. The road in front of them tapered into a walkway as they left the last of the homes behind, and they came to stand in front of an overlook at the edge of a glistening lake. The sun was a suspended yellow flame, spreading its warm glow across scattered crimson clouds, transforming them into golden platforms that scarred the red sky.

The landscape took Gregory's breath away, but nothing

he had seen his entire life compared to the striking beauty of Margot as she stared anxiously into the horizon, the warmth of the sinking sun caressing her flawless features. He envied the sun and its arrant reach. He had fallen in love with her a thousand times today. Every time he looked her way, he was given a glimpse into her rare loveliness, and he found himself lost in a moment filled with her allure.

She turned to him, fierce eyes fixed on his. Very few women were tall enough to be at eye level with Gregory. He preferred shorter woman who were forced to look up at him even when they wore ridiculous heels. Only once before had he found himself on a date with a woman as tall as he was, and he had found her unnatural length repulsive. It was an entirely new experience to stand eye to eye with a woman he could hardly resist.

"You think we've traveled too far," she said.

"You're a regular Sherlock, aren't you?"

"What makes you so sure?"

"He is tired, hungry, scared. And the bugger is lazy. He would look for a pint of beer rather than get knackered walking."

"We checked every bar."

"Maybe he was in the loo."

"Okay."

"Just like that, you suddenly care about what I think?"

"We need to find him. It's already getting cold and soon it will be night."

Gregory jogged to catch up. "If he's so important, why are we the only ones here looking?"

"Do you know they killed Kiras?"

Gregory stopped in mid-step. The confirmation of Nathan's suspicion left him cold.

"Come on." She waited for him to take a step forward, then

continued. "Since our universe began to awaken, there has been no deliberate violence between Awakened races. Until this morning."

A knot tightened in the pit of Gregory's stomach. Blood drained from his face. He was suddenly hit by the gravity of their situation. He realized how lightly he had taken the events of the last few weeks — the false sense of security he had felt in the presence of these beings. Even seeing Nathan's bloody body this morning had felt somehow inconsequential.

"I didn't know," Gregory said, "that you *could* be killed."

"Well, they found a way."

Kiras was dead. An alien being — advanced and immortal — murdered by other aliens.

"But they made a mistake," she went on. "Before they killed Kiras, they told us how to stop them."

"How?"

"We find all three devices, lock them in the chest, then bury the chest where it can never be found."

"And Nathan?"

"Nathan's a joke. No one actually believes he can control the Moli-orath. Except Isha, of course. She's telling me I'm wrong. But I'm not. We've *seen* him. True, he might have some dormant potential that he may in time identify. That potential may even help him control the Moli-orath one day. But it's not going to happen any time soon. Certainly not in time to save Thaia."

"Do you even care if we find him?"

"Of course, we do. That's why you and I are here."

They walked in silence for a time. Then he asked, "Has Isha been with us all day?"

"Pretty much."

"Hello, Isha. Terribly sorry for ignoring you. Certainly

wasn't trying to be an arse, but I thought I was alone here with Margot. Is she getting all this?"

Margot shot him an irritated glance.

"Was that nasty look from you or from Isha?"

"It was me. Isha can't control my body. She's here as an observer."

"If this is so important to her, why didn't she stay to look? Not that I'm complaining about our time together. It's been lovely. Truly."

"Isha is our only Channel. Her abilities are needed elsewhere."

"What abilities?"

"You really know nothing."

"I am quite ignorant on the subject of aliens, if that is, in fact, what you mean."

"It's about vibrations. Everything vibrates."

"Quantum physics."

"Yes. But we all vibrate at different rates. And beyond that, we have different vibrational ranges. You and I, for example, have vastly different vibrational ranges, because we evolved on different planets. You and I have far fewer vibrations in common than you do with any other being from your own planet."

"And that matters?"

"What matters?"

"To have common vibrations."

"Of course, it matters. Being a vibrational match is vital for communication."

"But we are communicating fine despite our vibrational variance."

"No. We're using language, which is crude and primitive. It's imprecise. It's amazing actually anyone can communicate at all in this way."

"So, on your planet, you don't speak?"

"Sometimes. I mean it's still fun to create sound, you know? But speaking is not our primary mode of communication. When you can match the exact vibrational frequency of another being, information flows freely and instantly."

Gregory remembered the night he met Isha as a child. The way he knew all that there was to know without asking a single question.

"Knowledge," he said.

"Exactly." She smiled. "It's the instant transfer of knowledge. That's how we communicate. But Isha's range is much greater than the rest of us. It's very rare what she can do."

A thought occurred to him. "If that's true, why did she—"

"Hurt Nathan the way she did?" she finished his sentence. Gregory nodded.

"Channels are very powerful. She's very sorry about that."

"What she did to Nathan… could you do that to me?"

"No. I wouldn't want to either. Whatever pain she inflicted, she felt it too. That's how it works."

As they walked, Margot scrutinized every store. Most shops were small enough that they could see the entire space at a glance.

With the grace of a figure skater, Margot glided to a group of men and women laughing in an informal circle. Their surprise was apparent as they watched a barely clad supermodel approach them and chirp a series of sentences that Gregory assumed were in perfect Icelandic.

Their expressions softened and they laughed heartily, re-marking on her choice of garment. When she responded, they burst into another fit of laughter, and Gregory saw her satisfaction with her own cleverness in the coy smile she shared with him. Could it be that they were more similar than different? He would have to ask her if laughter existed where she came from and what form humor took when all beings communicated with knowledge rather than words, and all punchlines were known to all at the start of a joke.

When she spoke again, her musical voice had a serious edge. The group listened intently. When she was done, they murmured amongst themselves, and a tall man with a round face and a rounder belly spoke for them all. Gregory surmised that they had not seen Nathan. Smiling, the man said something else, pointing directly at him. Margot responded, mimicking the man's playful tone, and the group exploded once again into laughter.

Gregory allowed their cackles to fade into the distance before he asked her about that final remark that was clearly a jab at him.

"Glad you're having a laugh at my expense," he said, deliberately sounding wounded.

"Oh, don't be a sensitive human."

"And not be what I am?"

"That was very deep, Mr. Walsh."

"I am a deep man. What did they say?"

"They haven't seen Nathan."

"And what did they say when they pointed at me?"

"Who pointed at you?"

"The man. When the man pointed at me. What did he say?"

"Hold that thought," she said, walking into another bar.

All evening, she engaged locals and tourists in conversation, asking every person they encountered about the American friend she had lost. She stopped strangers on the street, walked into stores, sat at people's tables as they dined. No one seemed bothered by her. On the contrary, every person she approached genuinely wanted to help.

Slowly, they made their way back toward the harbor. Not a single person had seen the scruffy tall foreigner in his mid-twenties who had ventured into the city earlier that day. It was as though Nathan had stepped into Reykjavík and vanished.

The sun disappeared into the ocean. Gregory hugged himself against the sharp chill that accompanied the graying sky. Margot's conversations became short and humorless. As a slow, drawn-out dusk descended upon them, she stopped speaking at all and only broke the thick, palpable silence between them to exchange a few curt remarks with passersby, who in turn responded with apologetic shakes of their heads. More and more, Gregory felt Isha's presence within Margot — her urgency building a wall of tension between them.

They entered a bar a few blocks from the harbor.

"Do you mind if I grab a beer?" It was a long shot, but Gregory was exhausted and stressed enough to risk Isha's scorn. To his surprise, Margot grabbed two empty seats at the bar and placed her order with the freckled-faced, red-haired barmaid behind the counter.

"I asked her to bring you her favorite Icelandic beer," she said as she got up from her seat. "I'm going to look around."

Gregory melted into his stool. He could not remember the last time he had felt such satisfaction by the simple act of sitting down. Closing his eyes, he savored the buttery smooth lager as it glided effortlessly down his dry throat. For once, he was not glad to see Margot return to his side, and he privately mourned the imminent end of this much-needed reprieve as she repeated the same familiar series of questions to the bartender who listened intently.

As Margot spoke, a blond girl in an over-sized cowl neck sweater squeezed in next to her, her wide eyes fixated on Margot. Tentatively, she interrupted the tense alien in mid-sentence by placing a gentle hand on her wrist. Their conversation was short and percussive. Margot hopped out of her seat, her face alert. She tapped Gregory on the arm even as the blond girl continued to speak and dropped a hundred-dollar bill on the counter. "We have to go."

They sprinted to the harbor as Margot filled him in on what the girl had said. She had gone to her grandmother's house and found the American sitting in the living room, wrapped in a blanket. She fed him and dried his clothes.

"She said that he ran out without an explanation, but he was happy."

"When?"

"A while ago. Before sunset."

"We should have seen him then."

"She said that he ran down the hill, and he was in a hurry. He was coming back to the boat."

At the harbor, she ran at an impossible speed between the many docked ships, jumping soundlessly from one deck to another. Nathan was nowhere in sight. When at last she returned to his side, he felt the turmoil of her chaotic energy.

"I can't find him. Isha is coming back. Maybe she can feel him."

"If she can feel him, perhaps you can too."

"No. I've tried. I can't distinguish him from other humans."

"But Isha is inside you. If you allow her access to your—"

"It doesn't work that way."

"I'm not sure how it works. But if she can sense him, why

can't she do it in your body?"

She paused. "Maybe," she said, and hardened.

When she thawed out, her energy was different, more grounded. She beelined to the line of buildings, and stopped when she reached their shadow. Gregory followed her movements intently, looking around for clues.

She walked slowly in an ever-tightening circle, her steps deliberate, until she came to a stop in front of a dark puddle on the concrete ground. She bent down, studying the pool of thick liquid. Standing behind her, Gregory's heart accelerated.

"Is that... blood?"

Margot lowered her fingers into the puddle and closed her eyes.

"Yes," she said. "It's Nathan's."

30
kesi mora

The first thing Nathan noticed when he opened his eyes was the light streaming in through the thin curtains. The second thing he noticed was the lack of pain in his body. He thought of lifting his arm, and his hand floated upward effortlessly and swayed painlessly back and forth in front of his face. On its palm, a dark circle danced like the outline of an eclipsed sun. He noticed the lack of a sleeve on his arm, and touching his chest, confirmed that he was not wearing a shirt. The soft mattress beneath him hugged his body. The weight of the comforter that covered him somehow made him feel safe. A hand brushed his, and he looked toward it. The pale long fingers were attached to the dainty arm of a woman so pale her skin looked almost translucent. Her oval face was framed by long white hair that was not the white of old age, but of hair that had never known pigment.

The woman looked young with no wrinkles marking her face. Still, her light gray irises, which were almost the same color as the whites of her eyes, revealed the kind of wisdom that is acquired through age.

"I took the liberty of healing your wounds," she said with the musical voice of someone kind and gentle.

She brought a glass to his lips. Nathan drank the cold water, not minding that some of it ran down his chin and the side of his mouth. The cool liquid felt refreshing.

"I took care of the big stuff, anyway," she said. "The broken ribs, fractured skull, internal bleeding. That sort of thing. You'll have some soreness. And that scar above your eye."

Nathan reached up and touched his eyebrow at the mention of a scar.

"The other side," she said.

He felt the gash on his head. It ran from the middle of his forehead to his temple and cut across the far end of his brow. He felt where she had sewn the wound shut with tight even stitches. Then remembering, he said, "The kicks were unnecessary."

"My sentiment exactly!" She smiled. "What is your name?"

"Nathan."

"Nathan," she repeated, "I've always liked that name." Another bright smile revealed a flawless row of white teeth. "Do you know what's going to happen, Nathan?"

He did not speak, yet his eyes took in the room — the closed door behind her, the sounds of the ocean just beyond the balcony.

"You must know," she said, brushing his hair across his forehead and tucking it behind his ear. "You were at the landing site, and then those Nooritans found the device. That was unexpected, I must say."

"Kiras?" Nathan asked.

"Ah. Really unfortunate what happened to him. Also unnecessary. Gibson went completely overboard with that one."

"What happened to him?"

"You don't know?"

Nathan shook his head.

"I'm beginning to think you're as useless as Veda made you out to be. Tell me, Nathan, was it pointless saving your life, or do you have something of value for us?"

"I don't really know anything…"

"Let's start with what were you doing at the landing site?"

Nathan thought about this. He tried to remember the last time he had heard that question. More importantly, he tried to remember what his answer had been.

"I was following Isha. I was drawn to her. I followed her everywhere for weeks."

"She would have seen you."

"No. She was too preoccupied. Didn't even notice me."

"Preoccupied with what?"

"How would I know? Most of the time she was just sitting real still for hours."

"And you never talked to her?"

"No."

"Why not?"

"Talking ruins things."

Nathan was surprised by the ease with which the words flowed out of him. Truth mingled with half-truths to create a version of himself who just might be stupid enough to appear harmless.

"You couldn't have followed her to Viliov. Isha would have seen you. She would have changed her course long before she arrived."

Nathan's lips spread into a smile. "Yes, but she never checked the trunk. She didn't know I was with her until we were already in the woods."

"Do you know what she is?"

"You mean *who* she is."

"No. I said *what* and I meant *what*."

"A woman?" Nathan watched the expression on the woman's face become rigid.

"How did you heal me?" Nathan asked. She studied him in silence.

"I don't believe you," she said. "You know exactly what she is as you know exactly what I am. And yet you choose to align yourself with them. You choose to deceive us. It is no wonder your planet is doomed."

"My planet is fine." Nathan sat up and pushed aside the comforter. Wrapping the sheet around his nude body, he climbed out of bed. He felt a sudden anger bubble up inside him. "Who are you to judge us? Who are you to decide our fate? Of course, I'm going to align myself with whoever's trying to save my planet. Where are my clothes?"

"So, you do know something."

"I know you're planning to harm us."

"I can see you don't have the full picture."

"I don't need the full picture to understand what's going on."

"Oh, but you do."

"Where are my clothes?"

"Sit down, Nathan. You're not going anywhere."

Nathan stood at the foot of the bed. A warm breeze touched him, and he knew he was no longer in Iceland.

"Did they tell you why we're here?" she asked.

"To make sure Earth wakes up."

"Did they tell you what happened to your sibling planet?"

Nathan stared at her, unsure what she was talking about.

"They told you that planets awaken?"

Nathan nodded.

"But they didn't tell you that they awaken in pairs?"

"Probably wasn't important."

"But it is. Your sibling planet is the reason we're here. About 4,000 years ago, he was on the brink of awakening. He was going to be the 13th planet to join us. Then, at the last moment, in the height of the violence and chaos that often precedes the Awakening, the planet was highjacked by Kesi Mora, one of its politicians. He wasn't even very high ranking — a clerk who happened to be in the battle chamber when he synced with his planet. But he was ruthless."

As she spoke, Nathan's mind zeroed in on one single word. "What do you mean *hijacked*?" he asked.

"When his mind synched with the mind of his planet, before he lost his own will to the will of his creator, he activated a doomsday battle sequence that destroyed half the planet and killed billions. The planet was weakened, and Kesi Mora overtook its consciousness. In one day, billions of sentient beings were destroyed. Thousands of lifeforms went extinct. Have you ever heard a planet cry out for help? It's dreadful."

"What's this got to do with Earth?"

"Thaia is his sister, and sibling planets have a special bond that connects them across galaxies. They can sense one another. We came here to prevent what happened there from repeating itself on Thaia. But as it turns out, we can't."

"You're wrong. Earth is good. That won't happen here!"

"It doesn't matter. Kesi Mora has located Thaia and is on his way here. We were hoping to shield Thaia's location from him until her awakening. But even there we failed. Now, the only thing left to do is what needs to get done. "

She paused, but no words came out of Nathan. He tried to

make sense of what she was saying.

"We can fight," was all he could muster up.

"It's adorable that you think that. But you can't. He will destroy everything beautiful, and he will take over Thaia as he took over his own planet."

"Can he do that?"

"He's willing to try, and that's all that matters."

"We can warn people. Get in touch with governments. Make them see the threat."

"You're not the brightest of them, are you? That's exactly the kind of mass hysteria that will ensure Kesi Mora's success."

"We can stop him. *Together.*"

The woman laughed as though he had told her the funniest joke she had ever heard.

"You can't destroy an entire planet based on speculations. How are you any different than—"

"There's nothing we can do," she snapped. "You can't fight an evil that's willing to destroy itself."

"It seems to me *you* have that same kind of evil in you."

"This planet is already condemned," she said. "It has been since Kesi Mora came into being. Believe me, this is not what we wanted. We thought we could change Thaia's fate, but we were wrong. This sacrifice is a small price to pay for the safety of the universe."

Nathan looked to the balcony. He would collect all the information he could, he decided, then he would make a run for it. He would find Isha. He would tell her what he knew, and they would find a way to stop this madness. There *had to* be a way to stop this!

"And your solution is to blow us up?" he said. "Very original."

"Have you ever seen a solar storm, Nathan? They are quite spectacular. They always remind me of my home. You know, Pari Pa'ari has the most beautiful solar storms in all of the universe. It has something to do with the way our twin planets reflect light back and forth between them. It's quite a sight."

"So, there's going to be a solar storm?" he asked, eyeing the street. He would have to be fast. *No hesitation.* As soon as he had the information, he would have to run. As she answered, he tightened the sheet around his waist, trying to look casual.

"Oh, yes. At first light tomorrow."

"So what? Our ozone has protected us from things like that for billions of years."

"Your magnetosphere." She smiled. Her eyes seemed to be mocking him as she said, "Are you sure it will protect you?"

Nathan's eyes shot toward her.

"What do you mean?"

"Suppose there were millions of microscopic organisms that were programmed to penetrate the core of your planet and cause a very sudden and very rapid expansion of its radius. It wouldn't be hard for them to do, but their effect... do you know what would happen?"

Nathan stared at her, puzzled.

"I guess physics wasn't your strong suit either?"

"What would happen?" he snapped.

"Well, your planet would start to slow down. Just slightly, but that would be enough to throw everything off balance. Eventually, it might even stop spinning all together. A dead rock just hanging there in the middle of nothingness. But that wouldn't be for a long time. By tomorrow morning, it would spin just a hair slower than it needs to, and that's all we need."

Her words sank into Nathan as his realization spread inside

him. Even he knew that life on Earth depended on the planet's exact rotation. His knees softened beneath him, and he caught himself on the edge of the dresser.

"Why?" he asked breathlessly.

"I've told you. It's a terrible thing, but it's necessary. But don't worry. The Moli-orath are fast. The worst will be over even before dawn."

He looked up at her.

"You know, earthquakes, volcanoes, severe weather events," she said. "Good news is, the solar storm will shorten the suffering. We want to save the universe, not torture Thaia."

Nathan could see it now: the rain of fire, the destruction, the screaming children and their hysterical mothers. He could see the ground splitting angrily, and people being flung into rivers of lava like rag dolls. His vision became blurred. His voice became prisoner to his shock and remained in the back of his throat where a lump of despair cut off the passage of air to his lungs.

His body slid to the ground. He saw before him his planet transformed into dust. There would be no recovery, no chance of survival.

She knelt down in front of him. With the tip of her fingers, she brushed the hair out of his face. Then she leaned in and kissed him on his cheek where a moment later a tear slid and dropped onto his bare chest.

She stood and walked to the door. With the door ajar, and her hand on the knob, she turned to him once more.

"By the way, what is that mark on your hand? The circle?"

Nathan's mind was a shamble, but even in his compromised state, he understood that he had to respond with care. He glared at her for a long time, trying to pull together his thoughts to produce the right lie. It took him all of his resolve to speak.

"I got it in college on a dare. I was drunk."

She shook her head reproachfully. "Humans," she said and stepped out of the room.

When he heard the door lock, Nathan's body jerked forward. He vomited and wept until he felt there was nothing more left in him to expel.

31
children of spain

Nathan lay in the fetal position at the foot of the bed with his face inches from a puddle of his own vomit, trying to make sense of it all. His body had melted away and was no longer functional. The agonizing helplessness inside him was more intense, more paralyzing than any physical pain he could have endured. He felt an endless hollowness inside him as though he was nothing but an empty shell. His mind held only one image: Earth as a dead, barren rock where all beautiful things had long ago turned to dust.

The scene of his nightmare played in Nathan's mind. There was nothing metaphorical about the fire that engulfed the planet in his dreams. All of it was real — the chaos, the turmoil, the annihilation. It wasn't a dream at all. It was a premonition. All of it was coming.

You're only paralyzed by fear if you are standing still, he heard Isha's voice inside his head. The voice was faint, but it fought its way through the despair inside him. He strained to hear the words — to understand them. *You're only paralyzed by fear if you are standing still.*

"Yes," Nathan whispered in response as he clawed his way out of the darkness and back into his body.

You can't stand still, he said to himself in his mind. *Get up!* It was too painful lying there. If this was going to be the last day of his life, he could not spend it in some hotel room, waiting to die.

Slowly, he sat up.

Once he was on his feet, he rummaged for his clothes. Every drawer was empty. They had taken his clothes as a precaution perhaps. Or maybe, they didn't think he would need them. He used his teeth to make a small tear in the bed sheet, and pulled the fabric apart, splitting it with ease. He tied the smaller of the pieces around his waist like a towel and stepped onto the balcony.

A warm breeze greeted him. Nathan scanned the streets, balconies, and rooftops for familiar faces. He wondered if the woman who had visited him earlier would regret saving his life once she saw he was gone.

He climbed over the railing and sank his butt onto the ledge of the balcony. From there, he lowered himself toward the one on the floor below him. His foot slipped on the lower railing, and he found himself dangling from his hands. He pulled himself up and swung one foot onto the balcony's edge, then stood on it and threw the other over the railing to come to safety. Once he stood on the balcony, he was startled by a set of eyes staring up at him from behind the sliding glass door.

The little girl must have been four or five years old. With a chocolate-smeared face, hugging a stuffed elephant, she looked more curious than surprised. Then, as Nathan took in the sight of her, the expression on her face changed into something more serious. Worry entered her eyes. She separated her right hand from her stuffed toy and pointed to a space beyond Nathan's left shoulder. He followed her finger, and his gaze came to rest on the sea.

"They're at the beach?" he asked, keeping his voice low. She nodded. Then she became childlike again and ran off.

Nathan did not have time to process what had just happened. He looked around and saw a drainpipe running at the side of the balcony and grabbed onto it. It creaked and threatened to separate from the wall, but this was not a time to hesitate. He put his weight onto the brackets securing the pipe, careful not to slice his bare feet, and used it to climb down.

Once he reached the uneven pavement below, he became uncomfortably aware of the people roaming the streets. Couples strolling, children chasing, a woman smoking behind an open window. Three teenagers spoke in Spanish and burst into laughter.

Spanish! On some level, Nathan had already known he was in Spain. Still, the thought had not solidified in his consciousness until this moment.

According to the Brit, the last device would be somewhere off the coast of Spain. What town? He could not remember. Nathan thought about Isha — about how close she must be. He needed to find her. He had learned what the devices were meant to do, and now he had to tell her. He tightened the knot of his sheet and ran toward the sea.

The density of tourists increased as he got closer to the water. Nathan squeezed through swarms of people at an irritatingly slow pace. When he reached the beach, he walked straight into the sea, and came to a stop when he was thigh deep in the warm water. Where were they?

He closed his eyes, trying to feel her energy, but it was hopeless. The sun burned his exposed back; the noise that surrounded him amplified the chaos inside him. He wanted to scream at everyone — make them disappear so he could focus.

He stepped out of the water and made his way to the shadow of a wall that supported an elevated boardwalk.

Nathan was hyper aware of his surroundings as he walked down the beach, periodically glancing behind him to make sure he wasn't being followed. An abandoned pair of blue and white men's trunks and a pink bikini top on a rumpled towel caught his eye. He grabbed the trunks and walked backward until he was, once again, in the shadow of the boardwalk. He slipped on the bathing suit under his sheet, wrapped the half-wet sheet around his shoulders like a cloak, and stepped onto the boardwalk above.

He looked around for familiar faces and kept an eye on the children that passed him by. He had noticed that younger kids became silent as they approached him. He could count on all of the two- and three-year-olds to stare at him with humorless eyes, while only one in ten teenagers did the same.

Impressive trick, Nathan thought, *though it would be a lot more helpful if they did something other than just stare.*

Still the children did nothing more until a very small, blue-eyed boy ran to him and came to a halt directly in front of him.

"Hide," said the kid and ran away.

Hide. Nathan's senses were on high alert. He looked behind him, and in the distance, he saw two silver heads, moving quickly through the crowd. He jumped down the stairs onto the beach, ducked underneath the boardwalk, and ran, looking for a cavity or a door or any opening he could cram himself into. He found a collection of unattended towels laid out on the sand. With one swoop, he grabbed one, dropped his sheet, and kept running. He dropped onto the sand, a few feet away from a girl asleep with her hand resting on a book, threw the towel onto himself, and lay still beneath its cover.

He remained in his cocoon for what seemed like a long time and reemerged when he felt the threat had passed. Nathan sat up, draping his towel over his head, watching beachgoers gather their towels and stumble across the sand. As his breath steadied, the helplessness of his situation began to sink into him. He had nowhere to go. The person he needed to see he had no way of contacting. He didn't even know where exactly he was or how much time had passed since he had last seen Isha and Conrad. Now, it occurred to Nathan that Reykjavík could have been weeks ago. There was a real possibility that Isha had already been there, found the device, and left.

He looked at the sun, large and orange in the sky and was suddenly aware that this was most likely the last sunset anyone would ever experience. Soon a never-ending night would fall on this planet. He was struck by how beautiful everything was. The glistening water in front of him that stretched for miles, the scattered pink clouds in the distance that hung like islands in the vast blue sky.

"There's no use," said a familiar voice. "I thought maybe you would lead us to your friends, but you're proving to be as useless as you look."

Nathan's heart pounded inside his chest. Directly next to him, less than a foot separating them, sat the ghost-man.

"Don't look so shocked," said the man.

"They will stop you."

"Oh, I'm certain they would if they could. You know, I've been thinking about what to do with you. And I have decided, the best thing to do is nothing at all. That way, you can determine for yourself the futility of your actions."

Nathan tried to suppress his anger. "Why do you hate us so much?"

"I don't hate you," the ghost-man said almost kindly. "I am actually quite fond of Thaia. I even enjoy being here."

"Then why destroy us?"

"Because I don't believe she will awaken. Humans — they're not ready. And the influence of Kesi Mora is too strong. Believe me, I don't take pleasure in destroying her. But I do take comfort in knowing that I am saving our universe from the evil that will ensue if Thaia is allowed to carry on."

"You don't know that."

"But I do. The twin planets of my home have the gift of vision. They are the oracles of many galaxies, and they have foreseen a future laden with war. This future must not happen."

"The future is not set in stone. It can be changed."

"Yes. That is why we came here. To change the path of a doomed planet. To help her awaken despite her destiny. And we have tried to course correct for more than three thousand of your years. Yet her fate remains married to darkness."

"You have to call this off. This is madness. We have changed our fate. I promise to you that we will awaken. This planet will join your ranks, and we will help you heal our universe of the disease that is Kesi Mora. Together we will be stronger. Thirteen is better than twelve."

As Nathan spoke, he recognized that the words flowing out of him were not entirely his. It was as though he was translating — putting into words — information that was presenting itself to him. Could this be Earth pleading through him?

"You have given us much," Nathan continued, "and because of you, *we will* awaken. Call off this senseless massacre and you will see."

"If we wait, it will be too late."

"We can stop him together."

"Waging war against him would be suicide for us all."

"You *are* waging war by destroying Earth! You are stealing from him. And at once, you are stealing from yourself the possibility of a stronger alliance."

"No! Sibling planets share a fate. Even if Thaia — by some miracle — does awaken, the bond between her and her brother will grow stronger. It will be painful for her to take action against Kesi Mora. As it will be painful for Kesi Mora to endure the death of his sister. Thaia must be destroyed because Kesi Mora must be destroyed. "

"This isn't about us at all."

"Your sacrifice will strengthen us and weaken our enemy."

"It's not a sacrifice. It's genocide."

"The universe is a big place with billions of life forms. Your friends can attest to this. There are young species in this universe who are still a million of your years away from developing intelligence. There are ancient species so wise each being is a world. And there are species in between at every stage of evolution. I know it must be difficult for you to understand, but we are trying to protect life."

"Protect us."

"Protecting you would mean condemning the rest."

"No," Nathan said, but his voice was faint and distant. There was no changing the ghost-man's mind.

"Ah," said the man looking at the distant cliffs to Nathan's right. "I guess I'll see you there."

The man got up and walked away.

Off the shore to the right of where Nathan sat, the ocean was glowing. Nathan stared at the bright pulsing light for a while before he realized it was no ordinary light he was seeing — this was not a light that humans were meant to see. Pushing himself onto his feet, Nathan ran toward it as though his life depended on it.

32
three lanterns

The familiar light of the mechanics remained suspended in the ocean as Nathan hurried along the coast toward the cliffs closest to it. He ran across small beaches and climbed over the jagged rocks that separated them. Whenever he could, he swam past rising cliffs instead of risking his footing on the rough terrain. When waves broke against his back, he held on to the boulders around him, and when they retreated, he trudged on with great haste. Like a mirage, the suspended light seemed to slip away the closer he got to it. Still, Nathan moved toward it with a great sense of urgency, hoping it was his friends and not the violent, homicidal aliens who had possession of the thing.

In the distance, he saw the silhouette of a tall figure, standing on the ledge of a high cliff. Nathan felt the figure's identity before he could make out any features.

"Veda," he whispered so softly the sound barely reached his own ears. Yet the figure turned its head toward him.

I'm too far away, he thought. *Veda can't possibly see me.*

Yet he knew that neither distance nor the absence of light

could keep him hidden from the piercing glare of Veda's all-seeing eyes. In the direct line of Veda's stare, Nathan felt exposed, naked, *ashamed*. He had left the ship in such haste — without regard for any consequences. Worse, he had convinced others to do the same. Was it his capture that had pulled Veda out of the safety of their camp into the open, where the risk of exposure was so great? Nathan's cowardice had put them all in danger.

Veda's energy retreated, and Nathan understood he was being given permission to approach. If he admitted it to himself, he was glad to see Veda. He bowed his head slightly in gratitude as he hiked from the beach along the ridge where Veda stood. Relief washed over him when he looked over the other side and saw several dozen alien allies standing in a clearing at the foot of a small rise that tapered into the black wall of a forest. When he sensed her familiar energy among them, Nathan felt he could finally breathe again. Her unmistakable current guided him down the backside of the rocky ridge and into the clearing. Soon, he stood in front of her, staring down into her eyes. Her beauty moved him. This could be his last night alive, and he had almost spent it apart from her. He placed his hands on either side of her face, sliding his fingers into her silken hair and allowed his lungs to fill with her scent.

"I'm sorry for running away," he said.

"You were afraid, and you didn't stand still."

He kissed the top of her head, aware with his entire body of the gentle electric current that seeped into him from where her hands rested gently on his hips. He recognized the familiar vibration of his own energy, flooding out of the depths of his chest. He observed it as it spread into the limbs of his body. Their intertwined currents swirled inside him — their effect less chaotic than he remembered.

Nathan wrapped one arm around her waist and pulled her into a tight embrace. How he had missed her body so close to his. Lifting her off her feet, he lost himself inside an infinite, safe nothingness as he buried his face in the nape of her neck.

I'm glad you're alive, he heard her voice inside his head.

How are you speaking to me? he asked with his thoughts.

I don't know... I... this... is not possible.

Yes... he thought and held her more tightly, crushing her into himself with all his strength, as though he could force their bodies to meld into one.

When he let her go, his body continued to vibrate with the force of their combined energies. He stepped back, noticing the tingling residue of their encounter beneath his skin. He looked at her, aware that she had been inside his head. They had communicated with their thoughts. Then, in one brief instant, the intimacy of the moment evaporated as a voice he had come to despise pierced through the illusion of safety created by their embrace.

"Impressive."

Nathan turned toward the voice and saw a dozen figures emerge from the dense forest, led by the ghost man.

Senator Ian Gibson, Nathan's mind put an identity to the humorless face. *How do I know this?* He must have seen the politician on the news, he decided. Or read about him on social media.

"You were holding back," chimed in the albino woman by Gibson's side. Nathan recognized her as the woman from the hotel who had saved his life. Her human identity, too, revealed itself to him. She was Patricia Kraven, Senator Gibson's sister and wife to Supreme Court Justice Sidney Kraven. The knowledge came to him so automatically, with such ease, as though he had always known who these people were.

Behind Nathan, Veda came to life with a surge of energy so intense, both Nathan and Isha grasped for each other's hands. In the hush that fell over them, Nathan became aware of a clamoring sound — a buzzing — that had grown steadily louder. When he turned, he saw a handful of new silhouettes standing next to Veda atop the hill. One of the aliens held the device, whose blinding light penetrated Nathan like a thousand daggers and forced him to avert his eyes.

"Honestly Veda, I don't understand why you've gone through such trouble," said Senator Gibson. "I guess you thought you could control them. How disappointing it must have been for the great Veda — the Kouri — to fail."

The snaking arms of Veda's energy whipped through the air violently, each splitting into strands that merged together in different configurations, creating flashes of light that were at once beautiful and terrifying.

Deep inside the forest, another alien light came into view and became brighter as it floated toward them. Nathan squinted. *The third device,* he thought. *The one they took from Kiras.*

For the first time since seeing the mechanics, Nathan realized what it was that made their light look so *alien*: despite its brightness, the light that the mechanics emitted did not *illuminate*. It was not reflected by the sea that surrounded it; it did not dance upon the foliage of the forest or change the color of leaves; it did not disturb the shadows cast by the moon. The light seemed to exist independently from the physical world. It fluoresced like an x ray sun that dissolved into the objects rather than being reflected by them. With his eyes averted, Nathan *felt* the tingling presence of the light both behind and in front of him, but without looking directly at the light, there were no visual clues of its existence. The night that stretched out in front of him was as black as any.

Gibson looked behind him toward the alien device, then at Nathan, his expression one of curiosity.

"Oh, that's different," said Patricia. "This one's full of surprises."

"Can he really see them?" asked Gibson.

"It appears so."

"I guess nothing is impossible. Borden, how about we let our friend join the threesome? I think he's earned a front row seat to the fireworks. Don't you think?"

Nathan followed Gibson's gaze and saw three burly men whose approach he had neither seen nor heard.

Private Detective Stanley Borden, the name came to the forefront of his thoughts as he recognized the man in the center. *A man who can topple governments... and has.*

These were the same neckless ogres whose unnecessary kicks still echoed inside Nathan's ribcage. As they closed the distance, Nathan detected two extra sets of arms outlined beneath their coats.

"Come on, guys. Let's not do this again." Nathan stumbled backward.

Veda's erratic energy tore through the air, its intensity threatening to crush him even as he clasped Isha's hand.

It took Borden nothing more than a glance to activate the two devices. The mechanics within them came to life, and swarming toward them, they formed a buzzing cloud of light directly above Nathan.

All the Favadani were on their feet then, ready to fight. Isha tightened her grip on Nathan's hand and stepped forward.

"Veda!" yelled Gibson, his voice stern. "Tell the Favadani to stand down!"

Isha's kin stepped forward. Veda's current whipped through the air and engulfed them in an invisible storm. Nathan felt his body being stretched in every direction — threatening to be split apart. He fell to his knees and felt only slight relief when Isha wrapped herself around his body. Even as he struggled to breathe, he noticed Gibson and his race of ghosts writhing in pain.

Veda is killing them, he thought.

Yes, he heard Isha's voice respond inside his head.

"Do it!" yelled Gibson. "NOW!"

The voice of a woman Nathan had only heard in his nightmares echoed inside his head as millions of mechanics darted into him, the agony of their collective attack making him instantly long for death.

"Stop this madness!" Veda's many voices pierced through the deafening roar of the machines inside him.

Nathan's mouth popped open, and he let out a horrible scream. His mind was occupied with nothing but pain and a longing for it all to be over.

We're sorry, he heard the crystalline voice of the woman who Nathan now realized was trapped inside the mechanics. *We're sorry.*

He saw her clearly then. A woman with a round face, soft almond-shaped eyes, a strong nose. She looked no older than he was.

We're sorry, said a second voice, this one of a man.

I know you. Nathan saw their faces in his mind. He recognized them. Night after night, these faces had bit into him, attacked him from the depths of the ocean. These were the faces of the monster that haunted his dreams.

Nathan's body twisted in pain as he pushed against their advances with all his might. This could not be the end. He had to fight. He could not be taken hostage and forced to participate as they destroyed the planet he loved. He could not be a part of this!

Like an answer to his prayers, the mechanics stopped their attack and began to withdraw. At first, Nathan thought it was he who had caused their retreat. Then, he saw the stream of light leave him and enter Veda, turning Veda's body into a glowing crucifix against the black of the night.

"You are making a mistake!" yelled Gibson, who was also on his knees. "You cannot control them."

Even without looking at them, Nathan could feel that the Guardians around him had hardened. He guessed they had joined their Elder and were helping save Veda's life.

"There is no point," said Gibson, with genuine concern. "You must release the Moli-orath before they harm you."

Veda's body continued to glow as the light slowly retreated to the center of Veda's chest and began to fade. Nathan felt the relief of victory within their grasp. Veda would smother the life out of the mechanics thereby destroying the devices and saving Earth. Tonight would not be his last night. He would be allowed to live. Earth would be allowed to awaken. There would be a sunrise tomorrow — beautiful and warm — which would signal not only a new day but a new age in the history of mankind. He raised himself onto his knees, waiting for the dimming light inside Veda's chest to burn out completely.

"You leave us no choice, Veda!" Gibson yelled. "Borden!"

Borden hesitated.

"Borden! Now!"

"I... can't," responded Borden. "It's... Veda."

"I know who it is! Do it! Now!"

One moment the light within Veda was nearly snuffed out, the next, Veda's entire body vanished inside a blinding cloud of light that collected into a pulsating cluster where Veda had stood seconds ago. The statues around him jolted into life, their panic and collective outrage palpable. Nathan tried to make sense of what was happening.

"I warned you!" Gibson yelled, his voice hysterical. "I warned you! Borden, finish it!"

"Gibson," Isha said. "Do not do this."

"It's the only way!"

Nathan could not peel his eyes from the ball of light that remained suspended where Veda had stood at the top of the hill. This is not how it was supposed to go. Veda was supposed to destroy them — not the other way around.

"Borden, you don't have to do this." Isha pleaded. "You don't want to…"

"Yes, he does!" Gibson cut in. "Do you think Veda will let them complete their work? Veda will find a way to override their will. To control them. And what happens if they spit out Veda's cells now? Veda will reassemble and try something new. No. This is the only way."

There was a wave of protest around him. Borden hesitated, then raised his head toward the mechanics and nodded once, his face taut with restraint.

The mechanics' glow became brighter. Nathan could feel their intense heat, could hear their excited chatter. He was surprised when he realized that, even at this great distance, he could see them. Tiny insect-like creatures, each with four or six or eight legs. Moving in frantic circles, bumping into one another. Nathan saw gray dust separate from each and sift through their many bodies and fall to the ground. He understood the pieces were Veda being expelled in a form that would be impossible to reassemble. How could he know this? How was he able see them with such clarity?

Tears filled his eyes. The despair he felt within him was amplified by the dense grief that surrounded him. He knew then that the same had happened to Kiras. Isha's reaction to Kiras's death had nearly killed him. Now, he found himself surrounded by Guardians who witnessed the death of their Elder. Still, even though he felt the force of their collective outrage, his body remained unharmed as it allowed their chaotic currents to pass through him.

How is any of this possible? he thought.

A heavy silence fell onto them as the mechanics, having completed their horrendous task, retreated into their respective devices. Gibson's grief-stricken voice was the first to break the silence.

"Veda's loss is a great tragedy," he said. "We shall mourn."

With that he turned and disappeared into the forest. No one objected when, one by one, Borden's men reached down and grabbed hold of the three devices, leaving behind the heavy chest. They wrapped the devices into cloth that subdued their shine only slightly, and walked after the albino couple into the black of the forest, three lanterns, slowly disappearing in the distance.

33
the hum of the guardians

A strange note hung in the air like mist, cloaking the Favadani in a shroud of melancholy as they sat in a semi-circle around the rock where Veda had stood. It wasn't exactly music, but it wasn't not music either. Nathan wasn't even sure that the song he was experiencing had any sound at all, or if it was a feeling that his mind was attempting to translate into something audible.

The song was somehow deeper than music — more ancient, more *real*. If pure, unadulterated grief could have a sound, this would be it.

Nathan allowed the steady hum to pulse through him, blurring his vision as he blinked his tears away — an inadequate response to the beauty and agony encapsulated in the note. This was *his* fault. *He* was the one they had wanted. Why had Veda made this sacrifice? Why save *his* life when there were so many more at stake?

Perhaps the mechanics were supposed to have taken him apart. Once consumed by the monster, he could have tried to control it. He could have forced it to resist orders.

Or perhaps it wouldn't have mattered. It was more likely that he would have failed and followed the same orders that the three-headed monster carried out even against its own will. Nathan had felt resistance among the mechanics. He had tasted their regret.

He finally understood his dream — the three-headed monster biting into his leg then exploding into a firework that engulfed the planet. Isha was right. He was the key. But they had all misinterpreted what that meant. He saw it so clearly now against his closed eyelids. The events that were set in motion would come to pass. There was no turning back from them. It was time to accept the inevitability of it all. *Acceptance*, Nathan thought. All this time they had spent fighting, thinking there was another way. How wrong they'd been.

It would all be over soon. In a few short hours, he would witness one last sunrise before his eyes were closed for good. Wiping his face with the heel of his hand, Nathan began to laugh. It was the private chuckle of a man who realized the absurdity of his entire life.

"What a joke," he snorted.

His body shook with laughter. Soon, the convulsion intensified and slowed until it turned into the spasms of a man weeping. Nathan collapsed to the ground. He bellowed in anguish, his face a mess of tears.

For the first time since this whole thing began — it now seemed a lifetime ago — he wondered what his family was doing in that precise moment. He would give anything to see his parents one last time, to smell his mother's homemade peach pie, to watch his dad fix a cabinet no one knew was broken. Hadn't his friends wanted to meet with him before this whole mess began? Had he let them down?

Was this his punishment? Had Earth brought him here to die alone and helpless and filled with regret as punishment for living such a selfish life? What was the point of it all? What was the point to any of it, if it was going to end like this?

The hum of the Guardians ended as it had begun, dissolving gently into the darkness until no remnant of it remained. Nathan lay on his back feeling like he might be swept away by the brisk evening breeze. His tears carried away his pain, and a sense of lightness spread within him. He realized his emotions had been heightened by the alien note. In his periphery, the Guardians came to life, and the moon reemerged from behind the clouds, illuminating their softening bodies.

Someone had gathered Veda's ashes inside a piece of cloth and bound it with long strings of grass and strips of fabric. Now they passed Veda's ashes from hand to hand, each Guardian contributing a strip and taking time to wrap it around the bundle. Isha approached him with the pouch and held it out to him. Nathan sat up.

"What do I do?" he asked.

"You bind yourself to it with something that belongs to you. To show we are all one."

"I'm not one of you."

She sat down next to him, wrapping her hands around his as she placed the bundle into them.

"This isn't how it was supposed to be," he said. "I wish... I wish there was more time. I wish I could go back and see my family. I wish I had never known you."

He regretted his last words as soon as they left his lips. "I'm sorry. I'm just... so tired."

"Tie around it something of yours," she said. "We are all one, Nathan. All of us."

When she was gone, Nathan stared at the bundle inside his palms, and with his fingertips, he traced the dozens of protruding knots, each signifying an allegiance, solidarity.

"It was supposed to be me," he said to the pouch. "Why did you step in? It was just like my dream. It was supposed to be me."

He received no answer from Veda's ashes. He pulled the string belt from the trunks he was wearing and wrapped it several times around the bundle. He didn't know if he was supposed to say anything, so he whispered, "With this string that I have stolen and hence is mine, I bind myself to thee." It seemed like an appropriate enough thing to say. It certainly did not feel wrong.

Isha returned when he was done.

"Come on," she said. "I have something for you."

Handing Veda's ashes to one of her kin, she led Nathan into the woods. There was a time when walking into an unknown forest in the dead of night would have frightened him. How far away that time now seemed.

Nathan slipped his hand into hers, allowing her energy to enter him.

"I'm sorry for what I said earlier," he said. "I don't regret knowing you."

"It's okay. I know what you meant."

"I wouldn't trade my time with you for anything."

She squeezed his fingers, sending a current of warmth into him.

"Where are we going?"

"It's a surprise," she said.

"Here we go again." He smiled.

She smiled too. "You'll like this one."

They walked to the edge of a road where a car waited for them. Its driver was, to Nathan's surprise, human. They sat in the back seat together and caressed each other's palms as the car entered a sleeping town.

Only a few more hours. Nathan thought of the millions of unsuspecting people safely tucked away in their beds, asleep behind dark windows. An intense sadness pressed against his chest.

The driver stopped in front of a small hotel. They pulled up to the oversized entry of the three-story stone building with its rows of cozy balconies adorned by fresh flowers. The doorman was expecting their arrival.

"Your room is ready, Ms. Kennedy," he said, handing her an envelope.

"Thank you, Mateo. We got it from here."

"Ms. Kennedy?" Nathan asked when the elevator doors closed in front of them. Isha tore the envelope open and pulled out a gold-plated key.

Their room was on the top floor at the end of a narrow hallway. It was cozy with a queen size bed and a view of the town stretching into the black of the sea.

Standing at the door, he watched as she walked to the center of the room and turned to face him. Her arms opened in a gesture of welcome as though it was her home he was entering.

"What are we doing here?" he asked. How could she think of sex at a time like this? It wasn't that he didn't want to. If tonight was his last night alive, he would love nothing more than to slip into oblivion at the height of ecstasy. But how could he? How could he give himself over to bliss when he knew darkness was looming just beyond daybreak?

Nathan was unable to take a single step into the room. He felt nauseous as though his body too was rejecting the option to make love when everything worth loving was on the verge of destruction.

"Are you coming in?"

"Isha... I..."

"Come in and close the door."

With the door closed, the room felt too small, too claustrophobic. The pressure of her request made him sweat nervously. How was he going to reject her? How would she react if he did?

"I don't think... I'm not..." He pointed at the bed. It was a subtle gesture but the realization on her face was instant.

"Oh. Oh, no. That's not why we're here."

"We're not?"

"No. We're here so you can call your family."

34

the ultimate sacrifice

"I don't know why no one's answering." Nathan hung up the phone. "What time is it over there?"

This was the fourth unanswered call in a row, the fourth person to let his call go to voicemail. He had not left any messages, but he began wondering if he should call back to do so.

"A little after four thirty," Isha said from where she sat with her back to the window.

Nathan's hand remained on the receiver. What other numbers did he remember? He had already dialed his parents' home, Pic's home, Pic's cell, and Joyce's cell. He had met Gray after he'd gotten a smartphone and as a result had never memorized his phone number.

Mistake. Gray was probably the only person who had his phone on him at all times and would answer a call from a foreign number without hesitation.

"No one's picking up. Something's not right. I can feel it."

"You tried everyone?"

What a senseless question. Of course, he had tried everyone.

He looked at the phone and twisted his face into a frown as he thought. *Who else?*

There was one other number he knew by heart, although it was a long shot. Years ago, when his dad had taken up carpentry as a hobby, he had built himself a shed on the far end of the backyard, with enough distance separating it from the main house to drown out the noise of power tools and loud music. The problem was that whenever his mother wanted to speak to him, she had to stop whatever she was doing and trudge across the yard to the shed. After several months of complaining, Nathan's father installed a phone in the shed, and the communication problem was solved. In the last decade, the shed had become a storage space for the nick-knacks that Nathan's father did not want to throw out but was forbidden to bring into the house. Nathan didn't even know if the phone line was still functional. He couldn't imagine his father dishing out ten or twenty bucks a month for a line that never got used.

Still, he picked up the receiver and dialed the number to the shed, expecting a generic recording telling him it was no longer in service. The phone rang and kept ringing. Nathan considered hanging up, but the repeated ringing was somehow comforting. Nathan imagined the phone as it used to be — dirty and stained, its original ivory white no longer visible through layers of grease and dust — the sound of its ring filling the small crowded space and even bleeding into the yard where it might reach the ears of an eight-year-old Nathan with his brother and best friend, Pic.

There was a click on the other end. Nathan wondered if the connection had been severed. Still, he didn't hang up.

"Hello?" The raspy voice sounded older than Nathan remembered it, somehow more *broken*, but there was no doubt about it, this was the voice of his father. Nathan's heart raced in his chest, and he sat up on the edge of the bed unsure of what to say.

"Hello?" his dad said again, and Nathan could feel the sadness in his voice.

"Dad? Dad, it's me. Where's Mom? Why isn't she answering her phone?"

It seemed like a long time before his father spoke.

"Nathan?" There was rustling on the other end, the scrape of furniture against the concrete floor. "Nathan? You're... *alive*?"

"Of course, I'm alive, Dad."

"Oh, my boy, my boy." His father's voice broke. "You're alive. My boy."

"Dad, what's going on?" Nathan tried to wrap his mind around what his father was saying. Why did they think he was dead? What had happened? Why was his father in the shed, and why was he *weeping*?

Nathan had never seen or heard his father cry. He could not even imagine the sight of it. This was a man whose regular gym was a boxing gym, a man who knew every part of a car engine even though he wasn't a mechanic, a man who built cabinets and tables even though he wasn't a carpenter. To everyone who knew Nathan's father, he represented an ideal of masculinity and practical skill. An impossible ideal that existed only in movies and the imaginations of women which no human male — including Nathan — could ever live up to.

This man did not cry, he did not know weakness. If he didn't know how to do something, he figured it out. If he needed a raft, he built it.

There was a long pause during which Nathan's father blew his nose.

"You tell me, son." His father's voice became the manly growl that Nathan knew. "We found your jacket in the ocean. Your cell phone, your wallet, all your belongings were still in your pockets. The cops said you had drowned. We found your car — abandoned with the keys in it. *You* tell me what's going on. You tell me why you couldn't call and let us know you were all right. Your Mom nearly had a heart attack. Your brother tried to kill himself—"

"Dad, slow down."

Nathan's head was a shamble. Images of the night he jumped into the ocean came to him. Had that actually happened? Had he been wearing a jacket? He must have been. The worst part about his father's words was they made him realize that since that night, he had not thought about contacting his family a single time. How long had it even been?

"Pic tried to…" was all Nathan could say. The world was upside down. It was all wrong. Nathan gripped the edge of the side table. He wanted to throw something — break something. A reality in which Pic, whose love of life was contagious, would attempt suicide did not make any sense.

"Your mother's at the hospital with him."

"Is he okay?"

"I don't know. I couldn't… Not after losing you…"

"Dad… I'm so sorry."

"You should be sorry. We raised you better than this."

"Dad, can you tell Mom I'm alive?"

"I think you need to go to the hospital and tell her yourself. And tell your brother, too, while you're there."

Nathan wished he could go to the hospital. He wished he could be held by his mother one last time. That he could sit by Pic's bed and tell him everything would be alright. The words he spoke next were the most painful he'd have to say to anyone in his entire life. "I can't go to the hospital, Dad," he said. "I wish I could go. I really do. But… I'm too far away." He waited for his father to speak. When there was no response, he went on. "Dad, there's so much that's happened. I wish I could tell you about it. I wish there was more time…"

"Where are you? Are you in trouble?"

"No. It's not like that."

"When are you coming home?"

Never, Nathan said in his mind. *No one is ever going home. Not after tonight.* Instead he said, "Tomorrow. I'll catch the first flight out. I'll be home tomorrow." It was a lie, but he felt comforted as the words left him. This story would give his parents hope. It didn't matter that what they looked forward to would never come. What mattered was for them to know he was alive.

"Just, do me a favor, Dad. Let Mom know I'm alive. Go to the hospital now and tell her in person. And tell Pic, too. Tell them I'll be home tomorrow, and they can yell at me all they want then. Promise me you'll go now. I don't want them to worry any more. They can be mad at me. But at least they'll know I'm not dead."

"Do you need money?"

"No. I'll tell you all about it when I come home."

"Okay. I'll take my cell phone. Do you have the number?"

Nathan told him that he did not and took down the number.

"You call my cell if you need anything. You call if you're not going to come tomorrow. You call if there is any change in your plans. You hear me?"

"Yes, sir."

"Okay. I'm going to the hospital now. I'll tell them you're alive, and that you'll be coming home tomorrow. But that means you're going to live up to that."

"I will. I promise."

"I'll see you tomorrow then."

"Yes." Nathan tried to keep the knot in his throat from revealing the truth behind his empty promise. "I'll see you tomorrow, Dad. I love you."

"I love you too, son."

The line went dead. Beyond the window, the town looked peaceful in the light of the full moon. It was hard to believe that tomorrow at this time, this very sight would be one of ruin. He would take his last breath here, in this room.

"You know," he said more to himself than anyone else, "that albino psycho is right. We are a selfish race and violent, too, which doesn't really make for the best combination. Who knows how many planets we'll destroy if we're not stopped now." He could feel her gaze on him and turned to meet her eyes. "At least this way there won't be any more suffering. There won't be any survivors to keep this cycle of violence going."

"The heightened violence is an indicator that the planet is ready to awaken."

"Maybe. But we won't. He said that evil planet is preparing for an attack."

"Gibson told you about Kesi Mora?"

"Yes. You weren't going to, were you?"

"Gibson is confused."

"He said Earth is linked to that planet. If Earth is destroyed then it is weakened. You can take him down by sacrificing Earth. This way, you can save the rest of the universe."

"It doesn't work that way. If we destroy Thaia, we've destroyed us all."

Nathan snorted. "Without Earth, the rest of you are safe."

"That's not true. We're all connected."

"It's no use, Isha. It's over."

She sat down next to him, her hand on his arm. "It's not over. *You* can change what happens."

Nathan stared at her in disbelief. After a long pause, he brushed her hand away.

"You don't have the full story," she continued, trying to explain this new reality to the shock on his face. "It's true that Kesi Mora is Thaia's sibling, and it has been overtaken by a great evil that is slowly destroying the planets surrounding it. But—"

Nathan laughed. "But what? What else can possibly matter?"

"The only way to save us all — the only way to truly save this universe — is to save Kesi Mora from the tyrant who holds him prisoner. Do you not see that? We *need* Thaia to awaken because as Kesi Mora's sister, she is the only one who can get close enough to do this."

He was tired of her expectations. He was tired of being responsible for the fate of billions of people. And now, was she actually asking him to save the entire universe? How could he possibly do this when he wasn't even able to save himself?

He had tried to control the mechanics when they entered him, and he had failed. He still felt the unruly, uncontrollable force of their collective energy rushing through him. It had taken all his might to keep them from tearing him apart. All of his concentration had bought him mere seconds. Had Veda not interfered, they would have destroyed him. He was certain of this.

"I'm not strong enough."

"Yes, you are. You were chosen for—"

"What? A reason? It's like in my dream. Once I stop fighting, everything gets better. Maybe that's why I was chosen. To convince you that *this* is the only way. There is nothing we can do to stop this from happening. And we shouldn't stop it. I think Earth wants to sacrifice herself for the good of the universe. The only way to weaken Kesi Mora is with this sacrifice."

He felt her energy intensifying as he spoke, like a pot of water about to boil.

"That is not why you were chosen. I didn't spend the last three thousand years protecting this planet so you can let her be destroyed."

"That's why she chose me. Don't you see? She knew you'd be resistant. She wanted you to have peace before the end. So you wouldn't think your mission was in vain."

"No planet wants to die. Especially when she's so close to awakening."

"You're not the one who has a direct line to her thoughts. You don't know what *this* planet wants."

"Neither do you."

"But I do. I finally understand. Since this whole thing began, I've been asking myself *why me*? And I finally know the answer. She chose me because I'm the perfect example of how selfish humans are, even ones with great families and non-violent lives. Everything we do is self-serving. I don't think Earth is very proud of her children. I don't think she believes we can wake up. And here's a chance to change things. To be remembered for our sacrifice rather than our violence."

"What you're saying cannot feel right to you. It's not what Thaia wants, I can guarantee it. Allowing her to die is self-serving and by killing Thaia you're killing us all."

Nathan shook his head. They were going in circles. How could he make her see the truth?

"Earth's sacrifice will save the universe," he said. "It will be remembered as the ultimate sacrifice. The species that gave their lives so that the rest of the universe could thrive."

"You're a coward, Nathan." Isha got up. "I don't know why she chose you. Maybe she wanted to prove a point, maybe she saw a glimmer of something that was worth gambling on. The worst part is that I bought into it. I thought if Thaia trusts you, so must I. You're right about one thing. She was wrong about you. She should have picked someone else."

Her last words took him by surprise. He watched as she crossed the room and opened the door to the hallway. She looked inanimate, foreign, and cold. There was sadness in her eyes mixed in with fury.

"Gibson and Borden didn't kill Veda," she said. "You did."

She didn't slam the door, yet its gentle click shook Nathan violently as though she had. He stared at the door, anxiety rising in his chest. She wasn't right. She couldn't be. Earth had to be destroyed to protect the billions of life forms across all galaxies. Doing nothing, allowing the plan to take its course, *felt* like the right thing to do.

Or did it feel like the only option he had? Was it cowardice that he was justifying with inaction? Was he taking the easy way out because he didn't know what else to do?

He sat on the windowsill confused, his head swimming with opposing thoughts and endless unanswerable questions.

35
battle of the guardians

The first time he got lost in the woods, Nathan was five years old. Unlike his father who often told stories of running through the woods barefoot, swimming in lakes, and sleeping under the open sky, Nathan's mother's idea of camping included plush beds with feather comforters, spa treatments, and yoga classes. Thinking back, she had most likely succumbed to peer pressure when she agreed to participate in a more traditional camping trip. All her life she'd managed to never put up a tent, let alone sleep in one. Nathan doubted she even knew where in the garage they stored their tents before that trip to Yosemite.

How he found himself in the middle of the woods several miles away from their campsite, Nathan kept from his parents to this day. All these years, he never told them that he had followed the three teenage children of their friends into the woods. Two boys and a girl, giggling and shoving each other, whispering and exploding into laughter. They were furious when they discovered him on their tail. For a while, they teased him, dared him to eat whatever they found, and tried to rid themselves of him.

When they did lose him, they did so with such success that it took him until nightfall to be found.

They had taken Lizzy with them, too, on that trip. It was the last time they would travel together before the accident. When he was finally returned to their campsite by a forest ranger, Lizzy refused to even come out of the tent to say hi. He learned afterwards that she had refused to eat all day.

That night, when his mother asked him why he had wandered off into the woods without telling a grownup, Nathan told her he'd seen a dragon and wanted to check it out. Lizzy had cocooned herself in her sleeping bag with her back turned to them, but at the mention of a dragon, she sat up and turned to face them.

"A dragon?" She said excitedly. "Like a *real* dragon?"

"There are no such thing as dragons, honey," his mom said.

"Yes, there are!" Nathan proclaimed.

"Yes, there are!" Lizzy echoed.

Lizzy, Nathan thought. *Why am I thinking of you now?*

Only a few months after that trip, Lizzy left him for good. It took another three agonizing years before Pic moved into the neighborhood, and Nathan learned to love another person again. With Pic by his side, Nathan would never again feel as alone and helpless as he did on that day in the forest, or as ashamed of being alive as he felt during the years that followed Lizzy's death. From their very first encounter, Pic stood up for him and protected him. He took beatings from older, stronger boys, stole back his favorite toys, and talked back to the teachers who tried to punish him for things that weren't his fault. Pic took a beating for him any day, and then he'd take his own beatings when he went home to his mother and her many boyfriends.

Nathan tried to remember Pic's mom, but the image was

distorted behind a cloud of smoke that seemed to follow her wherever she went. He remembered thinking she was beautiful, probably the first time he met her, before he knew her. She had died young. Pic had once told him that his mother was only seventeen years older than he was. Seventeen when she had a child; twenty-nine when she died of an overdose.

She was only a year older than I am now, Nathan thought, and he wondered how many people would die today who hadn't yet reached thirty.

It was Pic who had found his mother's lifeless body sprawled across a tangle of sheets. By then, Pic spent more nights at Nathan's house than his own. He was the first and only person who was allowed to sleep on the small mattress Nathan's parents kept in their den for when Lizzy spent the night. After Pic's mom died, they went into battle for him. For two years they were in and out of courts until, finally, they were allowed to adopt him and Pic officially became his brother.

The idea of Pic laying half dead on a hospital bed made Nathan think of Lizzy's tiny body, attached to contraptions and tubes, fighting for life. He could still hear the sound of Pic's booming laughter. Nathan often wondered how a child could be so bruised from beatings and still remain so happy. They had death in common, and together, they had found a way to cope with losing the one they loved most in the world. If Pic died, what was there to live for? Who was there to remind him how to be alive?

It'll be over soon, he thought and adjusted his position on the windowsill.

Halfway between where he sat in the safety of his hotel room and the glistening black ocean in the distance, he saw the familiar, green alien light come to life in the top-floor window of a building. Getting to his feet, Nathan strained to see. He opened the balcony door and stepped into the chilled air.

Then the light was on the roof, carried by a figure Nathan recognized. His heart raced inside his chest. It was Isha carrying all three devices, trailed by Conrad and half a dozen other Favadani. Everything — every movement — was accelerated, but Nathan had no trouble following them with ease. It was as though time slowed to allow his human senses to perceive their actions. Nathan was transfixed.

Isha ran toward the side of the building that faced Nathan. The eight-limbed Borden crawled out of a window three floors below and climbed toward her with great haste. Nathan leaned into the railing. He wanted to warn her. What was she thinking? Did she really think she could stop the inevitable by stealing the devices?

Borden emerged onto the roof and startled her. Despite the distance and the incredible brightness of the mechanics, Nathan could make out her icy features and her defensive stance. How was it that he could see such detail at such a great distance? Why did he feel no discomfort staring directly into their light? For a moment, she glanced right at him, then she turned and ran in the opposite direction. Borden launched himself at her. She dodged his attack, and he rolled to a halt several feet away. Nathan held his breath when she climbed onto the ledge, terrified that she might jump.

More than a dozen of Borden's burly men emerged seemingly out of nowhere and surrounded her. Nathan was so preoccupied with Isha that he hadn't seen them approach. She got down from the ledge. The rest of them closed in around the Favadani, forcing them to the center of the roof. There was no hope for escape.

Nathan recognized the ghost-like Gibson and his female counterpart Patricia as they emerged onto the rooftop through the door that Isha had used. The icy echo of Gibson's laugh shot across the empty space separating Nathan from the scene. Isha's face twisted into expressions that were not quite human as she spoke words he could not hear. Then everything happened at once.

Isha dropped the devices and leapt at Gibson. In that same instance, the Favadani flew, like bullets, into the clasps of their challengers. A battle, the like of which Nathan had never seen, ensued.

They resembled strange beasts as their bodies distorted in unearthly ways and collided into each other. Fists pierced into torsos and emerged on the other side. Heads and limbs were torn off of bodies that continued to fight despite being dismembered or decapitated. Pairs of bodies, locked in the clutches of battle, rolled off the roof and plummeted to the ground with thumps that made Nathan lean forward and strain to see the still-struggling mess on the sidewalk. They were killing each other, yet they were not dying when Nathan expected them to. Rogue arms and legs continued to fight as did headless and limbless torsos.

Borden dragged himself into a corner, undetected by the rest. He was missing his entire lower body. He pointed at the three devices at the center of the roof. Nathan's heart sank as the light of the devices began to expand.

Everything fell silent. The fighting ceased as the cloud of light loomed over them like a storm. The mechanics split into several tornadoes that swept across the fallen piles of broken and dismembered bodies. A moment later, the mechanics darted to Borden and engulfed him completely. The alien became taller as his missing limbs grew out of him. He stood up and stretched.

Nathan saw Isha struggle to her feet. She was unable to stand. Borden said something to her. She yelled something in return. Then Borden pointed up, and a beam of light, thin and sharp like an arrow, shot out of him into the sky. The light bowed across the night sky, dove into the ocean, and disappeared. Nathan felt a jolt inside his chest when the beam was swallowed by the black of the sea.

Nathan did not have to be told what this meant. The end had begun. The mechanics were now on their way to the center of his planet. He wondered how long it would take them to reach her solid metal core. How were they going to cause its expansion? What would be the aftermath of such an operation?

He heard Patricia's voice in his head. *Earthquakes, volcanoes, severe weather events.*

But that was only the first wave. There would be worse — much worse. And what was it she had said about a solar storm? Was it possible that in just a few hours, the planet would be in such bad shape that its magnetosphere could fail to protect it from a solar event?

Earth would become uninhabitable. Billions of people dead. It was the collective scream of the human race Nathan had heard so many times in his dreams.

The ground shook. A mild earthquake. Sporadic lights flipped on in various buildings. Nathan grasped the railing of the balcony, his eyes glued to the ocean.

It will be over soon, he thought, holding his breath. All he had to do was to get through the next few hours. And then it would all be over.

Coward, he heard a voice inside his head. It wasn't his voice. Nor was it Isha's. It was the voice of a child. In all the buildings across from him, children appeared behind closed windows, their features visible in the moonlight. They stared at him with accusing eyes. More and more of them appeared until a child stood in almost every window.

You are killing us, they seemed to say.

Another small quake shook the building. Nathan held on tightly.

I would stop it if I could, he said to them helplessly in his thoughts.

Their expressions did not change. Nathan's impulse was to retreat into his room, shut the curtains, crawl into bed, and stay there. How could he possibly stop what was happening? It was too late. He had already tried to fight the mechanics when they entered him, but he was not strong enough. It did not matter what he did. There was nothing he could do to change their fate.

The children raised their right hands toward him in unison, showing him their palms in a gesture that could universally be interpreted as "stop." The ground shook a third time. More lights came on. Behind a few of the children, Nathan could make out the bodies of adults emerging from corners, doubtlessly looking for their kids. The children remained frozen. He wished they would all drop their arms and run back to their beds.

He felt Isha's energy reaching out and lifted his head. She was struggling to stand. As they locked eyes, he felt something he had only felt in her arms, something so foreign to him that he hadn't at first recognized it. He felt that he was home. He was exactly where he was supposed to be, doing what he was supposed to do. He understood then what the children were trying to tell him. He looked down at the mark on his palm. When he looked up again, the kids had dropped their arms and were retreating.

The imprint on his palm became hot as though he was holding it over an open flame. The circle glowed in a golden hue.

Nathan held his palm toward the ocean and wordlessly called the mechanics to him. The ground shook more violently than before, causing protest from car alarms in the distance. Still Nathan persisted.

"Come on!" he yelled.

The mechanics came to him, rising from the depths of the ocean, and descending onto him from the heavens above. He held his arm out to them, and they circled around him. Nathan closed his eyes and willed them into his body. They entered from the portal inside his hand, their heat burning through him like wildfire, their energy spreading inside him, filling him. He heard Borden's voice echoing in them, telling them to destroy him. He felt Borden's frustration, his confidence that nothing could derail this plan.

Nathan projected into them the memory of Veda's death, and felt in them Borden's anger and his shame.

It doesn't have to end this way, Nathan said to Borden, his voice filtered through the beings that occupied him, and he felt Borden's confusion. *I guess we're not that primitive after all.* He said to Borden in his mind.

It was short-lived, Nathan's sense of victory. He did not anticipate the power of Borden's will when he ordered the mechanics to devour him. His authority was so complete that it took Nathan incredible effort to push back against it. The mechanics, unable to decide between conflicting instructions, bounced around noisily inside his body, their frantic movements attacking him from every part of his breathing matter. An intense heat that was previously concentrated in his arm engulfed his body.

Nathan dropped to his knees. Through his pain, he stole one last glance at Isha. He wanted to tell her that he couldn't hold on any longer. He had done his best, and once again he had failed.

He wished he was stronger. He wanted to tell her that he loved her. He loved her in a way that he didn't think was possible. Her presence — her very existence — made him feel complete. It made him realize how lonely he had been before he found her. His life started to make sense once she entered it, and it would stop making sense when she was gone.

The intense love he experienced shifted something inside Nathan. A gateway opened inside his chest, through which he saw the truth of what he was. He was this love that he felt for her. And this love was the infinite space that existed through and beyond his physical body. It was the very consciousness that occupied him — vast and formless. All thought left him then. In its stead, knowledge seeped into him from his source, his creator: his planet. Without having to remember Isha's words, he suddenly knew what she had meant: The death of Earth would be the death of the universe, because all things were one and the deliberate destruction of one was the deliberate destruction of all. This was why Veda had saved him. Because in a universe of connection, there was no justification for Earth's sacrifice.

He saw the mechanics for the first time as they truly were, each a complete being and each a part of a whole. He saw the melded consciousness of three humans dispersed among billions of mechanical entities. He understood that these humans had been fed to the machines whose sentience could only be derived through such integration.

The choice of using human consciousness inside these mechanics was Borden and Gibson's ultimate defense to ensure no other Nooritan could control them. Only Borden, their creator, would be able to get close enough. But they had made a mistake. Even Borden's control over them was limited. These Moli-orath's true master could only be another human. In their haste to destroy Earth, they had underestimated her lifeforms.

Nathan recognized the three figures, knew them as well as he knew himself. He felt their will to live, their defiance, their hatred of what they had done. Three prisoners, consumed by machines, stripped of their humanity and enslaved for eternity. The young woman had lived hundreds of years ago. He saw her life — hard and filled with physical labor. One of the men had been a soldier, fatally injured in battle and left to die when Borden found him and offered him immortality. The woman and the soldier had chosen this path, though they had not known what they were choosing, but the third man had been ambushed at night and taken against his will. Unlike the others, this man lived in more recent times. His wife had been pregnant at the time of his capture. His outrage was palpable.

Seeing them this clearly, Nathan no longer feared them. He understood their confusion, their desire not to participate in this violence, and was able to pry their will apart from Borden's. He recognized the helplessness they felt at being forced to destroy what had been their home. When Nathan ordered them to reject Borden's orders, he heard their collective sigh of relief. The Moli-orath were eager to obey him; suddenly aware of the damage they had inflicted on Nathan's body, they stopped moving. His slightest desire for relief from his physical pain prompted them to repair his body. They wanted to make him whole.

Can you carry me? he asked, and they knew exactly what he meant. They lifted his body, carried him across rooftops that separated him from her, and set him down in front of Isha. He willed them to return to their devices, and they obeyed.

Isha was missing an arm and a leg. There was also a large gash in her abdomen.

"Let's get you to your recovery pod." He picked her up with

one easy swoop, feeling stronger than he ever had.

Nathan walked past Borden toward the stairs, ignoring the look of disbelief on the alien's square face. Close to the door that led to the stairwell, a wounded Patricia sat leaning against a wall, surrounded by a large puddle of her own blood.

"I knew you were lying about the mark," she said.

"Yeah?"

"Gibson told me to not save you. But I couldn't take the chance."

"What chance?"

"That we might be wrong about Thaia."

36

connected

By the time Nathan emerged out of the building on ground level, the dark cobble-stone streets were swarming with apparitions whose swift movements blurred them into the lingering shadows of the night. Nathan observed how easy it was for him to follow the rapid, unnatural activity of these strange figures despite their incredible speed. Time and light seemed to yield to his eyes, slowing and bending as necessary to reveal to him what he wished to know. If he wondered about something shifting in the shadows, he could then make out the details of a wounded alien being lifted by another. If his attention was drawn to a subtle sound a block away, he suddenly knew that a van had pulled up that was to collect the severed limbs of Magirians. It felt like the most natural thing in the world, the way that information presented itself to him at will. As though he was meant to know every answer to every question.

All around him, alien beings carried distorted bodies into vehicles and cleaned up the mess of battle. He exchanged brief sideways glances with aliens who acknowledged him with imperceptible nods of their heads as they hurried past him. He saw them as clearly as he had seen the mechanics, as individual beings that moved and functioned as the limbs of a greater whole.

Among them, he recognized the various races he had seen represented at the Viliov — the image of their encounter in the woods now more vivid in his mind than he had remembered it before. A great number of them were tall, dark figures whose yellow eyes created a mesmerizing contrast against their glistening black skin. A phalanx of seven childlike figures whose adult features seemed out of place on their small bodies moved in unison as they carried limbs as large as themselves. There were aliens with auburn hair and skin that seemed to shimmer white in the light of the moon. To his surprise, he saw ghostlike men and women who appeared as eager to help as the rest. And there were also many who had Borden's thick neck, square torso, and additional sets of limbs, who scaled the walls like massive spiders and returned in the same way, carrying their wounded.

The battle scene was already entirely cleaned up, and the aliens were quickly disappearing into the shadows from whence they had come. Soon, it would be as though nothing had happened here, on this day that had so nearly been Earth's last.

Isha was a hardened statue in his arms. He guessed she had to harden to keep herself from further falling apart. He remembered how he had leaned on her the day he drowned. It had felt impossible to keep his weight to himself and had, at first, worried that she wouldn't be strong enough to help him up the hill. But she had practically carried him. Now, he could repay that debt.

Through the surge of shadows two figures emerged, moving at a normal human pace. They looked directly at him. One of the figures was Gregory, the man Nathan had disliked for reasons he no longer remembered; the other was a tall black-haired Guardian whom Nathan had seen on the boat but whose name he had never caught.

Margot, Nathan suddenly knew. Images entered him of Margot walking down streets that Nathan recognized, kneeling over a dark puddle of what he knew was his blood. How could he know all of this? The answer came to him. He knew because Gregory knew. These were Gregory's memories, accessible to him through his desire to know.

When the duo reached Nathan, Margot nodded and Nathan placed Isha's motionless body in her arms.

"Margot tells me you saved the world," said Gregory.

"Yes." Nathan smiled. "It was all me. These aliens were no help at all."

He was glad to see Gregory laugh. In reality, he knew that it wasn't he who had saved Earth. It was Earth who had saved him.

"Are you coming with us?" asked Margot.

"Not this time. I have some place to be."

She nodded and handed him some car keys. Nathan knew that Gregory would soon become the second human to ever see the Camp of the Elders and patted him on the back.

"You're in for a treat, my friend," he said, then turning to Margot, he added, "She is… going to be okay?"

"Yes. But I can't say the same for some of the others."

Nathan followed Margot's gaze and saw several ghost-like bodies being carried into a van. He recognized Patricia as she was deposited in the back of the van atop another body.

"Are they dead? Like… permanently?"

"Not all races handle physical damage as well as Nooritans do."

———

Nathan drove in silence, his mind a blank. He instinctively knew how to get to the airport, and so did not need to think. Instead, he felt his body which was filled with the force of an energy that had once overwhelmed his senses but now purred through him reassuringly. He felt the soft touch of the setting moon on his face and the gentle tingle in his palm that pulsed with the power inside him. He felt a deep gratitude that came from the heart of the planet he loved. He thanked her for her will to live and for teaching him how to be alive.

A Favadani Guardian — *Mateo* — greeted him at the airport and led him onto a private jet that sat on the runway, awaiting his arrival. He watched the sun rise over a blue horizon from high above the cover of clouds. His heart ached with love for the planet that had given him so much. To think that he had almost let her be destroyed… He sent her a private apology and felt instantly lighter as the realization spread inside him that Earth did not hold on to grudges.

"Would you like to freshen up?" asked Mateo. "There's a shower in the back and some clothes."

The bathroom on the plane was as big as the one in Nathan's apartment. He was still wearing the stolen trunks, though they were torn and laced with dirt. His body was covered in sand, dirt, and splatters of fluids he guessed were both human and alien blood.

He let the hot water wash it all away as he sat on the floor of the shower and shaved his face. The green long-sleeve t-shirt and jeans they'd left for him fit him better than any clothes he owned. He brushed the tangles out of his hair with his fingers and made a mental note that it was time to get a haircut.

He slept through most of the flight and found himself parched and famished when he awoke, refreshed from the first

restful night's sleep that he'd had in a long while. A simple breakfast of eggs, vegetables, potatoes, and orange juice was delivered
to him without him asking for it. He ate slowly, allowing each
bite to fill him with an explosion of flavor and energy. As he
chewed with his eyes closed, he could see the chicken who had
given her eggs for this meal. Nathan thanked her for giving him
this incredible gift of nourishment. He saw the cauliflower, the
carrots, and the potatoes emerge from the earth and the many
hands they touched before arriving in the kitchen to those who
would prepare them with butter and crushed pepper. Nathan
thanked the earth and the sun for infusing them with nutrients
that would give him strength.

You are the limbs of the same body, Isha had once told him.
He understood now what she meant. It wasn't just he and Gregory who were one. He was the same as the chicken and the potato
and the worms in the ground. He was one with the farmer and
the earth, with the ray of sun, the grain of wheat, and the drop of
rain. Nathan felt this in the deepest depths of his being.

———————

When they landed at LAX, all Nathan had to do was walk
down the stairs of his private jet into a black limousine where a
red-headed freckle-faced Guardian driver shook his hand vigor-
ously and said, "Well done."

The starless night sky was illuminated with city lights. He
had forgotten about how bright the night sky could be in a city
that knew no sleep. As the limo drove out of the airport, Nathan
thought about visiting Pic. It would have to wait until the morning. Visiting hours would be over by now, and his parents would
be home. He leaned forward and started giving the driver the
address to his childhood home.

"Twenty-two hundred—"

"Mildred Avenue." The driver finished his sentence, glancing at Nathan in the rearview mirror.

Nathan leaned back in his seat and relaxed, hearing new voices among the familiar sounds of Los Angeles traffic. Other people's thoughts and memories and dreams trickled into him wherever his attention rested. Looking at a gray-haired woman in the car next to him, he saw her sitting at a kitchen table not her own — her daughter's. He saw a two-month-old baby being handed to her as the frazzled mother prepared a bottle. Nathan saw the child as an egg before it was conceived. He felt the sense of security and love the child felt in the old woman's arms. All around him people's lives opened up to him. He knew them as he knew himself. He felt one with the woman and child and the child's mother. They all existed within one infinite perfect whole.

He could also feel people who did not yet live or lived long ago. Among them echoed Lizzy's familiar, hearty laugh, not as a sound, but as a presence that, Nathan now realized, had always been there. He knew then what Isha had meant when she said that losing Earth would mean losing the entire universe. As long as Earth was alive, no one ever really died. All consciousness was preserved within her, continually shifting form, endlessly evolving and becoming more. The same way that humans were anchored into this planet, all planets were anchored into the universe. It wasn't just the planets and the beings inhabiting them that were alive. Consciousness lived within the entire universe. No. Consciousness was the universe.

"Thanks," Nathan said as he got out of the car.

Nathan found the front door unlocked. With tentative steps, he slipped into the house. His heart sank when he heard Senator Gibson's familiar buttery voice, and he ran down the hall and exploded into the sitting room. His momentary fear was confirmed by the image of the lanky albino sitting in his father's chair, wearing an expensive striped suit, sipping tea from his mother's good china.

"What are you doing here?" Nathan could not keep the contempt out of his voice as he addressed United States Senator Ian Gibson.

"Nathan!" His mother ran to him and locked him in a tight embrace. Nathan sank into his mother's arms while keeping a leery eye on Gibson. He felt the full extent of his mother's worry, the despair she had felt when, at the police station, she'd been told they would keep looking for her son. She had seen the emptiness of those words. Now, Nathan felt her terror at losing him. In her embrace, Nathan saw how Pic, her adopted son, had slipped into depression. He felt her pain at seeing Pic suffer and experienced her helplessness.

He saw other things too. Bits of conversation, moments frozen in time, emotions expressed or kept secret. He absorbed the emotions of a lifetime in one brief, endless moment. It all existed within him.

"Senator Gibson was just telling us about how you were helping on a national security matter," said his father. "Top secret. Wouldn't even tell us what you did."

Nathan was grateful for the story that absolved him of any wrongdoing, but why had they sent Gibson to speak with his family? They couldn't have found someone who hadn't wanted to destroy all that he loved only hours earlier?

When Gibson got up to leave, Nathan walked him out.

"You proved me wrong," said Gibson, before getting into the limo that had brought Nathan to the house.

"If it was up to you, we'd all be dead right now."

"Yes, and the universe would be much safer for it."

"Whatever you're planning — if you try to hurt this planet, I will thwart it."

"I believe you. Don't worry. We're past that stage now." His voice grew stern. "What you've done has set certain things into motion that cannot be reversed. If you think you've dodged suffering, think again. The torture you'll endure as a result of this will have no bounds. We the Pa'ari are the seers of the Awakened, and we have seen chaos and destruction unfold across the universe. The final battle will destroy far more than your precious Thaia."

"But now Earth can stand with you against this evil."

"Arrogance. That's your race's greatest vice. Do you know how long it will take for Earth to awaken fully? For every individual on this planet to be like you, so you have a chance at being *helpful*?"

Nathan shrugged.

"It can take hundreds of your years. Maybe thousands."

"So?"

"So, we're lucky if we have one year before he comes knocking."

Nathan watched the car until it turned the corner at the end of the street and disappeared from view.

The future is not set in stone, he thought as he walked back to his parents' house.

37
brothers

It was a week before Nathan saw another alien. He spent most of his time at the hospital, reveling in his brother's miraculous recovery. Pic had lost weight, broken several ribs, and suffered a concussion. It was a miracle his spine did not break during his fall. But his health returned quickly. Pic was more or less back to his old chipper self now, joking freely, hitting on the nurses who tended to him, and teasing his friends endlessly.

"Are you excited to come home?" Nathan asked.

"And give up all this? 24/7 room service, hot nurses at my beck and call, people sending me flowers and chocolate all day long?"

"Well, Mom's excited."

Pic's face turned serious. "Nate. I wasn't… trying to kill myself. I was just…"

"I know. Mom knows too. Well, now she does. Besides, if you were trying to kill yourself, jumping out of a tree is probably one of the worst ways to do it."

"Yeah! What idiot would do that?"

They laughed.

A gentle knock drew their attention to the open door. Isha stood in the doorway, looking as she always had, petite and intense, her pale skin perfectly smooth, her lips plump and purple. Only her eyes were a lighter shade than their usual forest green. There was a calmness in them that had been absent in all the time Nathan had spent with her.

A grin spread across Pic's face, and Nathan heard his brother's words before he spoke them. Nathan had gotten used to knowing people's thoughts. It felt natural somehow, as though it was a normal part of being human. If he had to explain it, he'd say it was as though he had lived his entire life with his eyes out of focus, and all that had happened was that he had gotten glasses and now could see. Still, even though he could not imagine a time when he was not privy to other people's private internal dialogues, at times like these, he did feel a bit like he was eavesdropping.

"I guess you didn't make her up," said Pic.

"Nope," said Isha. "I'm as real as they come."

The pulsating current of energy inside Nathan, which had become a constant presence within him, intensified. He wanted to step close, to pull her into himself, and to hold her there, their life forces melting into one another.

"I'm sorry," Pic said. "Should I leave?"

It was Isha who broke eye contact. She looked at Pic with a smile. "Oh, no. I wanted to meet you. Nathan's said so much about you."

Nathan had said nothing about Pic, at least not *out loud*, yet he felt the immediate effect that her little white lie had on his brother.

"Yeah? That's not like him at all. Unless he thought he was going to die or something."

Nathan laughed and excused himself, claiming he needed to get water. Did anyone else want something from the vending machine? In reality he needed some distance from her to get the intensity of her pull under control. They were magnets, he decided. She tugged at him, and he tugged at her. Now that the source of his energy was strong within him, the pull between them was mutual and almost impossible to resist.

He returned to Pic's room with three bottles of water.

"Your girlfriend tells me you are going to meet her parents."

"I am?"

"I thought it's about time." She smiled.

38
the kouri

Nathan and Isha held hands the entire drive to Viliov, the Camp of the Elders. Much of the two-day drive they spent in silent meditation interspersed with rough passionate love-making that shook them both and left them breathless for long stretches of time.

Nathan noticed that since he awakened to Earth, he didn't need to speak much. He was content listening to and feeling the life that was around him. Without needing any explanations, he grasped the inner workings of all beings. The thoughts of butterflies, the songs of birds, the logic of trees and flowers and bees. It was all revealed to him in the silence. He *understood* life, and in that wordless innate understanding was a sense of complete and unshakable peace.

He told Isha about this.

"Now imagine if *everyone* experienced what you're experiencing. That's how it is when she fully awakens."

Nathan tried to imagine this. What would it be like if everyone had access to the knowledge that unfolded within him so effortlessly?

"There would be no more conflict," he said. "No wars. All problems would be solved overnight."

"And that's when life begins," she said. "An awakened planet is a perfect organism. Perfectly healthy and in synch in every way. Every person knows exactly where to go, what to do, how to do it."

"And what happens to our individuality?"

"You tell me? Do you feel like you've lost your individuality?"

"Strangely enough, no."

She smiled.

"I actually feel like more of an individual now, if that makes sense. It's strange. I feel like I'm just one cell in this massive body with countless parts. All I have to do is focus on any one element, and instantly I know all I need to know about it. I feel one with it. But at the same time, I feel more like myself than ever. I am a unique entity, not better or worse than any other thing. But I'm also the same. It's hard to explain… Like I'm this person in my body, but I am also every person in every body, and, at the same time, I am no body at all. Does that make sense?"

"Yes." She squeezed his hand. "We have a saying, *become nothing and become whole*. You have become your whole self."

"There's one thing I don't understand. If this is how it feels to be awake, how could — I mean — all that violence between your people — it doesn't make sense—"

"You're right. What you witnessed were not common actions of the Awakened. But you have to understand, we have been severed from our homes for a very long time. Living among a primitive race who—"

"Hey!"

"Well, it's true. You are a primate race. And this is your Age of Violence that often precedes a planet's awakening. Even I struggle to maintain my connection with my planet, and Favadan is the oldest awakened planet."

"So, how do you reconnect?"

"It's different for every race. For my race, an easy way is to get remade."

"So now, after spending some time in your pod, you're—"

"Good as new."

When they parked, Nathan hesitated to get out of the car. There was one other question he had wanted to ask.

"Why did you choose to look this way again? You could have had any body you wanted, right?"

"I think you know the answer to that."

"I do?"

She smiled and kissed him on the cheek.

They walked to the camp through the woods. Nathan remembered his first clumsy steps through this forest. Now, he moved without stumbling. He knew the ground under his feet as though it was an extension of his body. Every step conformed to its unique environment to form the perfect relationship between his body and the forest, as though the step itself was co-created by his will and the will of the ground that supported it. He increased his speed to a steady jog and marveled at the way his body's natural instincts allowed him to travel through the forest with ease. She matched her tempo to his, and they moved together as one.

He saw the buildings in the distance and accelerated to a sprint. When they were mere feet away, they were greeted by a group of Elders who stood in a semi-circle as they had once done, blocking their path. Nathan recognized them. This time, they seemed glad to see him.

"Welcome, Nathan Bradley, the Elder of the Human race," said the booming voice of the yellow-eyed black man — *Otis*.

"The what of the what?" Nathan whispered to Isha.

"I believe proper introductions are in order," continued the man. "We are the Elders of the Present Seven. We have come here to protect your planet. And we nearly failed at our mission. If it weren't for your perseverance and Thaia's skillful selection, this day would have been remembered as the day our universe collapsed upon itself."

Nathan looked at the faces of the Elders. He counted only six. He felt the void of the tall powerful seventh member, whose tragic death he had witnessed only a week ago.

"I am Otis of the Gronien race," continued the black man. "You have met Thoma of the Pa'ari race and Ma'ona of the Magirian race," he pointed at the ghost-like man at the head of the line-up and the spider woman next to him. "Sabien of the ancient race of Sunju," he gestured to a petite woman who looked no older than 16 years old, standing next to him. "Uri, the great Zartok," he said, gesturing to a gray-haired frail man with piercing alert eyes, standing next to Sabien. "And Celena of the Chelis race," he gestured to a yellow-skinned woman at the other end of the arc, whose wavy hair seemed to have been forged out of fire. "We are honored to welcome you into our circle as the Elder of your people and the voice of Thaia. You shall join hands with us and partake in decisions that will guide this young planet to her inevitable awakening."

It would have been important for Isha to have mentioned this, Nathan thought.

"Do you accept?" said Otis after a short pause.

Nathan did not know how to respond. Isha leaned into him and whispered, "Say yes."

"Yes," Nathan said.

Nathan and Isha walked at the back of the procession as they made their way to the cabins. The group came to a halt in front of Veda's house. There they stood, waiting. After a time, the door to Veda's cabin opened and Conrad stepped out, wearing nothing but a piece of cloth wrapped around his waist.

"It is done," he said and stood to the side.

The door opened, and Nathan saw a row of Favadani Guardians, dressed identically, lining the walls of the long hallway. From inside the ground, half-way down the corridor, a figure emerged with hair as black as tar, wearing an orange kimono. Nathan felt the familiar weavings of Veda's energy. He grasped Isha's hand, less for protection than to hold onto someone in this moment of joy.

Veda was alive, appearing in the genderless body of a child, standing no taller than four feet. As Veda approached the door, the energy fields that surrounded Nathan intensified, and Nathan knew all the Elders shared in his awe. Veda emerged through the door, standing powerful in a new body that seemed as appropriate as the previous one had.

"The Kouri is reborn," said Conrad.

Veda looked at the Guardians through all-knowing eyes. Nathan knew in that moment that Veda was the most powerful being in the whole of this universe. The being whose consciousness was so complete it could resurrect itself out of ashes.

Kouri, Nathan thought, *the being who is all beings.*

The circle was complete.

acknowledgements

Thank you for reading this book. There are so many incredible individuals without whom it would not be what it is today. If you loved The 13th Planet, you have these people to thank. Mahnaz Shahrestani, my mom, is at the top of this list. Thank you, mom, for reading multiple versions of the manuscript and for your generous praise, which fueled me as I worked through my doubts.

No one has had more of an impact on the contents of these pages than my editor and friend Carrie Paterson, who provided thoughtful notes on multiple drafts. Also a huge thank you to David Zucker, Debra Kushon, Jen Lhanie, Anahita Naderi, Layla Khamoushian, and all of Hot Crazy, who have been my personal cheerleaders for many years and whose faith in me seems unwavering.

Thank you to my family and friends who read early drafts of this book and provided invaluable feedback. Patrick Tyrrell, Noah Levin, Hans Jörg Neumann, Jeff Berkman, Katy Reese, Angie Engelbert, Jon Zelazny, Aaron Zerah, Timothy Gaer, Dan Reynolds. You are all so awesome for taking the time to read and provide notes! You might recognize your suggestions in these pages. I hope you like how the book turned out.

Also a huge thank you to all my friends and family who provided support and cheered me on, even if they weren't able to read and provide notes. There are too many of you to name individually, but you know who you are. Thank you for your belief in me and your encouraging words.

If you love the cover of this book as much as I do, you have Zsófia Vera to thank. Thank you, Zsófia, for your vision and for designing this wonderful cover all the way from the other side of the globe.

A massive thank you to my business partner, friend, and fellow peace trainer, Neloo Naderi, whose vision and enthusiasm continue to expand the possibilities of Peace Unleashed. Thank you for being.

Lastly, to every person prioritizing inner peace, thank you for doing the individual work that connects us all. As Rumi so beautifully said, "You are not a drop in the ocean. You are the entire ocean in a single drop." Never do we feel this truth more profoundly than when we are at peace.

Also known as the "Modern day Rumi," Ellie Shoja is an award-winning writer, mindset expert, and motivational speaker. Her fascination with spiritual realms, her deep love of humanity, and her passion for helping others connect with their inner peace are at the root of her desire to bring unique stories to life.

Ellie is also the author of the *Your Heart Knows The Way* oracle card deck. Visit www.PeaceUnleashed.com for more information.